NAKED TRUTH

A Thriller

Rick Pullen

VIRGINIA BEACH
CAPE CHARLES

Naked Truth
by Richard G. Pullen

© Copyright 2018 Richard G. Pullen

Cover Design by Brad Latham, Latham Creative

ISBN 978-1-63393-724-6

Published by

köehlerbooks™

210 60th Street
Virginia Beach, VA 23451
212-574-7939
www.koehlerbooks.com

Most truths are so naked that people feel sorry for them
and cover them up, at least a little bit.
—Edward R. Murrow

For Jill

1

She unhooked her bra and dropped it on the hotel carpet, standing before him. He gazed up from the bed, admiring the Lord's bounty.

Damn if he didn't have a good life. He'd slept with some of the most beautiful women in the world, and now another stood ready to do his bidding.

The nation groveled for his approval. He mattered. Better yet, he truly believed in the integrity of his calling. Can life get any better?

She climbed on top of him and clamped her thighs around his hips. He grabbed her waist and the bed rocked. His aging body felt born again. God, he thought he'd died and gone to heaven.

And god, twenty minutes later, he had.

2

Beck Rikki glanced at his watch again. *Where's Castiglia?* This was his idea—his request they have breakfast at this god-awful hour.

He gazed at the ruggedly elegant dining room—nearly empty thanks to last night's revelry. The chief justice seemed to have a particularly good time. He'd slipped out early, leaving with a slender blonde who'd sat at his elbow looking enthralled and hanging on his every word all evening.

West Texas subtlety, Beck thought. *No attempt at pretense here.*

Had this been back in Washington, it would have caused a minor scandal. Not even the attention-craving jurist wooed that kind of publicity. But wooing beautiful blondes? Yeah, he was good at that.

Beck checked his watch again. *Why does US Supreme Court Chief Justice Nino Castiglia want to see me anyway?* Beck assumed it had to do with one of his old stories. *What other reason would Castiglia have to talk to a washed-up newspaper reporter?*

"Sir?"

Beck looked up at the waiter.

"Would you like more coffee while you're waiting for your party to arrive?"

Beck had been staring through the large window that framed the rippling glare now awakening on the white desert floor. The rattlesnake-infested wasteland radiating through the massive windows complemented the wobbly trickle of aging business and political titans being attentively seated, one by one, in the dining room.

Beck wore a sports coat over a golf shirt but still felt a chill. *The air conditioning must be cranked all the way up,* he thought. It was as if Texas had to prove it could conquer all, including Mother Nature.

"No, I'll wait," Beck said. "He may have overslept. I should call his room."

"Allow me, sir."

Beck hesitated. Even at thirty-nine, he'd never gotten used to this brand of white-glove service. Yet he should have expected it at a private resort like this, even if it was a ranch in the middle of nowhere.

"Chief Justice Castiglia," he said.

The waiter nodded and stepped over to chat with the hostess. The hostess lifted her modish phone off of a small stand, said something, and then hung up. Beck again looked at his watch. It was seven fifteen.

The waiters in their long-sleeve white shirts scurried to fill their guests' orders and coffee cups. A round of bloody marys would fortify the morning before the group gathered for trap shooting to compare their sawed-off virility.

It felt like a gentlemen's club. Not the dirty kind with strippers but the private, smart kind Beck was familiar with back in Washington where self-important intellectuals gathered to discuss the world's problems and their investment portfolios.

Beck quickly felt out of place at an affair fueled by high-octane testosterone and masculine resolve. He had been to his share of kiss-ass and back-slapping receptions at the White House on so many occasions that he had grown immune to their allure. This party, however, had been different. The shear machismo of the event bothered him. He found the virility phony and crude. But the penetrating conversation at the dinner table was dead serious.

About thirty full-throttle businessmen, lawyers and politicos—along with a fistful of arm candy—had filled this very room the night before. This morning it looked so different. Weaker, perhaps. More human. Yet little but the time of day had changed. Its white tablecloth formality, the pungent, woodsy aroma of fine cigars and the elegant bite of fine brandy and Scotch would, no doubt, return in time for dinner. But for now, they were memories put away, replaced with unadorned, sumptuous, broad-shouldered grandiosity—and there was no arm candy on retainer within sight. They were called "ladies of the evening" for a reason.

From his seat across the room last night, Beck saw an old nemesis, Jackson Oliver, who had retired from the Justice Department while Beck was investigating his involvement in a sleazy land deal. Oliver was one who got away.

But it was Kevin Kelly, sitting at Castiglia's table, who garnered Beck's attention. Last year, Kelly was a junior law associate sitting with several other attorneys across the conference room table from Beck and his editors. The lawyers were trying to persuade Beck's editors to kill one of his exposés. Yet last night Kelly had been sitting at the table with the chief justice. *How do you go from legal flunky to dining with the most powerful jurist in America in just a matter of months?*

The waiter returned. "Mr. Rikki, I'm sorry but Chief Justice Castiglia does not seem to be answering his phone."

"That's not good," Beck said.

Last night, Castiglia seemed unusually cordial, even effusively kind. They had never met and only talked for a few minutes over the phone. Castiglia made a point of interrupting another conversation with a prominent politician to cross the room and greet Beck. Even though he was a good five inches shorter than Beck, he awkwardly wrapped his arms around him in a bear hug as if they were long-lost relatives. Beck was almost overcome by the chief justice's hair tonic. He would be blowing his nose for at least a week.

It was as if Castiglia wanted everyone to see a bond between him and Beck. Whatever it was the chief justice was selling, it must be important. Beck was flattered and at the same time flabbergasted. *Why? Why me? Why does the chief justice of the United States want to meet with me?*

Beck rose from his table, leaving his napkin in his chair and his coffee cup half empty. He walked to the front desk in the lobby and noticed another example of Texas grandeur: a painting as big as a Cadillac, depicting cattlemen rounding up a herd of longhorns, hung on the wall high above a diminutive clerk's head. Since Beck's arrival yesterday in Texas, the woman was the smallest presence he had encountered. *Not everything here is outsized,* he thought.

Stop it. Beck interrupted his East Coast smugness. His prejudices would not play well with his Texas hosts, who had been more than gracious. He was on edge playing in someone else's sandbox. *Relax,* he told himself. *Enjoy being on foreign soil.*

He asked the clerk for the chief justice's room number.

"I'm sorry, Mr. Rikki. For security reasons we don't give out our guests' room locations." She drew out the words in what Beck realized must be the local accent. While he had heard a smattering of Southern drawl at last night's reception and dinner, much of it was overwhelmed by a forced, Harvard-bred dialect; and none of it matched the young lady's.

"Look, we were supposed to have breakfast a half hour ago. The dining room hostess called his room and there's no answer. I just want to make sure he's all right." Beck paused and then asked, "He hasn't left, has he?" That would be the ultimate insult. Make Beck spend an entire day and thousands of dollars to travel here from his home in the Bahamas and then stand him up. *Could Castiglia be that petty?*

"No sir. We still show him as a guest."

"Can someone check on him? I'm hoping he just forgot about breakfast." Beck knew better. At seventy-eight, the chief justice appeared just as sharp as he was when he was appointed to the Supreme Court twenty-eight years ago. Then Beck thought about the beautiful blonde Castiglia had left with last night. *A good excuse to sleep late,* he thought.

"I'll see what I can do," the clerk said, flashing him one of those broad, *fuck-you* smiles. She turned her back to him and made a quick phone call.

The resort's owner, Michael Trowbridge, stepped from around a corner. "May I help you?" Then he recognized Beck. "Oh, Mr. Rikki. Hope you enjoyed the party last night."

They shook hands, and Beck explained the situation.

Trowbridge glanced at his clerk, his disapproval reflected in her demur expression, and then he looked back at Beck and smiled. "Come with me," he said.

Beck followed him to the elevator and up to the second floor. The owner knocked on Castiglia's room door. No answer. He knocked again, then pulled a key from his pocket, cracked the door and called for the chief justice. Still no answer. Finally, he swung the door open all the way.

"Oh Jesus."

3

Beck looked over Trowbridge's shoulder. Castiglia was splayed on the bed, his eyes and mouth open. The resort's plush sheets partially covered his naked body.

"Oh Jesus," Trowbridge repeated. He approached the body and touched Castiglia's wrist.

Beck's stomach churned. Whatever the chief justice wanted to reveal to him was lost forever. He touched Castiglia's cheek with the back of his fingers to reassure himself this was really happening. Castiglia's skin was cold.

Trowbridge looked at Beck as if to ask, "What do we do?" But then he transformed into a determined man-in-charge. "Wait here while I call the sheriff," he told Beck. "Don't let anyone in the room." Trowbridge closed the door behind him.

"Uh, okay," Beck said in a barely audible voice to the door. *Funny*, he thought. *Why not just call from here?* Obviously Trowbridge didn't want to make the call in his presence.

Beck took in the silence. He turned and heard a *shush*—like someone telling him to keep quiet. It was his shoe shuffling the depths of the thick carpet. He stood motionless, feeling his heart pounding and listening to his own lungs contracting. As he looked at Castiglia's lifeless bulk—so vibrant the night before while dominating the attention of his dinner companions—Beck felt a chill knowing he was now the only living presence in the room.

His old reporter's instincts kicked in. He scanned the bedroom and the corpse. Castiglia's expression was neutral, neither anguished nor at peace. His clothes were neatly folded or hung in the closet. *A heart attack perhaps? In his sleep?* The dead man's hair was a thick, tangled mess, not the slicked-back style Beck and the world had grown accustomed to on news sites and TV.

We're all human, thought Beck. *Not always perfect. Even the giants.*

Then he spied the stains on the sheet. *At least he died happy.*

Reading glasses sat atop a dog-eared novel titled *Naked Ambition* on the bedside table next to a half-filled water glass, a couple of cigars and a box of tissues. There was one of those sleep apnea machines—a continuous positive airway pressure breathing machine, a CPAP—on the far edge of the table. The chief justice had sleep apnea.

Beck had seen a similar machine once in the bedroom of a sexy reporter from a rival newspaper. She refused to spend the night with him after sex because, she finally admitted, she snored. "Who gives a shit?" Beck had blurted. After several months, he finally slept over at her place and pretended to fall asleep early. It was only then that he felt her rustling on the mattress and heard the soft white noise of rushing air into the machine. When he was sure she had fallen asleep, he rolled over to see a long tube hooked to a mask strapped over her face. It wasn't attractive and it gave him the push he needed to finally break up with her a few weeks later. Yes, sometimes he was that shallow.

The CPAP wasn't strapped to Castiglia's face—like he would care if someone knew he snored. The connecting hose and mask were on the floor next to the bed with a long hose affixed to the machine, which was plugged into a wall socket behind the bedside table. He pressed a button on top with his knuckle and air whooshed through the long plastic tube into the breathing device. He pushed it again. The air stopped. He looked at the machine and, using his handkerchief, carefully lifted the lid. He found a small, clear plastic water chamber. So the thing not only spewed out air but humidified it too. *Interesting,* he thought. If Castiglia had used the machine last night, he had turned it off.

Beck looked over at the bed. The stains were on the far side, which meant his companion had stuck around last night after the first act. But was there a second coming? *Oh stop,* Beck chided himself. *Stop the crude, noxious wordplay in your head. You're looking at a corpse, for Chrissakes. Okay, just acknowledge this makes you nervous; maybe even feel a bit creepy. Now get on with it.*

He needed to focus. Maybe Castiglia had fallen asleep after sex without putting on the apnea device. That could explain why it was on the carpet.

Could the pretty blonde have caused him to have a heart attack? If so, where is she now?

Beck looked around the large, well-appointed sunlit suite. *Curious*—the curtains had never been drawn. But, then again, there was nothing outside to look in but horned toads, prairie dogs and rattlesnakes.

The window was like a lens, focusing rays of morning sun on a large leather couch facing a small stone fireplace in the corner. The obligatory longhorns hung prominently above the fireplace, giving the room what Beck liked to call "the full cowboy." He chided himself again for his Washington elitism. It was a city he had grown to despise, yet he couldn't shake its influence.

He walked to the bathroom and eyed an open leather toiletry bag on the marble countertop. A parade of pill bottles, perfectly aligned in two neat rows, stood on the other side of the sink. One face towel and washcloth had been used. Apparently, Castiglia hadn't had time to shower before dinner. Or maybe before sex.

Standing alone in a room with a corpse was disconcerting—a ghoulish scene that humor couldn't erase. Beck had investigated dirty politicians for his old newspaper. But he'd never been a police reporter at the *Post-Examiner*, so he was spared the carnage of shootings, car accidents or drownings. In fact, Castiglia was his first dead body up close, other than at funerals.

Beck was anxious, but he needed to absorb everything he could before Trowbridge returned.

He grabbed his cell phone from his back pocket and took pictures of the drugs and paraphernalia in the bathroom, careful not to touch anything.

He returned to the bedroom. The faint scent of death fell on his nostrils, just like the chief justice's hair tonic. Beck reasoned Castiglia must have been dead for several hours. He began photographing the body, the CPAP machine, the bedside table, the stained sheets and the rest of the room.

He heard a key in the door and stuffed his phone back in his pocket as Trowbridge re-entered.

"The sheriff is on his way," he said. "Should be here in ten minutes or so. We got lucky. He's nearby. This county is so damned big; he could have been an hour away. You okay?"

"Yeah."

"This must be uncomfortable for you, but would you mind staying here a little longer so nothing is disturbed? I need to notify my guests. Just a few more minutes, if you don't mind." Trowbridge pulled the door closed behind him as he left, not waiting for an answer.

Protecting his ass, thought Beck. This could not be good for business, especially among this crowd. A dead Supreme Court justice amidst a gaggle of high-wattage individuals in a private meeting would surely draw hordes of media attention. Each attendee would have to explain what he was doing at the secluded Texas retreat. Which was? Not even Beck knew that. Not yet, anyway.

The thought roused him. *What if this wasn't a natural death?* He turned and eyed the body and the scene again. *Could it be more than a heart attack?*

He examined the CPAP machine. He went back to the bathroom and emptied a small bottle of mouthwash into the sink. He looked at the three-ounce container for a moment, wondering if it would be better to rinse it out or let the alcohol in the bottle do its thing. He rinsed it thoroughly.

He re-entered the bedroom and grabbed his handkerchief from his pocket. He used it to lift the water container out of the machine and walked back to the bathroom sink. He filled the mouthwash bottle and closed it tightly and then returned the water container to the CPAP. It still had water in the bottom. No one would miss a few ounces. Maybe he would have the water tested, just in case this wasn't a heart attack.

He slipped the bottle into his pocket. Then he noticed the water glass. He headed for the bathroom to look for another bottle and heard the key in the door again. He froze and turned just as Trowbridge entered. A man in uniform followed. Trowbridge introduced him as Sheriff Luke "Biggs" Johnson.

Big Johnson, thought Beck. *You've got to be kidding me.* He tried not to snicker.

"Now, you didn't touch anything, did you Mr. Rikki?" asked the sheriff.

"Not a thing."

4

Cinderella Rivera thought it a bit ironic that she, a lowly justice of the peace, was assigned the most powerful justice's last legal decisions—his death certificate. But still, she liked that both she and Chief Justice Castiglia had *justice* in their title, even though she was near the bottom of the judicial totem pole and he was at the top.

As a part-time county justice of the peace, she was constantly on the road, where cell service often vanished. So, now, she pronounced him dead from a battered, gray pay phone near the jukebox in the far corner of a disgusting diner in the middle of nowhere.

Cinderella figured she had the privilege of conducting the first long-distance virtual death pronouncement in Texas history. Talk about phoning it in. She couldn't wipe the Cheshire-Cat grin away. She had just become a legal pioneer.

—ᴍ—

Beck listened to Sheriff Johnson's side of the telephone conversation with the justice of the peace. The sheriff shook his head, shifted his feet back and forth, and stuttered into the phone at a desk against the wall of Castiglia's room.

"Can you do that? . . . Well, I don't know now, Cinderella . . . I guess so."

Beck couldn't believe what he was hearing. Castiglia was being pronounced dead—over the telephone. Big Johnson and Cinderella. He turned his back to the sheriff and walked up to the window so he wouldn't laugh. He felt like he was in the middle of a Fellini film or a Disney set. *Is this real?*

He spied three guests from last night's dinner directly below him on a sidewalk he hadn't realized was there. Beck recognized them. They had been seated at Castiglia's table. Three men argued; one man's arms flailed. The third man's index finger was buried deep in the chest of the roaring man, his face no more than a few inches from the other's nose. Finally, flailing man threw his arm up with his thumb extended as if to signal someone out at home plate. Suddenly, as if they had rehearsed it ahead of time, they all turned and walked back into the building.

Beck couldn't hear any of it through the thick, insulated bedroom window. He could tell one thing: the trio was leaving. Beck turned and saw Trowbridge looking at him. Then he understood. The proprietor had notified his staff to tell all of the guests about Castiglia's death.

"So, death by natural causes—a heart attack," repeated Sheriff Johnson.

Beck stiffened and focused on the only half of a conversation he could actually hear.

"Or maybe a stroke?" Johnson said into the phone. "Well, take your pick. It don't really matter, now does it? The man's dead."

And lucky for Cinderella he is not just dead, thought Beck, *but officially dead of natural causes*. That would save a lot of paperwork. The chief justice would have appreciated that. Beck knew how much he hated bureaucracy.

"What about an autopsy?" the sheriff asked. "Huh . . . No need? . . . Okay." He glanced at Castiglia's body. "Well, there's certainly no evidence of foul play."

Beck realized this would keep the faint smell of sex out of the public record. *How convenient.*

Beck followed the sheriff's gaze to Castiglia's bloated body. The chief justice probably had a dozen ailments his family might rather keep private— as they had every right to. Why drag all of that out in the open? Beck got it. Everybody deserved some privacy. He knew that only too well. He'd been through the public ringer himself, and not that long ago.

Had Castiglia not called him personally and asked him to meet at this sprawling ranch, he might very well have readily accepted Cinderella's ruling without question. But the justice had wanted to talk. It was important enough to Castiglia that he convinced Beck to trek two thousand miles to meet him. Beck didn't believe in coincidences. Whatever it was Castiglia wanted to tell him must have been damned important. *Could it have been important enough that someone would kill him to keep him from talking?*

Beck thought of the scene he'd just witnessed—of three rich businessmen arguing on the patio below Castiglia's window.

What am I missing?

5

Beck turned at the sound of a knock on the door. Two emergency medical technicians stepped in, carrying aluminum cases with red crosses on the side.

"We got a situation?" asked one. They were dressed in navy blue T-shirts and gray cargo pants. They approached the body matter-of-factly. One searched for a pulse on the neck and wrist. He pressed the back of his hand against Castiglia's cheek. Finally he pulled a stethoscope from his pocket and listened to the justice's chest. He shook his head. "Nothing we can do here."

"Yes, there is," said the sheriff. "I need you to move the body."

"We're not allowed to transport a stiff. That's a job for a funeral director."

"Rigor's already setting in. This could get uncomfortable for everyone," the sheriff said. "Trowbridge, you got a walk-in refrigerator or freezer in your kitchen?"

"Well . . . sure."

"Good. Wheel him down to the cooler."

"But—"

"What? Your steaks more important than our esteemed chief justice?"

It took several minutes for the medical technicians to grab a stretcher from their vehicle, complaining the whole time how this would leave them short of equipment. They pulled the bed sheet away and both struggled to transfer the rotund justice to the stretcher. They used their own clean sheet to cover the body, leaving the stained one crumpled on the bed.

"That's it?" Beck asked Sheriff Johnson. "You don't cordon off the room or bring in techs to examine the scene?"

"Son, I don't know where you from, but you been watching too many police shows on TV. You in the middle of nowhere, and we don't have SWAT teams and special investigative units—no CSIs—those crime scene techs you so fond of. If there was any suspicion the justice died of anything but eating too much sausage, or spaghetti, or whatever it was he liked, I might make a few more phone calls. But we've got, what?" The sheriff looked over his paperwork. "A seventy-eight-year-old, overweight Italian who loved his lasagna? Cinderella's gettin' ahold of his doctor. I'm sure she'll find physical and medical issues to back up her cause of death. The man had a heart attack. That's pretty obvious. At least he got to die in his sleep. That's better than most of us."

Beck wasn't going to argue, but the sheriff's logic seemed too convenient—and expedient.

"I'll have the maid come in and clean up," said Trowbridge.

"Let's wait until I have my certificate of death in hand. Just in case," the sheriff said, glancing sideways at Beck. "Let's get this body downstairs."

When everyone was in the hallway, the sheriff pulled the door closed and tried the latch. It was locked.

For all his rough talk, the sheriff wasn't stupid. He was still taking precautions. Beck figured with a high-profile case like this the sheriff was beginning to recognize he didn't want anyone second-guessing him when this became public.

They left Beck standing in the hall. Ignoring him, Trowbridge guided the EMTs to a service elevator at the other end of the hall. As Beck turned to walk back to his room, he remembered the blonde with Castiglia the previous night. *Where is she?* He took the stairs, heading to the front desk.

"I hope you can help me," he said to the clerk. "I guess you're aware of what's happened."

She nodded.

"There was a lady with the chief justice yesterday. Can you tell me if she's left? Someone needs to notify her of what's happened."

The clerk opened a drawer with visitor files. "Yes, she checked out very early this morning. I remember something about a family emergency at home."

"Could you give me her contact information? I need to call her. She was the chief justice's niece." Beck hoped the clerk believed him.

This time the clerk was more than friendly. She gave Beck the blonde's address and phone number. Beck wondered if the prostitute had forged everything. *Probably.* It wasn't likely she would give out real contact information.

"Do you have her license plate number? This is going to get out quickly and the authorities may want to track her down before she hears it over the radio."

"Oh, that would be bad," the clerk replied. She hurriedly scanned the registration again and gave Beck the number.

"I'm sorry, I forgot her first name. This will be a sensitive call. You mind?"

"Denise. Denise Fiori," the clerk said.

"Right. Thanks." He hoped he had what he needed to track her down. Time to go.

He went back to his room and packed, not bothering to check out at the front desk. As he approached the lobby, he encountered Trowbridge.

"Leaving so soon?" Trowbridge's smile was gone and he shifted his weight from one foot to the next.

"Without the chief justice here there's really no reason for me to stay. It really is a tragedy. I'm so sorry."

They shook hands, and Trowbridge thanked him for his assistance. As Beck reached his car in the parking lot he saw a vehicle pull up to the front entrance. Two very stern-faced, uniformed federal marshals stepped out.

Jackson Oliver emerged at the front entrance and greeted the marshals at the door. Oliver had been a highly-ranked official in both the Justice Department and White House before he managed to escape indictment in a money-laundering scam.

What the hell is Oliver doing with the marshals?

Beck dropped his luggage in the trunk of his rental car, closed the lid and walked back toward the building. When he stepped into the lobby he saw Oliver holding the elevator door and pointing the marshals toward the kitchen.

When it closed behind him, Beck took the stairs two at a time. He arrived on the second floor in time to peer around the corner and see Oliver at Castiglia's guestroom door. Oliver pulled a key from his pocket and opened it.

Where did he get a key to the chief justice's room?

Beck waited, peering around the corner at the end of the hall, and thought about finding the sheriff but decided against it. He didn't know what was going on and didn't think ol' Biggs Johnson would take kindly to Beck's questioning the macho privileged class. And he certainly didn't want to draw the attention of the marshals. But if he left now, he could get a jump on them. Maybe he could get to the prostitute, Denise Fiori, before they did. The clerk said she was from El Paso—a good three or more hours away.

Down the hall, Castiglia's door opened, and Beck stepped back around the corner, unseen. He heard steps squish on the carpet and then the sounds of the elevator. When the doors closed, he looked down the hall again. Nothing. Oliver was gone. Beck turned and walked back down the stairs.

In the lobby he spied Oliver standing at the front desk with his back to him, talking to the clerk. Beck hurried across the small lobby hoping to escape unnoticed, but both Oliver and the clerk turned to look. Beck smiled and nodded but did not stop as he opened the lobby door. *Dammit*, he thought. Surely, Oliver must have recognized him.

Back in the hot sun, Beck noticed the department store scion from last night's dinner closing the trunk of his Mercedes at the other end of the small parking lot. The lot, which was full last night, was now half empty. He looked off into the distance at a private runway. Yesterday afternoon when he arrived, three corporate jets were on the tarmac. Today there were none.

The rats are scattering before word spreads, thought Beck. *Just what in the hell am I witnessing?* In less than an hour, half of the guests had fled. He started to have second thoughts. *Should I stay behind or chase after my most promising lead?* Soon word would leak out, and the place would be swarming with media. Obviously, the guests had no interest in being on-site when that happened. Beck didn't either. Right now, he was more interested in a beautiful Texas blonde.

6

Beck drove for more than an hour surrounded by scrub brush and barren flats. Cactus, mesquite trees, and sand framed his view of scorched asphalt divided by a broken yellow line—mile after mile of passing zone, with virtually nothing to pass. It was hypnotic. More than once he shook his head to stay awake, watching the torrid air evaporate in waves above the asphalt.

Why some people thought the desert was beautiful was beyond Beck. He preferred the renewed turf of Washington's famous Mall to this. These roadside vistas were so remote he couldn't find cell phone service. He eyed a gas station ahead with a phone booth. *A phone booth? Do they still exist?* He reminded himself that out here, away from the cluttered coasts of America, there were still rural areas without smartphones and constant social contact. People lived here to escape that stuff. For a fleeting moment, he reveled in the idea but then thought better of it. He had the best of both worlds—a beach and a babe back home, and he could fulfill his need to stay abreast of the world through his laptop. Once a newspaperman, always.

He pulled into the station, grabbed some loose change from his pocket and tried to remember the last time he'd used a pay phone. *What was I? Fifteen maybe?* It had been a while.

He called Nancy Moore, his former city editor at the *Post-Examiner*. She sounded surprised to hear his voice. Even though they were close, they hadn't talked since shortly after he departed the newspaper and Washington six months ago under a cloud.

He told her about Castiglia.

"Holy shit," she said. "Can you give me details?"

He told her what he knew, not mentioning the prostitute or that he had borrowed a sample of the water from the chief justice's sleep apnea machine. No need to admit to his former boss he had tampered with evidence at a possible crime scene.

"I need a favor," he said. "I've got a car license plate I need to run down. It's probably out of El Paso."

"Beck, what are you up to?"

"You know me. I've got a suspicious nature."

"Beck—"

"Look. If I find out anything, it's yours. You know I have no place to publish a story anymore, no matter how hot it is."

"Beck—"

"Right now I haven't got much. Only suspicions."

"You think he didn't die of natural causes?" Her voice sounded scratchy over the ancient phone.

"I don't know. Give me a few days."

"I'll call the Dallas bureau. We'll have that license plate for you in the hour. Matthiesen has a great relationship with the Texas authorities. I'll also have to get him out there. Where, again, exactly is this place?"

Beck gave her the name and directions to the private resort. "And by the way, you'll have to leave me a message," he said. "Cell phone connections are bad out here. We're in the Wild West. I probably won't be able to use my phone until I'm within sight of El Paso."

"Will do. And Beck, thanks for the tip. I'm going to use your information to put out a bulletin. We'll do it out of the Dallas bureau so it doesn't raise quite as much suspicion about our source."

Beck hung up and jumped back in his car. He felt the same rush he once got when he worked with Nancy, back before it all went to shit. He'd been fired for writing a story about his girlfriend's employer. And she'd helped him do it. The problem was, he hadn't known who her employer was until it was too late.

Nevertheless, he was guilty of a conflict of interest.

God, he wished he still worked at the paper. He had owned Washington. Now, he had no platform, but he still had the drive. He had to find that blonde.

Beck checked the gas gauge. Plenty of fuel to get to El Paso. At this point he just hoped he was moving in the right direction to find the Fiori woman. He plugged his phone into the power port and set off for the nearest city, still many miles away.

—⁓—

About thirty miles outside of El Paso, his phone dinged and picked up a signal again. He checked. A voice message from Nancy. He punched the key and listened.

"The car was a rental." Nancy's voice was clear. She gave him the name of the company.

"Shit." He'd gotten lucky. He decided to try the telephone number Denise gave the resort clerk. He punched it in while sitting at a traffic light and got an immediate response—a non-working number.

Well, of course. The address she'd given would be fake, too. He was sure of that. His only recourse was the rental agency. He pulled off the road into a shopping center parking lot and did a Google search with his iPhone. The agency was maybe ten minutes away.

While he navigated El Paso traffic, he worked out a story to tell the rental clerk. A few minutes later he found a small franchise for one of the giant companies. There were maybe five cars in the lot. He was lucky again; no customers were in the office when he walked in. He noted the place could use a facelift and so could the clerk behind the counter.

He stepped up to the counter where a middle-aged, overweight woman with a diamond stud shimmering from each ear was typing on a laptop. She didn't look a decade over sixty even if she wasn't a day over fifty. He was being kind.

"Hi. My name is Beck Rikki," he said. "My fiancée, Denise Fiori, dropped off her car today and thinks she left her engagement ring in it. She's so upset. I told her I'd come check on it. Please tell me you found it. She must have dropped it on the floor mat, or it fell in between the seats or something. Could you check?"

The clerk leaned under the counter and pulled up a thick brown accordion file folder. She thumbed through small, tan envelopes filled with the lost legacies of so many road warriors. Nothing.

"I'm sorry," she said, concern in her eyes. "The car was just rented out or I'd have the crew check it over again."

"Thanks. I guess the only thing to do is mail it to us if you find it," he said. "Oh, but did she give you our new address?

"I don't know. I'll check." She found Denise's information on her computer screen. "That's an apartment at 221B Baker Street?"

"No. That's not it," Beck said. He gave her the address of an apartment building he'd passed on his way over. "So, if you find it, you'll send it there?"

"Certainly. But maybe she lost it elsewhere."

"I sure hope so." Beck thanked her for her concern. He jumped in his car, checked the GPS on his phone and headed for Baker Street.

While he was driving across town, the radio blurted out the news of Castiglia's death. It was now long past one o'clock, more than five hours since they had discovered the body.

He hoped Nancy had gotten the story out first. *Probably.* He knew she would be pushing her reporters relentlessly to get more information. God, he missed his days as a reporter. He felt like he was working a story again, and it felt damned good. *And what will I do if I actually discover something? Give it to Nancy?* But then it would no longer be *his* story. Or maybe he could sell it to the newspaper. *No, not a story this big. They wouldn't take it. A magazine, then? No, that would require a long lead time. Maybe one of the weeklies . . .*

He'd worry about that later.

Beck parked across from Denise's apartment building, a modern three-story brick walkup. She must be a high-priced hooker. Only the best for the chief justice.

He sat in his car, watching the building for a few minutes. He checked the address again, locked his car and set out to find her apartment. He scrolled the mailboxes just inside the entrance lobby door. There it was—*Fiori*. He skipped every other step up the stairs. He reached her door and paused to listen. Nothing. *What are the chances she's home?*

He rang the doorbell and waited.

"Coming," he heard. Beck held his breath.

The door opened as far as the safety chain would allow. He could see through the small opening that he must have just gotten her out of the shower. Her hair was wrapped in a white towel and she was wearing a thick, white bathrobe. Even so, he immediately recognized her.

"Ms. Fiori?"

"Yes."

"My name is Beck Rikki. I'm a reporter and I'd like to talk to you."

"What about?" she asked.

"There's been a murder. I'm not sure you're aware of it."

She gasped and slammed the door. The safety chain scraped against the lock and the door swung open again with such ferocity that her extended arm motion pulled loose her hastily tied belt. It fell to her sides and her robe gaped open. Beck gaped too, looking down at her exposed body. He fixed on her breasts, her smooth flawless skin and her taut belly. His eyes stopped there as she grasped at her robe with her free hand.

He tried to pretend he'd seen nothing.

"I'm sorry," he said. "I didn't—"

"Was it my sister?"

"Your sister?"

"The murder."

"Oh no." Beck regained his composure. "I'm not here about your sister."

"Oh, thank god."

"What about your sister?"

"She has issues. Never mind."

"That's not why I'm here. Chief Justice Nino Castiglia was murdered last night. I think you were the last one to see him alive."

She gave him a puzzled look. "What are you talking about?"

"I saw you at dinner last night, and then you left with the chief justice to go to his room."

He gazed into her wide, crystalline-blue eyes. Her face was delicate and flawless. Angled cheekbones offset the short narrow nose and sloped chin.

"Mister—Mister Rikki, is it?" she said.

Her tone changed.

"Mr. Rikki, I don't know what your game is or what you've been smoking, but I've never laid eyes on this justice of yours, and you most certainly did not see me at dinner last night. Please leave."

Beck hesitated. "But I saw you there. I was a few tables away."

"You obviously saw someone, but it wasn't me."

Beck knew better. *Why would she deny being there?*

"Now please leave before I call the police."

"Sorry. I didn't mean to upset you. Obviously, I've got the wrong person. Please accept my apology." *Damage control.* "I really am sorry," he repeated.

She shifted her weight to one leg, thrust her hip to the side and arched an eyebrow, giving him a look of disdain he'd seen in so many of the women he'd dated over his lifetime. He backed up, and she slammed the door in his face.

He stood in the hallway for a moment, staring at the door, angry with himself for mishandling the situation. He'd talked too hastily. He was too excited about finding a potential lead and he'd blown it. That or he'd been too distracted after seeing her half naked.

As he trudged slowly down the stairwell, he replayed their encounter. She was movie star material. He could not find a flaw in her appearance. *She's perfect. Classic*, he thought. He let himself out of the building into the blazing sun, shaking his head and searching for shade as he walked.

Fiori might be model material, but she's still a prostitute, he reminded himself.

Usually, the beautiful people have it so easy. Why would she turn to prostitution? The money? And why stay in a city like El Paso? Business is bound to be better in a bigger city like Dallas or Houston. She had the looks to go to Hollywood.

Beck slumped into his rental car. He needed to find out what was behind that beautiful facade. This woman knew something. She'd reacted too quickly when he mentioned the chief justice—but not in a way that suggested she really knew him.

Maybe the feds will soften her up. And the feds would be by, no doubt. There was plenty of evidence back in the hotel room that she had been there. The rich guys could cover up only so much. He sat there, looking down Fiori's street, wondering about his next move.

—⁂—

Beck drove away in search of a place to spend the night and found a mid-priced motel about a mile away, grabbing the last room on the second floor. He called his girlfriend, Geneva, and relayed the events of the last few hours, leaving out the unintended striptease, of course. Geneva expressed the appropriate shock about Castiglia's death and then asked him to hurry home to Abaco, their retreat in the Bahamas. She missed him, she said.

"I'm sitting here naked overlooking the water, just thinking about you."

He had no doubt she was, since that was her favorite state of being.

"I hope to be home in a couple of days. Obviously, this Castiglia thing turned out a lot differently than I expected."

Beck tossed his bag on one of the double beds. The springs protested a sour note. *E-flat?* He tried the bed. *Just flat.* Otherwise, the room was clean.

He had seen a Mexican restaurant a couple of blocks down that looked passable. He'd give it a try. He was looking forward to a beer and some good Tex-Mex while he ran his investigation through his head and figured out what to do next. That old feeling was back. The hunt was on. If only he were still working for the newspaper and his sidekick, Red, were here. *Oh, the possibilities.*

He felt a surge in his step.

About a block from his hotel, he passed a construction site while still thinking about Denise and what she might know. He heard scuffling behind him. He turned just as a giant wood splitter of a fist connected with his jaw. His head snapped back, and he began to crumble, his legs suddenly Jell-O.

"Hey!" was all he could muster.

His shoulder took the brunt of the impact as he landed hard on the concrete. He groaned. *What's happening?* Someone rolled Beck onto his back. He looked up at two blurry figures and tried to move. He needed to get up. *Must get up. Must . . .* He lay there, his arms and legs feebly thrashing. A hard boot slammed into his side. He shrunk into a fetal position. Fire blazed through his chest. He struggled to breathe. He felt a sharp jolt to his head. The boot again. Beck closed his eyes, covering his face and head, reeling in an anguish he had never known.

"Let this be a warning," said a male voice above him. "Stay away from what you don't understand. Got it?"

Beck said nothing. Another heavy boot slammed his back.

"I said, do you understand?"

Beck whimpered something that sounded like "yes." Then he heard footsteps and voices rapidly fading. His head throbbed, and he moaned again, his eyes tightly closed.

He wheezed, craving oxygen. Every gulp felt like barbed wire being pulled taut around him.

He struggled to open his eyes and gasped for small breaths of anything. After what seemed like forever, he felt the heft of his breaths subside. The burn in his lungs cooled to a rhythmic tide, slowly ebbing.

He tried to focus on his surroundings as he lay on his side. The gritty contours of the hot concrete sidewalk pressed his cheek and looked like small, abandoned children's wading pools. Pungent wild onions sprouted from a jagged crack barely six inches from his nose.

Then more voices.

He slowly turned his head. Two teenagers appeared above him.

"Help me," Beck gasped. He focused on one of the boys in a black T-shirt and dark jeans. The redhead, no older than fourteen, bent over, rifling Beck's pockets. Finding his wallet, he pulled out the cash and dropped the billfold on the concrete next to Beck. The two ran, laughing. Beck groaned again, and everything went black.

—∿—

When Beck awoke, a young woman in a sea-green tunic faced him.

"Are you with me, Mr. Rikki?" she asked.

Beck sighed and looked at her. *Who is she? Where am I?* He tried to remember. Yes. Someone on the sidewalk had hit him. He focused on the woman in front on him. "Who . . . who—"

"I'm Meredith. Your nurse."

"Nurse?"

"You were mugged. You're in the hospital. You were in the wrong part of town, but you'll be okay now. You've been given a painkiller, and we gave you a sedative to help you sleep last night."

Sunlight streaked through the blinds, reflecting off the room's ceiling. Beck began to turn his head toward the window but stopped when a sharp pain shot through his temples.

"Try not to move too much," Meredith said. "You'll feel better if you don't move right now. It will just take a little while." She squeezed his hand. "We'll take good care of you."

He looked at her and said nothing.

"We called your wife. Geneva said she'll be here later today. She's flying in. Now you rest."

My wife? "But I don't have—"

The nurse twisted a valve on the IV line and clear liquid ran down a transparent tube. He immediately felt himself fading.

7

"Beck? Beck?"

Beck heard the distressed tenor of a familiar voice and slowly opened his eyes. Her figure was blurred, but he knew the voice. As he focused, he couldn't mistake the soft line of her long brown bangs or the slope of her cheekbones cascading to her angled chin. He concentrated and managed to lock on her bright amber eyes. He struggled against the pain to crack a smile. She was actually here in El Paso.

Geneva leaned down and placed her cheek against his. Beck felt her warm tears sliding down his face.

Then a soft sob. "Oh, Beck. I was so worried." She backed away and held his hand. "You're going to be okay. The doctors said you'll be fine, but you'll have to take it easy for a while."

"What happened?" he whispered.

"You were mugged, robbed. I guess they left you on the sidewalk unconscious. A driver saw you there and stopped her car and called police."

He tried to remember. "Sit up?"

"Sure. Hold on." Geneva pushed a button that slowly raised the bed. Beck winced at the motion. She adjusted his pillow. Now he could see her clearly. She handed him a cup with a straw, and he took a sip of cold water. Then another. Then he finished the entire cup.

"That was no mugging," Beck said, barely audible.

"What do you mean?"

"It was a warning. Someone told me to mind my own business."

"About what?"

"This Castiglia thing. I'm sure of it."

"Oh, Beck. How? Besides, all of your money was stolen."

"Teenagers." He struggled to speak. "They came by after I was on the ground and couldn't move."

"All I care about is that the doctor says you're going to be okay. I've arranged for a plane to fly us out tomorrow."

"A plane?"

"I'll explain later. You just take it easy right now. We're going to DC. Stay at my place while you recuperate. Our doctors are there. Once you're feeling better, we can go home, back to Abaco."

"What will your ex think of us in your old condo?"

"Does it matter? It's not like the president of the United States hangs out there. He's got better accommodations seven blocks up the Avenue."

"Call Nancy."

"Nancy?"

"My editor."

"Oh, that Nancy."

—⁂—

A few hours later a uniformed police officer arrived and asked a lot of questions. He jotted Beck's answers on a form attached to a clipboard. Beck described what he could about the mugging. He was still groggy from the drugs but sharp enough to leave out the part about the attackers' warning. Whatever was going on, he didn't want the local cops involved. This was his investigation now. He owned it even if he had nowhere to publish a story. He was determined to find out what happened to Castiglia. The idea that he was in pursuit again made the pain bearable.

The next morning he was wheeled out of the hospital to a waiting taxi, which took them straight to the airport and to a private jet in the general aviation terminal.

Maybe forty yards away, he noticed a casket being loaded onto another larger plane. He wondered if it could be Castiglia. Then a man wearing a blue windbreaker with *US Marshal* in large white letters on the back stepped from the other side of the craft to board.

Beck sat in the cab, not moving. Just watching. He felt like he was watching his only clue—his only link to the truth—slip away. And he couldn't do anything about it.

"Beck?" Geneva asked. "Is everything okay?"

Beck looked at Geneva and then their plane on the other side of their taxi. "How the hell can you afford a private jet?"

She shook her head. "I said I'd explain later, and I will."

The flight to Reagan National Airport took nearly four hours. A limo whisked them downtown to Geneva's penthouse overlooking Pennsylvania Avenue. The driver carried their bags as Geneva helped Beck onto the elevator and into her condominium.

He had never been here before. His place was across the Potomac in Old Town Alexandria, which is where the two had spent most of their time together.

Geneva's condo was filled with sunlight. The furniture was light and airy. It reminded him of their place in the Bahamas. All it needed was a beach.

She led him to a bedroom with a queen-size bed.

"Rest."

Two hours later, he awoke and found his cell phone and wallet on the bedside table. He sat up slowly and turned to sit on the edge of the bed. Shards of pain raced through his sides as he moved very deliberately.

He thumbed through his wallet. Only cash was missing. He checked his cell. A message from Nancy. She would drop by tomorrow to check on his condition. Geneva had called as he asked.

He eyed his suitcase, on a luggage stand on the other side of the bed. Beck stood and pain seared his chest, making it difficult to move. He was in his boxers. Geneva must have undressed him.

Gingerly, he walked across the room and opened his suitcase. His clothes were situated just as he had left them at the hotel. He opened the toiletry bag. Good. The mouthwash bottle was still there. He would take care of that when he was feeling better.

He was starving and couldn't remember the last time he'd eaten. With some effort, he made it to the kitchen and opened the refrigerator. Pain followed each motion. Geneva had bought him some beer. She must have gone shopping while he was sleeping.

"Hey, good looking. Hungry?" Geneva stood at the kitchen door, naked and covered in sweat. "I've been getting a little sun. You're looking better."

"So are you."

Geneva smiled.

Beck didn't remember getting undressed or even crawling into bed. He looked back at the naked beauty in front of him and then down at himself.

"This feels familiar."

Geneva laughed. "You must be feeling better."

"I'm pretty sore."

"You should be. The doctor said they broke two of your ribs."

Beck winced. "I guess that will curtail our sex life for a while."

"Don't you be so sure, young man. I can get very creative." Geneva walked over and kissed him hard on the mouth, gently grasping his shoulders. It felt strange. Usually they embraced when they kissed. Beck tried to raise his arms, but pain zapped his sides again. He felt like a captive in his own body.

"Don't, hon," Geneva said. "The doctor warned against overdoing it. There's nothing you can do for broken ribs—and whatever else you broke—but rest. Come on. Let's go outside."

She led him through the door to the penthouse patio. Beck was blown away by the view of the city. It was all rooftops. He looked again at Geneva.

"Don't you need to put some clothes on?"

"Look again. We're on top of the world. There is no one within direct sight of us."

Beck surveyed his surroundings. Two lounge chairs with small side tables faced the National Archives building across the street. He walked to the edge and noted the Navy Memorial thirteen floors below. He turned. She was right. They were high up, by Washington standards, in a completely private space. He heard traffic below and a police siren in the distance.

"You and your oasis theory. You seem to always find one no matter where you are."

She just smiled. "You know me too well. Here, let me help you."

She held Beck's arm gently and helped lower him onto a lounge chair and then sat in the one next to his. She took a sip of red wine and gave him a guilty look.

"Sorry. Doc says no alcohol with your painkillers."

"Painkillers?"

"See what I mean. You don't remember taking them before your nap."

Great, thought Beck. *I feel like shit and can't even have a beer.*

"Screw the doc."

"Beck."

"Screw the doc."

"As you wish." She opened a small cooler next to her chair and pulled out a Corona Lite.

"Am I that predictable?" Beck shook his head.

"I'm required by law to give you the surgeon general's warning. But yes, you are that predictable."

"Damn." Beck was silent for a moment, popped the top on the can and took a swig. He hadn't had a beer in days, and it tasted extra strong.

"This is quite a place, but I feel weird knowing you lived here with your ex and he still owns it."

"Part owner and not for long. We've reached an agreement where I'll buy him out. It will be ours."

"Ours?"

We've been living together for less than six months, and she's talking about giving me half of this penthouse? That was a commitment he wasn't ready to make.

"Well, if you would like. I don't want to presume."

"If you don't mind my asking, where does all of this money come from?"

"Harv has family money. When we divorced, I settled for a smaller portion than I was entitled to in exchange for this place. And I've done quite well on my own in the stock market."

"I didn't know you played the market."

She tilted her head and look straight at him, a smirk on her face. "There's a lot about me you still don't know, Mr. Rikki."

"I'd sure like to explore you in depth right now."

She smiled. "I rather doubt in your condition you'll be exploring much of anything for a while." She learned over and kissed him and then picked up the day's *Post-Examiner.* "They're still writing about Castiglia's death."

"Does it say anything about him being murdered?"

"Murdered?"

"Yeah. I don't think he died of natural causes."

"My god, Beck. Who would want to murder the chief justice of the United States?"

"Beats me. But there are too many things that just don't add up."

"Like?"

Beck carefully adjusted himself in the chair, and pain jackknifed through his right arm.

"Like . . . he was with a prostitute the night he died. Like . . . Texas officials are too eager to call it natural causes. Like I saw my old buddy, Jackson Oliver, sneak into his room after Castiglia's body was removed. Like Castiglia was so concerned about something that he invited this ex-reporter out to Nowhere, Texas, to talk with him privately in a public place. What was that about?"

Geneva thumbed through the folded paper and looked up. "Like . . . the family opposed an autopsy?"

"What?"

"Says so right here." She pointed a red fingernail at the bottom of a front-page story.

"You just made my point."

"Glad I could help. You have a lot of questions but no answers. Do you really believe he might have been murdered?" Geneva set the newspaper down on her lap.

"Something was going on. Just the gathering of business giants and political heavyweights makes that clear. What were they up to? Just a weekend of big-boy fun with guns and prostitutes? If it was, would Castiglia have invited me? Something smells."

"Okay, suppose he was killed. Why?" Geneva took another sip of her wine, twirled the glass, examining its clarity, and then set it down.

"I don't know, but I think it has something to do with what he wanted to tell me," Beck said.

"And that was?"

"I have no clue."

"You're just full of answers, aren't you? So you really know nothing. Where do you begin?"

"I checked out the prostitute."

"Really?" Geneva sat up straight. "So you've already done some of your in-depth exploration. Just how deep did you probe?"

"Oh, come on. Don't be lewd. And don't sound surprised. I told you earlier what I was doing in El Paso. She denies she was even at the resort. But she was; I saw her, and I was mugged right after leaving her apartment."

Beck shifted and winced.

"You saw her with the chief justice? You sure it was her?"

"Yep. She's a prostitute. She lies. It's probably as simple as that. What I found interesting though is she seemed to be caught off guard by my questions—like she really didn't know what I was talking about. Her acting is very good. I would have believed her if I hadn't seen her for myself back at the resort."

"Think of what she does in the presence of a stranger—whether she's having sex with him or not," she said. "It's all acting."

"Good point."

Thinking about Denise Fiori naked made him feel guilty sitting here talking to Geneva in the same state. He wondered if Geneva had already recognized his distraction. She was good at subtleties. *Me? Not so much.*

"So what's next?" she asked.

"I need to check out Kevin Kelly and Jackson Oliver."

"I recognize Oliver. Who is Kevin Kelly?"

"Remember last year when lawyers from the presidential campaign were trying to kill one of my stories? Kelly was the junior associate who did the grunt work and the bulk of the lying." Beck's throat was dry, so he took another sip of beer.

"So?"

"So, guess who sat at Castiglia's table the other night?"

"From flunky junior lawyer to tablemate of the chief justice?"

"Precisely."

"It certainly raises questions." Geneva picked up the bottle of red and refilled her glass. She swept strands of her shoulder-length hair out of her face to take a sip. "I hope you don't mind. I invited your friend Nancy over for lunch tomorrow. I'd like to meet this other woman in your life—I mean besides Red, of course. But then, I have no reason to be jealous of Red."

"Don't be so sure." Beck smiled. He almost laughed, but he knew it would hurt too much. "When you meet Nancy, you'll think the same of her."

Beck thought of his condo across the river and Red. Even today he found it difficult to believe he had divulged his secret to a woman he hardly knew at the time. But somehow Geneva got the whole story out of him—how he had discovered his muse: his brown leather reading chair. Talking to his chair, which he had named Red, somehow helped him focus to put words in their proper place.

It was a complete embarrassment. Talking to a chair. Really? If word ever leaked, he would be the laughingstock of official Washington.

Now it was *their* secret. Geneva never judged him. Maybe that's why he had trusted her from the beginning. And yet, she had not always been honest with him. And after nearly a nine-month relationship, he still didn't know her as well as he thought he should. Geneva's high-priced surroundings raised even more questions.

Geneva handed Beck the newspaper and he read about Castiglia. The only thing that caught his attention was a line about US Marshals and the FBI taking the lead in the investigation over the objections of Texas officials. *Typical. The feds always want to meddle and take charge.* But at least it made sense this time since they were investigating the death of a man the marshals were supposed to protect. Come to think of it, the marshals were nowhere around when Castiglia died. They weren't even staying at the resort. *Where the hell were they?*

"Hon, it's time for a shower," said Geneva.

"What?"

"I've been perspiring and you haven't had a shower for at least two days."

Beck looked at the beads of sweat clinging to the curves of her body. God, she was breathtaking. And she was so confident. Even though he struggled with it, being nude didn't bother her at all.

"Hon, you're staring."

"Sorry."

"It's time I got you cleaned up," Geneva said. She rose and walked around the lounge chairs and placed her hand on his. "Come on. Need some help getting up?"

"I can handle it."

They stepped into the large bathroom with the walk-in shower. She turned him around so they were facing each other and pulled down his boxers.

"Ah. I see I've gotten your attention." She turned on the shower and tested the water. They stepped in together. She grabbed the bar of soap and began lathering both of them. Beck stood there and enjoyed the attention.

When they were done, Geneva toweled off Beck, being extra careful around his ribs. Then she led him to the bed.

"Lie down."

Beck lay on his back, looked at Geneva, and his heart pumped faster. She sat next to him. He instinctively raised his arm to caress her, but the pain made him think better of it.

"Careful, love. I don't think you should partake in any vigorous activity tonight."

"I'm fine," he said.

"You know, sometimes you need to accept your limitations. You're my Superman. That's all that matters."

"Don't you think Clark Kent, fumbling reporter, would be more appropriate?"

"Oh stop it. You might just be the best investigative reporter in the country, but you sometimes need to learn to accept others' help. It's not a sign of weakness; it's a sign of strength. You've got to learn to leave yourself vulnerable sometimes."

"Yeah, but it's been a long time, and I want you."

"That's not a problem." Geneva's eyes traveled down his body. "I'll take care of this."

8

It was the first time she had been dressed since she brought Beck to her condo. Geneva smiled at the thought. She wore a loose-fitting blouse and skirt, and no underwear. It was her preferred style now that she had become financially independent at forty-two, no longer had to go to the office, and had retired to a life of leisure and lust for the man sitting next to her.

They sat on her rooftop patio at a glass-top table under a large, green-and-white striped umbrella. A cold front had cleared the typical Washington summer haze. They finished the morning papers—the *Post-Examiner* and its more conservative rival, *News-Times*.

She had an urge to walk around the table and kiss him, but she didn't dare. She'd learned long ago that reading the paper was his sacred time. He grew irritated when she interrupted.

She liked the way he now swept his long brown locks back. When they met at that Georgetown party last year, his hair had fallen over his forehead. Since he moved in with her on the island six months ago, she had persuaded him to let it grow longer and comb it back. And, somehow, it went better with that droopy mustache, which she repeatedly failed to persuade him to even trim. He could be stubborn. But it was his face, and a handsome one.

The doorbell rang and he looked up.

"You sit tight," Geneva said.

"With these damned ribs, that's about all I can do," Beck said. "You know what I need?"

"No. What?"

"Some spareribs."

"That was bad. Really bad." Geneva shook her head. He could be such a dork.

She walked through the condo. She opened the front door to a stocky woman with close-cropped gray hair. Geneva guessed her age at about sixty.

"You must be Geneva," the woman said. "Nancy Moore." They shook hands.

"It's a pleasure," Geneva said.

"How's our patient?"

She led Nancy through the condo and outside.

"Hey, invalid. How you feeling?" Nancy smiled.

"Must admit I've been better," Beck replied.

Nancy walked over and wrapped her arms around his shoulders from behind. They hadn't seen each other in more than six months and Geneva detected a tear in her eye.

"I've missed you." Nancy stood and took a chair facing him. "No one worth yelling at in the newsroom anymore."

Beck smiled.

"Drink?" asked Geneva. "Ice tea? Lemonade?"

"Ice tea is fine," Nancy said. "Too early for the hard stuff."

Geneva poured her a glass from a tall pitcher on the table.

Nancy looked at Beck. "So, you've gotten yourself right in the middle of another big story."

"Seems that way. Can't seem to mind my own business."

"So what did Castiglia want with you?"

"I don't know. I never found out."

"Shit. I had Steve and Leslie do some follow-up on the justice's trip."

"And?"

"Seems our chief justice got himself a free trip to Texas courtesy of one of the biggest law firms in town, James Howell & Gordon—one that just also happens to represent our newspaper and regularly practice before the Supreme Court."

"Interesting. I'd say the chief justice had a bit of a conflict of interest."

"You'd think. But apparently there is no such thing on the court. Each justice monitors his own behavior."

"You mean his or her own behavior." Beck smiled broadly.

"Yeah, right. Whatever. But anyway, each one decides what's a conflict and what's not. Tells you how sad a place Washington is when they define their own ethics."

"Why not? They define everything else. That also explains their rulings on that Virginia governor who was on the take a while back. Rolex watches, a Maserati, expensive wardrobes, cash. You name it. Everything is acceptable these days. Can they set the bar any lower?"

"Only in the court of public opinion—and even that seems to accept most of the self-dealing these days. I think we call that ethics in this town," Nancy said. "So, anyway, Leslie found Castiglia actually flew to Texas with Kevin Kelly, that junior attorney who tried to buffalo us last year on your story."

"Interesting," said Beck. "He was sitting at the table with Castiglia the night before the chief justice died."

"Wonder what their connection is."

"I think I need to find out."

"He's not returning our phone calls."

"I think I can get his attention long enough to return mine."

Nancy sipped her ice tea and dabbed her mouth with a napkin. Geneva noticed she wore no lipstick.

"And then there's the Trowbridge connection," Nancy said. "He's the managing partner in the resort. Seems he and his fellow owners had a case before the Supremes two years ago, which they won. Castiglia cast the deciding vote in their favor. And Trowbridge gave him free room and board at his Texas hangout. Imagine that. And you'll love this one: After he died, someone at the resort called for a hearse. It came to the resort and left for El Paso around four o'clock in the afternoon."

"So what's so interesting about that?"

"There was no body in it. It was a decoy."

"A decoy?"

"That's what I just said."

"Why? What for?"

"We don't know. Perhaps it's just government paranoia. And get this—Castiglia's body wasn't removed from the resort until midnight, under cover of darkness. Then an entire caravan made the long trip to El Paso."

"What? They think some terrorist is going to attack a hearse? Kinda defeats the purpose," said Beck.

"Steve found that tidbit. The more he and Leslie dig, the more questions they come up with. We're slowly getting closer to writing a story, but we need more facts. But there's more I need to tell you." Nancy suddenly looked grim.

"Oh?"

"You're not going to like this one. It's newsroom chatter." She looked Beck in the eye. "Your beloved managing editor, Bob Baker, is wooing Kerry Rabidan to replace you."

"What? Rabid Dog? The bitch who got me fired? I can't believe it. Why would Baker do that?"

"Yeah. It's caused a bit of an uproar in the newsroom. You'd be surprised at how many friends you still have there."

Beck hadn't heard from any of them since the day he left the newspaper. Geneva noticed his pained look and wondered if there was more to this Rabidan woman than a job application and lost job.

"Baker was pretty frank about it," Nancy said. "He said he lost the best investigative reporter in town when you left, and Rabidan was the second best."

"Shit, I can't believe it. Sounds like Steve and Leslie are doing just fine without her."

"Not my call. All I can say is you have been missed. Terribly. Not only for that sparkling personality of yours and that mess of a desk, but for that dazzling skillset a few misinformed folks in the newsroom seem to believe you possess."

Beck smiled. Geneva felt uncomfortable. She and Beck had never discussed his departure from the *Post-Examiner* during their months together in the Bahamas. He'd never blamed her and she wondered why, since their affair had caused his firing. She got rich and he got fired. Not exactly a fair tradeoff.

"So I guess you won't be needing my help," Beck said.

"On the contrary. Baker hasn't landed Rabidan yet. Her paper has made a counteroffer, but I doubt it's enough to keep her there. Let's face it—the *Post-Examiner* is a far better paper, and we pay more. Everybody wants to work for us. She's playing one off of the other. She's going for the big payday. Can't say I blame her, what with the state of journalism these days. And Baker is likely to pay her whatever it takes. He's desperate for another you."

"I'm available."

There was a long, awkward silence.

"If only," Nancy said. She pursed her lips. "I know she's not on your Castiglia story yet, and I don't intend to put her there, although I don't know what Baker has in mind. Look, I know you can't write for the paper anymore, but maybe you can drop us a few tidbits. Become our anonymous source. I know you. You will pursue this and won't let it go. It's in your genes. I really appreciate you calling me from Texas. We were the first out of the starting gate with the story. That was huge."

Beck smiled.

Geneva looked at his eyes. Even in his current condition, she recognized the drive, the desire to investigate Castiglia's death. Beck had often talked about the thrill he got from tracking down threads of a story. But there was no newspaper that would hire him since his firing from the *Post-Examiner*. She felt for him. His career fiasco was more her fault than his. If she had just been honest with him from the start, he might not have been accused of a conflict of interest. But neither she nor Beck had any idea they would ever fall for each other.

"I'll see what I can do," Beck told Nancy.

"What do you have planned next?"

"Not sure. I'm hampered by my ribs. I can't move very well right now. I need to think it through."

"Let me know if I can help. Did the license plate work out at all?"

"Naw. Dead end."

———※———

After Nancy left, Beck gingerly rose from his chair. Geneva stopped him.

"I need my cell," he said as he slumped back down.

"Sit tight. I'll get it." She found his phone and brought it to him. "What are you going to do, sweetie?"

"I'm going to find Kevin Kelly and find out what his relationship is with Castiglia. Then I'm going to somehow find out what Jackson Oliver is up to."

"What was the license plate about?"

"Nancy ran the plates on the rental car driven by the prostitute, Denise Fiori. That helped me find her."

"Oh. She has a name."

"Duh."

"Why did you tell Nancy it was a dead end?"

"She's going to be working with Rabidan. I don't want to feed Kerry anything."

"But she says she's not."

"Oh, Nancy might think that, but Baker will put Kerry on the story. Nancy's the editor for investigations and Kerry is one vicious investigator. They call her 'Rabid Dog' for a reason. Just look what she did to me. To us."

"Beck, I'm sorry about that. We've never really discussed it. I know how much you loved your job at the newspaper."

"Let it go. I've got what I want right here." He smiled and their eyes met.

She felt herself melting and wondered how he could be so kind to her after she'd put him through hell. Worse, she still hadn't been completely honest with him. *Someday*, she told herself. *Someday I'll tell him everything.*

9

Beck tugged open the door of the K Street office building. He wondered why Kevin Kelly so readily agreed to meet with him. The smarmy young attorney must have seen him at the resort the night before Castiglia died, but even that didn't explain the eagerness Beck detected over the telephone. Beck was used to pushback and even having to threaten sources to get information. He figured Kelly must be curious to learn what Beck knew. Lawyers always had an angle to exploit or protect.

The building's mammoth lobby was three stories of green-and-black marble. It was meant to impress even the most jaded visitor and enabled its owners to charge equally impressive rents.

The directory behind the guard's desk showed four floors of lawyers for James Howell & Gordon. *How ironic,* thought Beck. Last year a partner from this very firm was defending Beck's newspaper from Kelly. At the time, Kelly worked for another, smaller firm. Lawyering was like baseball; players moved from team to team throughout their careers. Kelly, a minor leaguer in Beck's estimation, had just hit the majors—"The Show"—with James Howell & Gordon.

Beck scanned the long list of names. There had to be fifty lawyers. He stopped on one name: Jackson Oliver. Oliver must have joined the firm shortly after he quietly retired under a cloud from the Justice Department earlier this year. Well, at least Beck knew where to find Oliver when he finally got around to investigating the scumbag. The son of a bitch had gotten the best of him last year when Beck was investigating improprieties in the presidential race.

Beck took the elevator to the seventh floor where he followed the swaying hips of the pert secretary in her too-short skirt and too-tight blouse into Kelly's office. *God, I do love today's professional attire.*

Beck almost didn't notice the skinny young attorney. Kelly looked tiny, almost childlike, behind the oversized mahogany desk. Beck imagined him needing a child's booster seat and wondered if his feet touched the floor. At least Kelly was wearing an expensive suit. He'd come up in the world, for sure.

"This is awkward," said Beck. "First we're on opposite sides of a case and now you agree to meet with me."

"Not at all," said Kelly. "This happens all the time. It's the way the law works. One day we're fierce opponents, the next we are on the same side."

"Strange bedfellows," Beck said.

"In a way, yes. It's the law," Kelly replied.

Beck shook his head. "I'm here to ask about Chief Justice Castiglia's death and what you were doing in Texas."

"I figured as much. I saw you at the party the night before. But there's nothing really to tell. We traveled together to the retreat."

"I never saw any security for the chief justice while I was in Texas. Don't US marshals accompany him on the road?"

"Castiglia dumped his detail in Houston. We took a commercial flight to Houston and then hopped on our firm's corporate jet to west Texas."

"Why would you do that?"

"Dump the marshals? You tell me. One reason he went there was to talk to you. I assumed he didn't want the marshals hanging around when you guys met."

Beck leaned forward in his seat. "You assumed?"

"I have no other explanation. I guess it also could have something to do with riding on a private jet for free. Not sure the marshals would be allowed to do that."

"But the justice could. Interesting. Did he do that frequently?"

"Let's just say he did it more than once." Kelly looked down at his desk as he played with a rubber band.

"Isn't that a conflict of interest for him?"

"You want a conflict of interest, check out the owner of the resort. He just won a case before the court a few years back."

"So the chief judge rides down on a jet owned by a law firm that practices before him, and he takes free room and board from a plaintiff who recently won a case before him. That seems to be really stretching the whole professional ethics thing, don't you think?"

"It's not for me to say. The high court has its own ethics rules, which I will say are not really written down anywhere that I know of. Each justice makes his own decisions."

"So they police themselves?" Beck already knew this from his conversation with Nancy, but he wanted to hear Kelly say it.

"Yep. That's the way it works."

"Don't opposing lawyers complain about favoritism?"

"Not a good career move if you want to appear before the court."

It was so typical Washington. Once you moved inside the beltway, ethical behavior became relative behavior—all based on your own best interests. Beck tried to hide his disgust. It was time to move on.

"And what about the prostitute? The Fiori woman?"

"What about her?"

"Did you have anything to do with that?"

"Are we on or off the record here?" Kelly asked. "I don't want to sully the justice's reputation or do his family harm."

"We can go off the record." Beck figured the man's sex life was really no one else's business, although plenty of newspapers and magazines would be more than eager to print salacious details. Journalists had ethical issues, too.

"I traveled with the justice half a dozen times a year and each time he would have a companion waiting once we reached his destination. Sometimes I'd help him find one. Sometimes not."

"How did you become so close to him?"

"I clerked for him three years ago."

"You ever practice before the court?"

"I've assisted but not taken a case on my own."

There were definite gaps in Kelly's resume. The lawyer appeared to have one foot in the chambers of the Supreme Court and the other still in some expensive boarding school. "What was the justice doing in Texas?"

"I assume just having a good time. Meeting with old friends. He didn't really say. Again, the only unusual thing is he told me he was meeting with you. I found that odd. He'd never done anything like that before when I traveled with him."

"I figured it had something to do with stories I've written in the past," Beck said. "I thought maybe he was defensive about them."

"You didn't know Justice Castiglia. He wasn't defensive about anything."

"Do you know what he wanted to talk with me about?"

"Not a clue."

"You mean you traveled all the way there with him, and he never said a thing about why he wanted to talk with me? I find that hard to believe."

"Believe it. He didn't confide in me. All I know is at some point he planned to have a conversation with you. What it was about was his business, and he didn't share any of it."

Beck stared at Kelly, trying to figure out what was left unsaid. "What were you doing there? It doesn't make a lot of sense if the chief justice was just there for a weekend of fun and conversation."

Kelly rubbed his hands together. "Off the record again?"

"I'm listening."

Kelly stalled, searching for the right words. "The justice had health issues. He was elderly. Overweight. He needed assistance."

"He seemed awfully robust at dinner."

"Yes, but he was on a great deal of medication to keep him that way."

Beck thought about the neat lineup of pill bottles in Castiglia's bathroom.

Maybe he should look at his photos and read the labels. "He spent the night with a prostitute. He must not have been too unhealthy."

"True. He enjoyed the perks of his status and sometimes acted entitled. He liked someone like myself, someone he presumably trusted, waiting on him. We'd grown close when I clerked for him, so he looked to me from time to time for aid. He did not want the outside world to know his vulnerabilities."

Kelly looked resigned and every bit the junior lawyer.

"Exactly what were those vulnerabilities?" Beck asked.

"Nothing exceptional for a man hiding his age. Just the basics—high blood pressure, high cholesterol, the onset of diabetes. He liked the image of a more robust, younger man. You may have noticed how he commanded the attention of everyone at the dinner table that night. He loved telling stories and having an audience. I think he feared losing all of that, especially if he showed any weakness."

So he was human after all, thought Beck.

"Why was a decoy hearse dispatched from the resort in the afternoon and Castiglia's body not removed until midnight?"

Kelly sat up. "How'd you know that?"

"I may be unemployed, but I'm still a reporter."

"Politics," he said.

"Politics? What does that mean?"

"The marshals arrived within the hour after Castiglia's body was found," Kelly said. "They were handling the investigation until the FBI barged in. Then it became a jurisdictional smackdown. Mix into that crazy salad the unwelcome arrival of the fourth estate—which immediately began asking impertinent questions—and you had a real cluster.

"Castiglia's body, meanwhile, was in the kitchen's walk-in refrigerator during all of this," Kelly continued. "The wait and cook staff weren't exactly serving lunch and dinner at this time. In fact, the whole resort had been pretty much shut down by then. Trowbridge, to say the least, was growing more and more pissed as the hours dragged on."

Beck watched Kelly closely. This was a story about nothing. *Is he stalling for something?*

"The decoy hearse?" Beck asked.

"Yes, well, you see, they wanted the media gone. Nearly all of them chased after the decoy—mainly the TV and cable people. A couple of smart print reporters stayed behind to question the authorities. At first the feds ignored them, but then they realized they needed to throw the reporters a bone or they would never leave. Finally, they answered a few questions and the remaining press left."

That seemed logical. "Why the long wait until midnight?"

"Oh, that," Kelly said. "We couldn't find another hearse."

"You're kidding."

"We were hours from anywhere, remember. We'd used the funeral home's only hearse. Another mortuary agreed to send a loaner if we sent them the body to embalm."

"Amazing." Beck shook his head.

"Capitalism at its best. The justice would have loved it. Yet, as it turned out, the marshals and the FBI decided Castiglia needed to be examined by the coroner in El Paso. So he didn't go straight to the funeral home after all."

Beck had just confirmed everything Nancy told him, but the coroner information was new. It was time to wrap this up.

"So what brought you to this firm?"

"They offered me a partnership."

Interesting. Kelly was important to the firm as Castiglia's former clerk and lapdog. Now that the chief justice was dead, Beck wondered if Kelly had any future here. Capitalism at its best, indeed.

"I guess it didn't hurt being friends with the chief justice of the Supreme Court."

"No, it apparently did not." Kelly's overstated grin spoke volumes.

Beck could tell he'd hit a vulnerable spot. Suddenly, he felt sorry for the new junior partner. Kelly was much like Castiglia, the notorious hugger. They both had a confident façade but appeared vulnerable beneath the surface. *They must teach bravado in law school,* he thought.

Beck wound up the conversation and Kelly walked him back to the floor lobby. They shook hands one last time and Beck headed for the elevators.

—⟋⟍—

Jackson Oliver's elegant frame leaned against Kelly's desk, arms folded across his chest. He was still wearing his suit jacket.

"You think he bought it?" Kelly asked his senior partner.

"I think so. The key is to get him to publish something. We need to put Castiglia's reputation into play as soon as possible."

"With Castiglia's conflicts of interest big enough to drive a tractor trailer through, I would think Mr. Rikki would run with the information."

"He'll have to check it out first," said Oliver. "That's what reporters do. He won't take your word for it. But it should be easy enough to corroborate. Then he'll either give it to the *Post-Examiner* or write it up for some other publication. Wherever he publishes it, we'll be able to track his connections. We'll know who his friends are. That could prove helpful. But that, of course, is only good until he finds another job in journalism."

"Do you think that's possible after being humiliated so recently with his own conflicts of interest?"

"He's still licking his wounds in the Bahamas with that girlfriend of his," Oliver said. "But he'll be back. They always come back. America loves redemption. In this town it usually takes a year of silent repentance to let a scandal die down. Then the guilty party slowly reemerges—publicly humbled—and rehab begins. Right now, Rikki is still radioactive. It will take some effort for him to rebuild his reputation. He doesn't have professional handlers to do it for him. We'll just have to make sure he never gets that far. We'll keep our eyes on him. But, for the moment, we need him to do what he does best—for him and for us."

Oliver smirked. Kelly did not feel his confidence. This type of hardball was new to him. He loved Chief Justice Castiglia and he was not sure he liked any of this.

10

In a taxi on his way back to Geneva's condo, Beck thought about what Kelly had said about conflicts of interest, which dredged up his own past. Now the reporter who had destroyed him was about to replace him at the *Post-Examiner*. How could his old managing editor do that to him? He'd been loyal to Bob Baker for nearly two decades and Baker had treated him like a son. Now Baker was going to hire the woman who broke the story about his conflict of interest.

He thought about that as he dialed Kerry Rabidan's cell. She answered on the second ring.

"I didn't expect to ever hear from you again," she said.

"Bygones."

"Beck, by the tone of your voice, I'm not detecting any real sentiments of forgiveness here."

"Kerry, I need a great investigator and outside of me, you're it."

"That sounds a little more like you. Thanks for the compliment. I think."

"You interested in a story about someone else's conflicts of interest besides my own?"

"I'm listening."

He told her about Castiglia's ties to the law firm and the owner of the resort.

"I think I can do something with that," she said.

"I know the *Post-Examiner* is working on it, so you need to work fast."

"So you're deliberately screwing your old newspaper in hopes I beat them to the story?"

"Those are your words. Not mine."

"Okay. If that's the way you want it."

"It is. And you didn't get this from me, okay?"

"Gotcha there. No problem."

He hung up. Beck knew she would attack the story just as she had when they worked together years ago at the *Post-Examiner*, before she was downsized and snatched up by the *News-Times*. They had slept together once after spending a month working on a big investigative story. They realized immediately they were not a match made in heaven. *More like a match made in hell*, he thought, as was proven years later.

Beck felt no guilt at screwing his old newspaper. Baker had seen to that. He understood Baker's need to let him go, but to consider hiring the woman who outed his affair with Geneva was too much.

But he did feel bad about Nancy—and Steve and Leslie. He just hoped Kerry published her story before they published theirs. Leaking it to Kerry was a gamble. He was relying on her dogged nature. He'd figure out some way to make it up to his colleagues at the *Post-Examiner*. But, right now, he was formulating a plan he hoped would break this case open.

—⁂—

Two days later a two-column headline above the fold of the *News-Times* screamed the late chief justice's conflicts of interest. The story was the main feature on the paper's website, too. Nothing yet had been published in the *Post-Examiner*. Rabidan had beaten the competition.

The wire services, Internet, television networks, and all-news and talk radio networks picked it up. "Fly Boy" and "Free Loader" dominated several headlines. It was a slow news day, so it was the lead story everywhere. And it reflected on the justice's character just as the eulogies praising his legacy were about to begin. It was another of those awkward Washington moments where the news media were called upon to solemnly balance the sober occasion of a high-profile funeral matinee with the tabloid headlines shouting out the deceased's questionable character.

Castiglia's daughter-in-law stood in Castiglia's front yard before the cameras and expressed outrage at the stories. It was all about his place in history now.

Beck felt a bit of relief for having kept Castiglia's libidinous proclivities out of the press. The chief justice's family had enough to deal with right now.

Beck also knew, no matter what path he followed investigating this story, he was going to suck up to Rabidan. She could prove useful, and right now he needed all the help he could get.

After reading her story, Beck began to wonder why Kevin Kelly was so willing to expose his own law firm's favors for Castiglia. It just seemed like Kelly was setting the firm up for a round of bad PR.

He thought about that for a long time. For every political action there was an equal and opposite reaction in the nation's capital. But the key was the motivation behind that action, something that wasn't always apparent. *What good*, he wondered, *could come out of this for a prestigious law firm like James Howell & Gordon?*

He started to laugh to himself. Of course. They didn't care about the public's reaction. The public didn't pay their outrageous hourly fees. But potential legal clients would see the firm's close relationship with the court as an asset they could exploit. If Trowbridge could do it, why couldn't they? Capitalism was all about money, and the court was all about determining winners and losers. Getting that edge to ensure being on the winning side was every capitalist's dream.

Only in Washington did you promote your sleazy side to attract new clients.

11

Castiglia's funeral was by invitation only and filled the Basilica of the National Shrine of the Immaculate Conception. Beck used his old press pass, which had yet to expire, to glide through security. The event's organizers had safely quarantined the scorned media bloodsuckers on a balcony far above the city's political gentry to ensure there would be only storytelling and no truth-seeking. Beck was ushered to the nosebleed section behind the television camera crews and ink-stained working stiffs dutifully playing the role of sardines. They even tended to smell the same under the hot television lights. The smell of cheap cologne and sweat in the standing-room-only section reminded him of a locker room. Only the occasional whiff of perfume improved the assault on his nostrils.

The Basilica held more than a thousand. The crowd skewed more Republican due to Castiglia's conservative jurisprudence, but Beck saw the Democratic leadership there too. Many attended just to be seen, no doubt, but Beck had read enough about Castiglia to know, outside of his legal opinions, he was adored by just about everyone who had ever met him.

Beck felt sad now, knowing he had missed his chance to get to know Castiglia. He wondered if he too would have liked him. He got a small taste of it the night they met at the party. Castiglia had greeted him like a long-lost son.

Castiglia was old-school Washington where pols would tear at each other for hours and then retire to a nearby Capitol Hill bar in the evening to trade gossip about their day. Today's Washington was occupied by a helicopter Congress. Members dropped in for three days of votes and campaign fundraising, and then zoomed back to their districts or states for long weekends of backslapping. It was all about reelection, not representation. Fewer politicians moved their families to Washington and got acquainted with their colleagues—especially colleagues from the other side of the aisle. *A terrible rat race,* Beck thought.

He wondered about Kelly. The way Kelly had described his relationship with Castiglia, you would think he'd be seated with the family. Beck kept looking for him. It was difficult to find anyone in the sea of dark suits and black dresses. Finally, he spied Kelly about ten rows back, next to the middle aisle. Beck couldn't tell who was sitting with the young lawyer.

Beck scanned the rest of the National Shrine. Vice President Daniel Fahy had just arrived through a side door and was glad-handing everyone in sight, even with the security bubble surrounding him. Beck and Fahy had a relationship, strained though it was. They used each other from time to time.

Politicians made an art of using journalists to further their causes. Beck had heard enough grousing at the National Press Club bar to know it happened on a daily basis. Journalists, in many ways, were enablers. They were a cog in a system that kept Washington functioning. Beck suspected he was culpable, probably on more than one occasion. He just didn't like to admit it.

The music swelled and a cortege of robes strolled down the main aisle. The crowd stood and turned toward the procession leading the family. Beck saw Jackson Oliver standing with Kelly. *Lackey duty again? Or are they close?* Beck hadn't considered that. Both were in Texas at the same time. Both had moved to the same law firm. Beck's bullshit antenna engaged. He would have to be careful with Kelly. Maybe things weren't as they seemed.

Then he saw Oliver put his arm around Kelly. Even from his distant perch in the balcony, Kelly appeared stricken, his body shaking as the family walked down the aisle. A male family member stopped in the aisle and leaned awkwardly into the pew and around Oliver to give Kelly a hug and pat on the back as he passed. Perhaps there really was a strong connection between the junior lawyer and the deceased chief justice.

12

Back at Geneva's condo, Beck soaked his sore ribs in her hot tub. He had been in for about five minutes when Geneva climbed in across from him. He would never get accustomed to her beauty.

"What?" she asked.

"Honestly? I should be used to seeing you naked by now, but it still gives me a thrill."

Geneva smiled and slid next to him. "You say the nicest things." She nuzzled his cheek and kissed him. "How is your story—ah, investigation going?"

"Not sure what I have. Castiglia's got lots of conflicts of interest, and his so-called friends are trying to make him look bad by leaking every last questionable thing he ever did. I'm wondering if Jackson Oliver has something to do with this, but I have no evidence. I met with Kevin Kelly, the kid lawyer who flew around the country with Castiglia a lot. He was sitting next to Oliver at the funeral this morning. The two of them were also at the Texas resort. I don't believe in coincidence."

"Any idea what they were both doing there?" Geneva turned to him and placed his hand on her right breast.

"You're distracting me."

"I sure hope so." Geneva smiled into Beck's eyes.

"Where were we?"

"You were fondling me."

"You know what I mean."

They laughed together.

"You were musing about what both Kelly and Oliver were doing in Texas." Geneva looked away and skimmed her other hand across the water's agitated surface. "Anything to do with the prostitute? What's her name? Denise something?"

"She wasn't very cooperative. She adamantly denied even being at the resort."

"What if she's telling the truth?"

"She's lying. I saw her sitting at the table with Castiglia."

"You're sure?"

"Sure I'm sure. She wasn't thirty feet away. I'm not blind."

"Okay. Okay." Geneva raised her hands in mock surrender. "I'm just trying to come up with some explanation for her behavior."

"Sorry. Didn't mean to jump on you. I'm frustrated. I can't see where to go with this. I've got to think it through."

"Then I'll leave you in peace to think about it." Geneva rose and Beck watched her sway over to the pool and dive in. She began swimming laps. When they were back in Abaco, she would swim a hundred yards out into the ocean each morning. He was always impressed by how strong she was and how she seemed to slice effortlessly through the waves.

Beck closed his eyes and wondered if life could get any better than this. He began to stretch and was immediately brought back to reality. *God,* he lamented, *when will these damned ribs heal?*

He considered what Geneva had said. Maybe it made sense to give Denise Fiori another try. Throughout his career, he'd worn down others into cooperating. It just took time for them to trust him. He'd met her at an awkward moment. Perhaps he should try again, though he didn't look forward to flying back to Texas.

What else can I do with Kelly? And what about Oliver? Should I confront either of them? But with what? Suspicions? He'd caught Oliver sneaking into Castiglia's room. *But really, what does that prove? So he had a key. So what?*

No. He was at a dead end.

Then he thought of the water sample he had taken from Castiglia's sleep apnea machine. He needed to have it tested.

Beck stepped gently out of the tub—mindful of his ribs—and toweled off. He walked into the condo while Geneva continued her laps. He was hit with a blast of air conditioning. He sat down at his laptop and began searching for local laboratories. He found several and after five phone calls he decided on one. He told the lab he would be by in an hour with his sample. Beck dressed, struggling to minimize the pain of putting on his shirt. He walked out to the pool to tell Geneva where he was going and was out the door.

—m—

The Uber driver dropped him in front of the lab. Inside, he asked to speak to the technician he had talked with over the phone.

The tech looked at his container. "Mouthwash? It could kill bacteria."

"I rinsed it pretty thoroughly before I grabbed my sample."

"You said it's from a well at your farm?"

"Yes. It's an old dilapidated place that hasn't been used for years. I just bought it and I want to make sure the water's safe to drink. I heard a rumor from a neighbor that it might not be drinkable from ground pollution and illegal dumping in the area. So I want you to check for toxins. I'm into health and organic food."

"We have some basic tests for well water," the tech said. "We do them all the time. They cover just about everything—at least everything you'd be worried about."

He said it would take a few days at a minimum and much longer for some tests. It would cost several hundred dollars. Beck signed some paperwork and handed him his credit card.

13

"I think it's time you took Castiglia's place," President Michael Harvey said. He was sitting in the Oval Office with his predecessor, William Croom. The former president was a Democrat, and Harvey was a Republican, but they had been friends for years. Harvey thought it ironic how just nine months earlier he was Croom's guest in this office. Now their roles were reversed.

Croom had served two terms and sat quietly, avoiding the media, while his friend, Harvey, trounced Croom's candidate in last year's election.

"You sure you can pull this off?" Croom asked.

"You've got a lot of goodwill on Capitol Hill. You went out with nearly a 60 percent approval rating. Who can argue with that?"

"Yeah, but your party is in power now, not mine."

"Let me worry about them. They know you, worked closely with you, and they won't forget that. Many Republicans like you. I need a moderate to replace Castiglia. He was way too much the strict constitutionalist—and I'm a conservative. We need to move this town closer to the middle again. No more extremes. Both parties are getting beat up for not cooperating. We need to change that. Your approval as chief justice will be the beginning. I spent a lot of years in the Senate, and I can call in a lot of chits. We'll make this work. If not, the Senate will have the sorest set of balls in America. There won't be a road built, a post office constructed, or any other pork barrel showing up in their states or districts for years. I'll get what I want."

"I'm not so sure I want to get mauled on this one." Croom fidgeted in his chair on the other side of Harvey's desk. "I've spent years and a lot of political capital building my reputation. I don't need my legacy tarnished for the history books."

"Don't you worry. I've already made some calls," the president said. "I've got assurances from the leadership on both sides that even if things go awry, your reputation will not be touched. I think you've got better than a fifty-fifty chance at the moment, and I haven't even begun to call in favors. I'll announce your nomination to the public tomorrow, and we'll set up a Senate listening tour over the next few weeks."

"If you pull this off—"

They both nodded in agreement.

"Come with me to the balcony. I think I owe you a Cuban." They both laughed. It had been their tradition during the eight years Croom was in the Oval Office to meet for a Cuban cigar on the Truman Balcony.

Long ago, Harvey's then-wife, Geneva Kemper, had told him Croom had confided in her how much he liked her husband. When they split up, Croom had called Harvey to comfort him. Harvey hadn't forgotten.

The Secret Service scurried when Harvey told an aide he and Croom were going to sit on the balcony.

"Mind if the vice president joins us?" Harvey asked.

"Not at all. Haven't seen Dan for a while."

Harvey signaled an aide to contact the veep while POTUS and the former president strolled to the balcony. When they arrived, a closed humidor of cigars awaited. They lit up and relaxed on comfortable rattan chairs.

"You really think this will work?" Croom asked. "You know, we could literally change the course of history."

"That's the idea." Harvey said. "It's exactly what I have in mind. We must start thinking big."

"You've got the right man in place to do it," Croom said. He looked over at the door as Vice President Daniel Fahy joined them. "Speak of the devil."

Fahy went to the humidor for a cigar. He lit up and sat on the other side of Croom.

"I've been on the phone to the Senate majority whip," Fahy said. "He's finally on board after we talked about his behavior last year with those two Senate pages."

"It always helps to have an ace in the hole," said Harvey.

"And it helps even more if the whip puts his ace in more than one," Fahy said.

They all laughed.

Harvey was eager to put Croom on the court. It would be the linchpin in their larger plan.

"No problems having a moderate replace a conservative on the court?" Croom asked.

"Sure there are," Fahy said. "But you're a conservative moderate—at least that's what I'm selling on the Hill. That's what you're going to be selling during your confirmation hearings. And since you're an ex-president and a friend to many on the Senate Judiciary Committee, those hearings won't be very tough. You've got a lock on the Dems. You need a little more than a dozen Republicans to get the nomination."

Fahy waved his cigar dismissively in the air. The smoke drew bands of blue around his face and shoulders. "We know some will squawk. We'll just figure out how to squelch any protest when it comes. I've got an entire quick-response team in place to tamp down any messy issues."

"So let's pretend this goes as easy as we hope," said Harvey. "Let's look at the next phase."

He loved where this was going. It was all so deviously clever and yet good for the country.

"That would be?" Croom asked. He puffed on his cigar, his white mustache filtering the smoke.

Harvey turned to Fahy. "You haven't told him yet?"

"I thought I'd leave that to you," the vice president replied.

14

The more Beck thought about it, the more he liked the idea of trying to interview Denise Fiori again. He made arrangements to fly back to Texas— commercial this time. *And what about that corporate jet Geneva hired to fly me to Washington?* He needed to ask her about that. She said she would explain and she'd been avoiding it.

After seeing her penthouse with the pool, the patio and hot tub, he realized she was a lot wealthier than he had imagined. This was real money. He'd only seen her place in the Bahamas. It was nice, maybe cost a few million. But also owning a penthouse in the heart of the nation's capital took super big bucks. This was way beyond the reach of a mere well-paid lobbyist. She must have gotten one whopping divorce settlement or scored really big on Wall Street.

Beck had been spending so much time running down leads and nursing his ribs that he hadn't thought much about Geneva's bank account. Actually, he had been enjoying his life with her so much he frankly didn't want to deal with it. *And we're in a relationship that hasn't lasted a year yet, so how much of this is really my business?* Even though they were close, he still felt some distance. Perhaps it was his fault. His history of failed relationships with the opposite sex was telling.

One thing he liked about Geneva was how she didn't flaunt her wealth. She was comfortable, not ostentatious. It was just there and made their lives easier, but it didn't define her. She didn't spend extravagantly. Not on jewelry or clothes. She was no fashion plate, but she was fashionable. She dressed tastefully—the few times she actually dressed.

He hadn't grown up in the opulence that now encompassed him. His career had kept him comfortable. But Beck had a nest egg thanks to his bestselling books, not his old job as a reporter for the *Post-Examiner*.

Geneva was the daughter of a government spook. Her dad was an embassy employee and she suspected he was an undercover agent for the government. Civil servants usually didn't leave their kids big inheritances. *Geneva earned her money*, Beck reasoned.

They really needed to talk.

Beck realized he hadn't been himself. The almost constant pain from his busted ribs commanded so much of his attention he wasn't concentrating on the task at hand. It was time to get back on board. He needed to mentally recuperate. He worried that could take longer than his ribs.

He'd never been mugged before. Now, he was beginning to understand how unsettling it could be. His space had been invaded. He'd lost complete control. As a journalist, he'd always felt in charge, though maybe that was a delusion. Still, he knew it wasn't the story but rather the hunt that thrilled him because he was in control of the narrative.

The french doors opened behind him and Geneva emerged carrying a towel and wearing a wide-brimmed, straw hat, shades, sandals—and nothing else. She placed the towel on the lounge chair next to him and sat down in the shade.

"How are you feeling?" she asked.

"Confused."

"Oh?"

"About all of this." Beck swept his hand across the view of the pool. "I never realized you had so much money. You've told me about your family. Unless there was a rich uncle somewhere, I don't think you inherited this."

Geneva gazed silently straight ahead, hiding behind her dark sunglasses. Then she sat up straight in the lounge chair and swung her legs around, facing him.

"Beck, I haven't been totally honest with you." She removed her glasses and held his gaze. "I haven't lied to you directly, but I guess I have by omission."

Beck sat silently.

What is this all about?

Geneva seemed to be struggling to utter the proper words. "I stole it."

"You what?"

"I had a good salary, but not one that could afford this. Harv's and my lifestyle—the political thing in this town—required nearly all of our money. You have to buy your way to power in this city, one way or the other. The parties, the charities, the dinners, the nightly fundraisers—you know the bit. I wanted out. I just got sick of the whole damned hypocrisy. But I couldn't afford to leave. So I created an insider trading scheme, where I was the insider."

"You traded stock in your old employer, Serodynne?" Beck was dumbfounded. She was admitting to a crime.

"Yes. I set up this plan with an investment banker in New York and I made enough money to retire for good."

"You're not afraid of getting caught?"

"You're kidding, right?"

"Dead serious."

"Of course not. I was the wife of a US senator at the time. Anything I did, we did; it was perfectly legal even if he didn't know about it. Insider trading is against the law for everyone but members of Congress. Gosh, I thought you were going to chastise me for my deceitful behavior."

"That's next."

"I'm sorry. I should have told you long ago." She wrinkled her brow, seeking forgiveness.

"And you timed your trades based on my news stories dealing with Serodynne, which you knew about before the general public?"

"No. Well, maybe. Actually, I suppose yes is the proper answer." She bit her lip.

"So you were using me."

"I suppose I was. But that was before I fell for you. I never intended to use you. I should have told you what I was up to, but you were a journalist.

I didn't know you then. And, frankly, I was falling for you, and I didn't want to destroy what we had. I feared because you're a good man you would have totally disapproved of me and dumped me. I didn't know how to tell you then, and I don't really know how to explain it to you even now. This scares me. I don't want this to come between us."

Beck was burning inside. The woman he had fallen for had an ulterior motive for their relationship. They had been living a lie.

Now it was Beck's turn to look away. "Was our relationship based on you enriching yourself? Is that all this was to you?" He turned back to her for an answer.

"No, Beck. I love you. I admit I never intended to—I didn't want to—but as I got to know you, I came under your spell. I'm mad about you."

"I thought you were different from everyone else in this town." Beck grew enraged.

"Does it matter how two people met? Even if my intentions weren't honorable? I never dreamed I'd fall for you, but I did and I don't regret it for a minute."

"I don't know what to think."

"Beck, please don't judge my original intentions. Judge me now—us now. Plenty of people start off as adversaries because they don't know each other."

She was pleading, yet he didn't feel a thing for her at the moment.

"Maybe I can live with that. I don't know. But it's this devious side of your personality I never recognized."

"I'd like to think 'desperate,'" she said. "I was desperate to leave all of Washington's pseudo-jingoism behind me, and I would have done almost anything to get out. Yes, even something as unethical as insider trading. I guess Washington has rubbed off on me more than I'm willing to admit."

"I can see that. You live in this rathole long enough you start behaving like the other vermin. But I wonder about me. How I could have been so easily deceived? How did I miss it?"

"Perhaps you fell for me too?" Dread stretched across her face. "I hope I turned your head a little."

Beck saw the pain in her expression. Right now, he didn't know what to think. *Yes, I might be in love, but with whom?* Everything he appreciated about his relationship with her just became a giant question mark. Another part of him finally ached more than his ribs.

He stood, completely naked like her. He had reluctantly accommodated her apparel-free lifestyle—a show of solidarity for what he thought was their deepening relationship. He walked away and entered the condo without saying a word. He walked into the bathroom and took a long hot shower to wash away his disgust.

15

Jackson Oliver considered his next move as he walked the familiar corridors. Kelly had done well, luring Rikki into the smear about Castiglia. And he was right; Rikki had gotten the story published. But Oliver thought it curious who published it—the reporter at the rival paper who had destroyed Rikki's reputation. He wondered if Rikki's old newspaper refused to run it.

Whatever motivated Rikki at this point didn't matter. Oliver was happy. The story had triggered small rumblings about Castiglia's ethics. That would make it easier for Oliver's plan to work. The deceased chief justice would no longer be eulogized as an uncompromised conservative. He was a flawed man like everyone else. That would make an easier path to confirm the next chief justice.

Oliver wondered why Castiglia's extracurricular love life was not disclosed. Had Rikki kept that to himself or was the newspaper too prudish to publish it? Oliver decided to keep that in his back pocket if needed later. Right now, things were going so well he decided not to stir the pot.

The secret plan to rid the court of the extremist justice and replace him with a moderate was working. They needed just one vote to shift the court's majority and steer it on a more moderate course. The Judiciary Committee would be too embarrassed to question former President Croom's squeaky-clean moderate credentials with the Castiglia scandal hanging in the air. It was brilliant. They had tarnished Castiglia's reputation without ever questioning his brilliance or conservative credentials. It was about imagery, not jurisprudence.

Oliver had played his role well for his old boss and President Harvey's Supreme Court nominee. He was the setup man. This phase of his role was now over. It would be for others to steer Croom's confirmation through the Senate.

Oliver waved to the security guard on the second floor of the Old Executive Office Building next to the White House. He was just another familiar face to the Secret Service. He had been down these aging halls for nearly the entire Croom presidency, serving as one of Croom's chief legal advisers before returning to the Justice Department. An elevator trip brought him to the right floor, and a secretary showed him into the office where he sat on a couch alone. Waiting.

A side door swung wide with a Secret Service agent holding it open.

"Mr. Vice President," said Oliver, rising to greet him.

"Jackson, how are you?" replied Dan Fahy.

Oliver knew the familiarity was intentional. Until last year, Fahy had been working for him at the Justice Department. Oliver had tried to block Fahy's advancement. Now the tables were turned. *What was that old saw about climbing the political ladder? Be careful whose ass you kick on the way up because it may be the same one you have to kiss on the way back down.* Oliver was now kissing the backside of that equation.

They exchanged uncomfortable glances.

"Well," said Fahy.

"Yes, well, we've started things in motion," Oliver replied. "How long before the next shoe drops?"

"That will depend on the FBI," said Fahy. "But the new director assured me there would be something happening this week. Good job on the story in the *News-Times.* How'd you do it?"

"That reporter—or, I should say, former reporter—Beck Rikki. We gave it to him, and he apparently leaked it to a rival reporter, Kerry Rabidan, the one who destroyed his reputation."

"Funny how things go," Fahy said. "You never really know who's working for you and who's working against you around here."

Oliver smiled, not taking the bait. "Allies, then enemies, then allies again. You just can't take it personally if you want to be successful."

"Exactly." Fahy pursed his lips.

—⁓—

Oliver left and the veep immediately called the private line of FBI Director Patrick McCauley. McCauley owed his job to Fahy, and Fahy's constant attention ensured McCauley would never forget.

"How is everything on the Castiglia investigation?" Fahy asked.

"We turned everything over to the attorney general yesterday. It's pretty cut and dried. They're making an arrest tomorrow and will announce it the next day."

"That's fast."

"Believe it or not, sometimes we actually can move quickly."

—⁓—

Kevin Kelly arrived early at his office, wanting to prepare a brief for one of the senior partners, who had an upcoming case before the Supreme Court. The partner had wanted it on his desk in two days. Kelly was perusing files when his secretary called, saying the FBI wanted to speak with him.

About time. They were sure dragging their feet on the Castiglia case.

The door opened and three agents entered.

"Kevin Kelly?" one of the agents asked.

"Yes. Come in."

"We're not here for a social visit."

"Well, I assumed not."

"Kevin Kelly. You're under arrest for the murder of Chief Justice Nino Castiglia."

"What? Are you crazy? What are you talking about? This is all wrong. You don't get it."

"Hands behind your back please, sir."

Kelly left his plush office in handcuffs.

16

After he showered, Beck took some pain meds and lay down to think about his future with Geneva. Eleven drug-infused hours later, he awoke, groggy. The pain—physical and emotional—was so bad he had taken two pills. He grabbed the prescription bottle, trying to focus on the label. It said no more than one pill daily. Now he understood why.

His cell phone rumbled on the bedside table. Beck looked around. No Geneva. Her side of the bed had not been disturbed.

He picked up the phone. It was the young lawyer, Kevin Kelly.

"I need your help. Can we meet?"

"What's up?"

"I've been arrested. They think I killed Castiglia."

"What?"

"I loved that man."

"What was your arrest based on?"

"My fingerprints are all over his CPAP machine. The machine was full of poison. All I did was set up the machine. I never poisoned him."

Oh Jesus, thought Beck. *I'm dealing with a murderer.*

"I need a top investigator. I'll pay you anything you ask. I can't trust the FBI. I know I'm innocent and look what they did to me. You're the only one I know who isn't part of the system."

Beck wasn't used to compliments from lawyers. And he had been an *investigative* reporter. He was intrigued.

"You home?"

"Yeah. I made bail."

"I thought there was no bail in murder cases."

"This is federal court, and my law firm, as you know, is well-connected."

"Okay. I'll see you at your office this afternoon." He hung up and searched the penthouse. Geneva was nowhere to be found.

—w—

Kelly chose one of the firm's senior partners, Charles Curtiss, to defend him. Beck knew Curtiss from work he'd done for *The Post-Examiner*. Curtiss also taught some evenings at Georgetown Law School, which Beck suspected kept his name on the lips of the young graduates and gave him the pick of the litter when they were scouting for associates' jobs.

Curtiss was not only a big man, probably weighing more than three hundred pounds, but also a big name in town, known for his connections.

It had been about four hours since Kelly's call. Now the three of them were meeting in Curtiss's office.

Curtiss flipped a folder to Beck. "The attorney general's office has given us copies of all of their investigative files for this case as they are required to by law. These are the toxicology reports from the lab about the poison. Something I can't even pronounce. I looked it up. It's pretty deadly stuff. Traces were found in the water compartment of the CPAP sleep apnea machine on Castiglia's bedside table. My reading says the poison causes convulsions. He must have been in the middle of a spasm and ripped the device off of his face. He was found on his back but not attached to the device."

"Not a nice way to go," said Beck.

"Not a way I'd like to leave this world," Curtiss said.

They looked at Kelly, who said nothing.

Curtiss tossed another file. "Here are the crime scene photos. You were there, correct, Mr. Rikki?"

"I was."

"Good. Look these over carefully. See if anything jumps out at you." Curtiss stroked his white walrus mustache. "Oh, and here's another file. Seems Castiglia and his lady friend took a few selfies that night. The FBI pulled these from Castiglia's phone. Nice-looking lady. She's got, uh"—he paused, taking Beck's "guy" temperature—"quite a pair." Curtiss smiled.

Beck reciprocated to assure him they were fellow cave dwellers.

"Why is the prosecution being so cooperative?" Beck asked.

"Normally, they'd hem and haw for months to the point we'd be tempted to file a motion for a bill of particulars. But, well, you might say this firm carries a little weight in this town." He grabbed his giant gut and smiled at Beck. "Seeing as the government wants a quick disposition of this case, I persuaded them to cooperate from the get-go." Curtiss seemed pleased with himself.

In contrast, Kelly sat expressionless. It was as if he were in another place. Beck wondered how it must feel to be charged with murder. He also wondered if Kelly was guilty.

"So, right now," said Curtiss, "the case is all circumstantial. But the fingerprint evidence is pretty damning. It's not fatal. We can certainly explain it away. But we need to find something to knock down the government's case. I don't want this to ever go to trial. We either prove our client not guilty in the near future, or we settle with the government. Last thing you need, Mr. Kelly"—he looked at Kevin—"is a show trial. If you ever want to practice law again, we need to find clear evidence you didn't do this. If we go to trial, the public will convict you even if the court doesn't. It will be a media circus, and the odds of you working in this town again are slim to none."

Kelly held his head in his hands. "I can't believe this is happening. All I did was help the man. I didn't kill him."

"Problem is," said Curtiss, "the media mavens are now questioning Castiglia's ethics, which makes anyone close to him guilty by association. At best, the public will see you—and the rest of the firm, quite frankly—as an enabler of unethical conduct. At worst, you're viewed as a murderer. We need to control this."

He turned toward Beck. "If there is any evidence out there to prove our client's innocence, we need to find it and fast."

Beck shook his head. This felt weird. He'd been a newsman pledged to bring dark secrets to light his entire career. Now he was working as an investigator for a major Washington law firm to find facts that might bury the truth.

"Okay, we're done here," said Curtiss. "Mr. Rikki, call me if you find anything. I'll be drafting motions and trying to keep as much of this as possible out of my other client's newspaper."

Good luck with that, thought Beck. How ironic. One minute Curtiss was defending Beck's former employer when someone threatened a libel suit, and in the next he was trying to undermine it. *Lawyers are nothing but corporate sluts*, he reminded himself.

17

When Beck returned to the condo with his satchel of files, he found Geneva on the couch reading. She was wearing a T-shirt and shorts.

"Are we speaking?" she asked.

"I don't know," Beck said. "I'm still pretty disturbed about our conversation."

She came up to him and pressed her soft body against him, wrapping her arms around him, pinning his arms to his side. She kissed him, but he did not kiss her back. Then tears began to flow. *Definitely not fair,* thought Beck.

Beck dropped his satchel of documents on the floor and embraced her. He felt the pain of his ribs but held her anyway. He wasn't sure how he felt about Geneva's confession. He returned her kiss. Maybe that answered the question. They hugged and she continued to weep, her head resting gently against his chest.

"I need you to forgive me and accept me," she said.

Beck lifted her chin and smiled at her. "Me too."

If they were going to continue, he knew he must forgive her. He'd try. They hugged for several minutes until he couldn't take the pain in his side any longer.

"My ribs," he said, pushing back.

"Oh, Beck. I'm sorry. I was—"

"It's okay. Relax."

Beck could tell she was restless—like she didn't know what to do. It was like she felt she couldn't do anything right at the moment.

"Would you do me a favor?" he asked.

"Anything, hon."

"Help me into the hot tub. My ribs are killing me."

She helped him strip in the middle of the living room and she held his arm as he stepped in, flipped the jets switch and settled into the hot, churning water. The scent of chlorine exploded from the rumbling bubbles.

"Can I get you something to drink?" Geneva asked over the din.

"No. I think I just need to soak."

"May I join you?"

What Beck really needed was a soak in solitude to rehab his ribs and his psyche and mull over Kelly's case. Geneva was a beautiful distraction. But she needed this right now as much as he needed his alone time.

"Sure," he said.

She dropped her clothes on the patio and climbed in beside him. He realized he couldn't shake it. He was still angry with her but was surprised that insider trading didn't really bother him that much. She had used him and deceived him, and that was hard to forgive. He still struggled to understand how he felt.

—◊—

Beck's sides felt better an hour later. The hot tub only relaxed his muscles and probably didn't do anything for his broken ribs, but, whatever it did for him, the pain was gone.

For now.

He was sitting at Geneva's desk looking over the Kelly files. They were all pretty much the same photos Beck had taken with his cell phone—various angles of the room—with the exception of no dead chief justice in the bed since his body had been removed before the feds arrived. Beck opened the folder with the telephone records—a list of calls made from Castiglia's phone for an entire week before his death with identities for each call. Beck ran his fingers down the list of names. Nothing stood out, but then he didn't know what he was looking for. There was a call to Kelly the day before the flight to Texas. No doubt checking on their itinerary. A man in Castiglia's position wouldn't bother with such mundane daily life chores.

Beck flipped over the spreadsheet of numbers and names, and under it was the first of many eight-by-ten glossy photos lifted from the chief justice's cell phone by the FBI. It was a close-up of Castiglia from the chest up, smiling at the camera. He flipped to the next—a selfie of Denise with her arm extended toward the camera. She must have been on top of him. It was from the neck up. A third photo showed them in bed; Denise was in the foreground. Beck could see her arm extended. She obviously was holding the phone. The photo included both of them naked from the waist up.

Beck wondered about her. In some aspects, she was like Geneva. She had no compunction about her own nudity. The difference was Denise would sleep with a man for money. But in a way, Geneva *had* slept with him for money. He didn't want to draw that comparison, but it made him wonder again just who he was sleeping with. After all, last year she'd enriched herself by using her insider knowledge of his upcoming stories to make stock trades before the general public had a chance.

He looked closer at Denise. Her breasts were about the same size as Geneva's, but her nipples were smaller, lighter in color. They were—

Beck stopped and looked at the picture again. There was a small mole under her left breast, maybe a half an inch in diameter. Oddly, its outline resembled the Capitol dome. He was sure there was no mole when he had met her the day after Castiglia died. Her robe had gaped open when he met her at her apartment door. And he was a guy, for Chrissakes, who had a clear, if brief, view of a beautiful woman's breasts.

"Nice," Geneva said, looking over his shoulder. "You into dirty pictures now? I guess I'm not the only one with secrets."

"These are the prosecutor's photos of the prostitute. Apparently she and the chief justice were into selfies that night."

"Uh, may I?" She stepped around and motioned to look at the selfie photo.

He handed it to her.

"I can see what you see in her."

"Oh, stop."

"The dome thingy?"

"I was trying to figure that out. It's either a mole or a tattoo."

"Oh, so this is purely professional. A mole exam. Like a doctor. Hmmm. Nothing to do with her breasts?"

"This *is* professional. Thanks for nothing," Beck said. He shook his head.

"Oh, that's not nothing. That's a pair of something." Geneva gave him a very broad smirk while handing back the photo.

And now he was about to head back to El Paso to try to interview Denise again—mole and all.

When Beck returned from El Paso, he might have to do some damage control. There appeared to be a considerable amount of insecurity on both sides of their relationship.

18

Beck checked into a hotel in another section of El Paso, far from his previous stay. He'd done his homework and paid a little more to stay in a nicer neighborhood. He drove across town to Denise's apartment and parked a half block away.

He climbed the steps and rang her bell again, not knowing just what he would say. He heard footsteps and then saw a shadow in the peephole in her door. The doorknob creaked, and then there was a moment of hesitation. The door opened a crack until the safety chain was taut.

"I thought I told you I wasn't interested in talking to you," she said.

Beck could see only a portion of her face, but he could tell she was fully clothed this time.

"I just need a few minutes of your time. You may be in trouble, and I'd like to help."

"Really? What kind of trouble?"

He used a line he'd thought up during his flight. "The feds are going to show up at your door any day now. They think you played a part in Chief Justice Nino Castiglia's murder."

A groan came from her side of the door. He must have hit the mark. Then more silence.

"Please, I'm only here to help and find the truth."

She disappeared behind the partially opened door. It shoved close. *Good*, thought Beck, *she's going to open up and I can finally speak with her.* He waited to hear the chain scrape against the door and for the latch to click.

Nothing.

He knocked again. Nothing.

He pounded.

Nothing.

Damn it. He'd spooked her. This woman was tougher than he thought. After waiting five minutes, hoping she would reconsider, he left. He walked back down the block, sat in his rental car, and thought about what had just not happened.

He was sure he rattled her. But he wasn't expecting this reaction. He was sure the ploy would work. Obviously, he wasn't convincing enough. Dumb on his part. He should have crafted a better plan.

Prostitution, no doubt, had hardened her to life's challenges. He hadn't considered that. He was looking at this through his own eyes. He was used to sophisticated, self-serving Washington sources. He was beyond the Beltway now. He was dealing with a tough cookie who knew how to make her own way in the world. No doubt she didn't trust authority, and Beck must have represented that to her. He needed to figure out how to convince her he was really on her side—even if he wasn't. He was engaged in the hunt again, the thrill that energized him.

Just then, he saw her in his rearview mirror emerging from her apartment building. He watched her swaying along the sidewalk in her tight jeans, a large purse slung over her shoulder and bouncing off her hip. The motion was mesmerizing.

She opened the door of a silver Toyota 4Runner, casually tossed her purse across the front seat and then extended a long, lean leg up into the car. Something stirred inside him.

Beck started his engine, did a U-turn and began to follow her. He kept a safe distance so he wouldn't be noticed, trying to stay a block or so behind.

Traffic was sparse and the 4Runner was tall enough he could easily let other cars between them and still kept her in view—until another, larger SUV pulled in front of him as they meandered through a series of residential neighborhoods. He feared he might lose her after all, but soon she turned right at an intersection and he was behind her again.

He pulled up behind her at the next stoplight. He realized what he had done and hoped she didn't check her mirror. Finally, the light changed. She pulled out and he backed off. *Did she spot me?* He needed to be more careful and pay closer attention. He'd let his nervous energy overwhelm him.

She drove for twenty minutes and then pulled up to the curb on a side street in a manicured residential neighborhood. She had stopped in front of a bungalow with a wraparound front and side porch. Beck parked a half block away and could see only Denise's outline sitting in her car probably waiting for someone. He looked back at the bungalow and made a mental note of the location. Another blonde appeared at the front door. She turned to lock it and then hustled down the steps to the 4Runner and got in. She was slender and wore a light jacket.

Denise pulled away from the curb. Beck had turned off his engine, fearful of drawing attention in a nice neighborhood. He cranked it and the car sputtered. He turned the key again. It whined. "Shit!" He banged on the steering wheel. *Calm down*, he told himself. He was in an unfamiliar rental car and he didn't want to flood the engine.

He cranked the key again, popped the car in gear and almost laid a patch of rubber. The 4Runner was two blocks away and Beck sped to catch up.

About ten blocks of turns later, the 4Runner pulled into a shopping center in front of a chain restaurant. Beck pulled into the parking lot just as the two blondes entered the front door. After waiting a few minutes, he decided to enter. *What do I have to lose at this point?*

He scanned the restaurant and saw her in a booth on the other side of the large U-shaped bar that took up the center of the room. He took a seat on the far side of the bar with a clear line of sight. The other blonde sat with her back to him. The two women engaged in an animated chat. He ordered a beer and sipped.

Denise looked around the room, and Beck froze, worried she'd seen him. But she kept talking as if she hadn't noticed.

She stood and headed to the ladies' room. Beck didn't pay much attention until she returned to the table, then he realized something was wrong. She was wearing a flowered skirt. When Denise had left the house, she was wearing a white blouse and tight blue jeans. *Did she change in the bathroom?* He looked at her companion, the one with her back to him. He could see her leg under the table. She was wearing jeans.

Beck walked deliberately over to the table. Denise looked up at him.

"Can I help you?" she asked.

"What's going—"

"Do I know you?"

"We just talked." Beck looked at her companion, then back at her. They were identical. The blond hair. The beautiful skin and face. The bodies matched perfectly.

"Cara, this is the man I was telling you about," said the companion, who had been facing away from Beck.

"You're not Denise," Beck said, looking at the blonde who had just returned to the table.

"I'm Denise," said the other woman. "The one you've been hassling."

"Sorry," he said to the woman he had been staring at for half an hour. "I mistook you for—"

"Me," Denise said. "It happens a lot. We're used to it."

"But—"

"Cara, as I was telling you, this rude man has been pounding on my door accusing me of killing a judge," Denise said.

Cara looked up at him. "I'm Cara Beverly. Denise Fiori is my sister. What do you want?"

"Look. I'm not trying to bother either of you. I'm investigating the death of Chief Justice Nino Castiglia."

"We had nothing to do with it," said Cara.

"You were there. You have a small mole under your left breast," he said, looking at Cara.

Cara looked back at him, shocked. "And how would you know that?"

"The same way the police do. You took a selfie that night with the chief justice while you were in bed with him. They took it from his phone during the investigation. If you haven't received a visit from the FBI yet, you soon will. My client is going on trial for murder—a murder he didn't commit, so he is likely to implicate anyone else he can to defend himself."

Beck could tell Cara was bristling, fighting to keep her calm.

"Sit," Cara ordered. She slid across the bench to give him room. "Now, what do you want?"

Beck turned to Cara. "So it was you and not your sister who was with Justice Castiglia that night?"

"Yes, yes, I was there. So what? When I left he was still alive."

"What time did you leave?"

"I guess around midnight. One, maybe. He was an old man. He didn't last long."

"How long were you there?"

"I think he was asleep by eleven or so. I napped for a short time, made sure he wasn't going to wake up again and need more servicing. Then I got up, showered and dressed."

Beck could tell Cara was uncomfortable talking in front of her sister, and Denise's expression made it clear she didn't relish what she was hearing. Cara looked like she was mustering her thoughts about what to say next.

"After I left the room I dropped the key in an envelope at the front desk for Mr. Oliver."

"Oliver?"

"Yes. He told me to be out of there before morning to avoid embarrassing the chief justice. I was supposed to leave the key in an envelope for him and there would be an envelope of cash for me at the desk. Which there was. Three thousand dollars plus five hundred for expenses. Now, are you satisfied?"

"Did Oliver hire you?"

"Uh . . . yes."

"How did he find you?"

"I've worked the resort before. Management knows me. I'm one of several girls they call to entertain their high rollers."

"If you were told to leave before dawn the next day to avoid embarrassment, why did you sit at the dinner table the night before with Castiglia?"

"I don't ask questions. I do as I'm told. I met Mr. Oliver before dinner, and he gave me a room key for the judge. He said the judge was probably napping after his long trip and I was to arouse him, if you know what I mean. I did, and afterward the judge insisted I join him for dinner. And then after dinner, well, I entertained the judge again."

"For an old man, he seemed to do pretty well."

She smirked. "I know what I'm doing."

In all of his years as a reporter, Beck had never interviewed a prostitute. Fellow reporters would tell him stories about the high-priced hookers the lobbyists hired to service the needs of their favorite congressmen. That's as close as Beck ever got to this world.

He found it interesting that Cara was so matter-of-fact about her work. Denise, however, was looking away across the room at the bar.

"Would you be willing to testify to Oliver's involvement?" Beck asked Cara.

"Involvement with what? All he did was hire me to have sex with the judge."

"Yeah, but I'm sure Kelly's lawyer would like you to tell that story in court."

"For a price."

"They can compel you to testify for nothing."

"Someone's going to cover my expenses."

"That can be arranged."

"I have expensive tastes."

Beck shook his head and tried not to smile. This hustler was already trying to shake him down.

Despite their identical good looks, Cara displayed a coarser pedigree. Yet she exhibited a degree of sophistication and class—a necessity, Beck figured, to entertain her wealthy clientele.

Beck honestly couldn't tell them apart. They wore their hair the same and even sounded nearly the same.

"You both have different last names. You married?"

"No. I was adopted," said Denise. "Cara lived with our biological mother, who told us years later she didn't have enough money to raise two kids. We didn't even know each other existed until I kept hearing stories of people seeing me on the other side of town. After so many sightings, I began to look myself. Eventually I stumbled upon Cara and my biological mother. Neither of us knew the truth. She finally told us. It was emotional for both of us." She grabbed her sister's hand across the table and they glanced at each other with knowing smiles.

"Our real mom was a lady of the evening," said Cara, swirling a tiny plastic straw in what appeared to be a gin and tonic. "I took up the family business. She died of AIDS years ago."

"And you, Denise?"

"I have an accounting practice here in town."

He turned back to Cara. "Is that really a mole or a tattoo under your breast?"

Cara smirked. "It's a mole," she said. "It was the only way our mother could tell us apart."

"Did you ever meet Kevin Kelly?"

"Yeah, the young guy sitting on the other side of the judge at dinner," Cara said. "I met him and overheard some of his conversation with the judge and others. But that was about it."

"What do you think happened?"

"Just what I read in the newspapers. He died of a heart attack that night."

"But he was alive before you left?"

"He was."

"So, you were the last person to see him alive."

Cara was quiet for a moment. "I guess I was. Hadn't thought about that."

"I was supposed to meet Chief Justice Castiglia the next morning for breakfast."

"You know, he did say he had an important breakfast meeting. So that was you?"

Beck nodded. "Did he tell you anything else?"

"Yeah, well, before our second round, he got quite chatty. Well, at least for a while. We both had our share of red wine. He actually was a very nice man. He wasn't trying to impress me at all. He seemed quite worried, though. It concerned his meeting with you, but he didn't explain, and I didn't ask questions."

"What did he talk about?"

"Oh, nothing you'd be interested in. Some of it was sexual, some about what he thought of Texas."

"Nothing about the reason he was there?"

"Hey, I had him naked on his back. I was the reason he was there at the time."

Beck noticed she was talking more deliberately, careful with every word.

"What time did you take the photos?" he asked.

"I don't know. You tell me. You've got them. Look up the time stamps."

Beck hadn't thought of that. The phone would record the day and time they were taken. He hadn't bothered to look. *Was Castiglia deliberately documenting he was still alive at a certain hour for some reason?* He must have suspected something. *But if he actually thought he was in some sort of danger, wouldn't he have done something more proactive?*

Cara excused herself to go to the ladies' room again. Beck slid out of the both to let her pass and flashed a questioning glance at Denise.

When Cara was out of earshot, Denise explained. "She's having tummy issues."

"I gather you don't really approve of your sister's line of work."

"Look, I didn't know her when we were young. I don't totally understand the hardships she faced as a child. I admit it was a shock to learn about my biological mother."

"How come Cara used your name at the resort?"

"Her credit wasn't always the best. You need a credit card to rent a car, get a room, so I gave her one of mine. Her finances are better now, so I can only guess she uses it out of habit. And I assume she sometimes wants to shield her identity to make her more difficult to trace."

"Well, I mean her no harm," said Beck. "I'm trying to find the truth, that's all. If she had nothing to do with Castiglia's death, then she has no worries from me."

Beck watched Denise's eyes shift to the side. He felt her hesitance. He knew that look. He'd seen it often, when a source was on the verge of telling him something important but needed a nudge to jump.

"If there's anything you can tell me to help me prove your sister's innocence, I'd be very grateful."

She looked at him in a long silence. Beck had learned to wait out people to the point of awkwardness so they felt pressure to fill the void.

"She said something about a group," Denise said. "No. That's not right. It was *The Circle*. I think she used it as a proper noun."

Beck maintained his silence.

"She told me in the car she overhead a conversation during cocktails between a couple of older men, expressing concern Castiglia might tell someone on the outside about something called the Circle. Maybe that's why you were there."

"That would make sense. That could be why he was killed before he could speak to me."

"Please don't let Cara know I told you. She'd get really angry."

"Not a word."

Cara returned to the table. "Not a word about what?"

"I haven't heard a word about the food here. I was just complaining to Denise that no waitress has come to our table since I arrived," Beck said.

"Maybe that has something to do with you." Cara flashed a wicked grin.

Beck gave her a sheepish look. Maybe it was time he left. He'd just gotten a half dozen leads to follow. He felt like he'd hit the jackpot.

19

Beck tried to book a flight that night, but there was nothing available. It was the next day before he could grab a middle seat back to DC. It made him appreciate Geneva's private jet. He needed to stop resenting her money—if that's what he was doing.

During his flight, Beck thought about the different power players who had wandered in for breakfast at the resort that morning when the chief justice was found dead. *Were they the so-called Circle Denise mentioned?* All the guests appeared to be powerful politicians, political activists and politically connected business people. *Is politics what they had in common? If so, what were they up to?*

But now his ribs were hurting again. He popped a pill and slept for the remainder of his flight.

—⚊—

He was up early the next day sitting on Geneva's penthouse patio and looking through the evidence files. He checked the time stamps on each selfie. They were taken later than he thought. Cara said Castiglia fell asleep around eleven, yet the photos were taken at a quarter past one.

An hour later Beck was sitting in a conference room at James Howell & Gordon with only Kevin Kelly sitting across the table. Curtiss was in court.

"We know now Chief Justice Castiglia was still alive until at least after one. What were you doing at that time?" he asked Kelly.

"I'm not sure. I drank a lot of wine at dinner. The party broke up around eleven. And then I went up to my room. I crashed. I was alone."

"So you have no alibi at the time of the murder."

Kelly looked at him with a half grin and shook his head. "If only I'd hired a prostitute for myself."

Lawyers, thought Beck. *Always the smart-ass. Always splitting hairs.*

"I interviewed the prostitute. She told me you did not hire her, but Jackson Oliver did. Why did you lie to me?"

Kelly said nothing. Beck was pissed. *So this is the way it's going to be.*

"You want my help keeping your ass out of prison, then don't lie to me again. Otherwise, I walk and you're on your own."

Kelly looked pained but resigned. "Oliver told me to tell you I had hired them."

"Oliver? Prostitutes?"

"Several were hired for the evening. I didn't know who hired them."

That fit with what Beck has seen at the party that night and what Cara had told him the day before. Several young beautiful women were scattered throughout the dining room hanging on the elbow of several older men that evening.

"Why did you agree to say you hired her?"

"Oliver wanted to discredit Castiglia. Something to do with helping his replacement's nomination process go smoother. When you called and wanted to meet with me, he suggested I tell you I had hired the prostitutes."

Interesting. Oliver was helping President Harvey replace Castiglia. He'd have to think about that one.

"You're a lawyer. You know not to lie to your lawyer, and in this case, your investigator."

"You weren't my investigator at the time," Kelly said. "I didn't even know I was a suspect when we first talked."

The rotund Curtiss walked into the room unannounced. "Gentlemen, I hope you're building me a case. What have we got?"

"I thought you were in court," Beck said.

"We do what we nearly always do. Settled an hour before. Saves time, money and my day," he replied. "Any progress?"

Beck explained that Oliver—not Kelly—had hired the prostitute.

Curtiss looked sternly at Kelly. "You didn't think to bring this up? That was a stupid move. I'm not sure of its importance to your case, but it's something. I'll have to talk with Oliver. Find out what he's up to."

Curtiss turned to Beck again, his hands folded across his wide girth as he sat at the end of the conference table. "Anything else?"

"I met with the prostitute who slept with Castiglia that night. She told me Oliver hired her. That's all I've come up with so far."

Curtiss looked at Kelly with contempt at the mention of Oliver.

Beck decided he wasn't ready to talk about the so-called Circle yet. He needed to learn more.

"Not much new to go on. Keep digging." Curtiss turned to Kelly. "Have you anything else to share with us that you may have so conveniently forgotten?"

Kelly sat up. "I've told you all I know."

"Thank you, defendant Kelly. You may leave us."

Kelly stepped out of the room.

"So, Mr. Rikki, now we have a client who isn't completely candid with us and you're not finding a lot of new evidence to clear his name. I don't have a good feeling about this. I fear we may have to plead this case unless you come up with something new—and soon."

"Settle? So soon?"

"Look at our situation. Since his arraignment the public has all but convicted him. The media have splashed his name and photo all over the country. The sooner we plead, the better deal we'll get from federal prosecutors. The longer this percolates, I fear the worse it is likely to get for Mr. Kelly. We might be able to get Kelly off with fifteen years right now. Maybe twenty at worst. Remember, this trial has national importance. The world will be watching. The feds will want Kelly's head."

"We're dealing with a man's life. The feds don't even have a motive. Shouldn't we be trying harder?"

"Well, of course. You keep digging. It's really on your back to find us some evidence. In the meantime, I will feel out the prosecutors. See what they say. We might be able to get a decent deal for our guy."

Beck said he would keep digging and got up, pushed open the heavy glass conference room door and left, feeling a little disgusted.

As he walked through the lobby, the receptionist stopped him. "Mr. Rikki, isn't it?"

"Yes."

"Accounting would like you to drop by. They need you to fill out some tax forms so we can pay you."

"Well, I certainly wouldn't want to hold up that process," Beck said.

The receptionist directed him down the hall to the third office on the left. When he was done giving his Social Security number and his Alexandria home address, he ventured back to the lobby—he spied Curtiss through the glass wall of the conference room, arms flailing and mouth wide open. Then he spied the object of his discontent. Jackson Oliver slouched at the conference table, looking like a naughty puppy cowering before his master. Wow, Curtiss must be giving Oliver hell for hiring the prostitute. Beck slipped by, not wanting to be seen. Curtiss was not only a big guy, it was clear he carried a lot of weight in the firm.

"What the hell are you doing?" raged Curtiss.

Jackson Oliver sat defiant, looking up at his senior partner. "I had to do something. I didn't want this pointing directly at the Renaissance Circle."

"You didn't think to check with me first? What if this backfires and leads right back to us? Are you a fool?"

"It won't. Kelly is the fool. Besides, we don't need him anymore. With

Castiglia dead, I figured he's expendable, and what better way to expend him? He's a convenient dupe, and we don't want the feds looking anywhere else, now do we? And we sure don't want Congress to hold up Croom's confirmation."

"By staining Castiglia's legacy?" Curtiss shook his head and leaned over the table, palms on the shiny surface, staring down Oliver.

"Precisely. It will pave the way for President Harvey's nominee. Croom's opposition won't have a legacy to wave in support of appointing another Castiglia. The best part is we still have the prostitute in our arsenal if we need her later to destroy Saint Castiglia's reputation."

"Don't ever, ever go off on your own again," Curtiss growled. "The Renaissance Circle has survived precisely because we agree on our decisions. We don't need some cowboy running about. You've put us in danger of exposure."

"No. Castiglia did that. I tried to protect us."

"Enough excuses. I've said my piece. Don't ever do something like this again." Curtiss stormed out of the room, never looking back.

Oliver stood, making sure no one watched from the hallway. He buttoned his suit jacket, straightened his tie and strode back to his office. *That Curtiss,* he thought. *He's probably never been involved in anything more significant than some corporate lawsuit. He knows nothing about making history.*

20

Beck tossed his satchel of files in the backseat of an Uber car as he climbed in just outside the law firm. He gave the driver Geneva's address and began recounting his investigation. There was the prostitute, the CPAP machine, Kelly, Oliver, the so-called Circle and even the missing US marshals. All question marks.

He couldn't put it together. He bounced it around his brain a few times but got nowhere. Beck gazed out the car window at the tourists on the Mall. *What did I do when I found myself in a spot like this, back in the good old days when I was actually writing stories?*

Exactly, he thought.

He told the Uber driver, "Take me to Virginia instead." Beck gave the driver the address of his condominium in Old Town Alexandria. It took about twenty minutes. He entered the elevator and pressed the button for the third floor. It had been months since he'd been home. It felt familiar, comfortable. He realized he'd missed his place.

He buried his key in the lock and the door sprang open. He looked around. The place smelled musty. He closed the door behind him, walked over to the balcony and flung open the french doors. Six months of stagnant air seemed to rush out all at once. He turned to his living room and Red.

"Hey, old girl, good to see you."

Red did not answer.

Beck smiled. "It's time to get to work."

He entered his sanctuary and began to discuss the facts of the case. He was glad he was alone. Only Geneva knew about Red—and his former newspaper editor Nancy Moore probably suspected something. He had begun talking to Red when he was struggling with his writing more than a decade ago. His writing style was clunky and often pinged by his editors—until he started reading his stories aloud to Red. When he talked to his chair, his words and ideas flowed.

He was so embarrassed by his new writing crutch that he didn't tell anyone. And then—for some reason he still couldn't explain—he had opened up to Geneva not long after they'd met. Instead of ridicule, she embraced him. He figured that was the moment he fell for her.

"So, Red, I have a case. No longer a story. You know. No job, at least no permanent job. Working for a lawyer and his client—one of the law firm's junior partners."

He laid out the facts for Red—Castiglia's death, Kelly's arrest, Cara's . . . what? As he spoke, Beck felt the logic fall into proper order. He loved that feeling. It was the same as writing a story where the facts needed an orderly flow to explain a complicated tale. And the holes needed to be filled. One by one.

He walked through everything and found numerous unanswered questions. Then he opened his satchel of files and pulled out the stack of selfies. *Is there anything in the photos that's different?* He grabbed Denise's photos—*oops, no, Denise is now Cara.* He had to keep them straight. Cara was the prostitute, Denise the accountant sister, and, for the moment at least, he was the only one who apparently knew that.

He looked at the photos. In the selfie shot at one fifteen in the morning, he saw the bedside table in the background. The CPAC machine was there along with Castiglia's glasses, a newspaper, a box of tissues and a water glass. The hose to the CPAP was folded neatly on the far side of the bedside table.

He clicked on his phone and heard his printer humming, printing out his own photos of the death scene. He compared Cara's selfies from Castiglia's phone with his own. Everything looked the same except for the location of the

CPAP hose and facemask, which were on the floor.

He noticed how different Castiglia looked. Alive one moment, all red-faced and happy with Cara, and then dead the next, his lifeless body now pale. Castiglia could have even been dead before Cara left. *How would she know, if she thought he was asleep and she was tiptoeing around trying not to wake him?*

He placed the pictures next to a third set taken by the FBI. He examined them closely. Nothing. He walked to the kitchen and opened his refrigerator. *Oh Jesus.* The smell. He had left so quickly six months ago; he hadn't bothered to empty it. Beck poured the sour milk down the disposal and threw everything into the trash, tied the plastic bag tightly and headed for the trash shoot in the hallway.

That chore done, he opened the fridge again and found six-month-old beer. He popped the top and took a swig. Tasted fine.

He walked back to the dining room and examined the photos again, this time looking at the FBI's fine craftsmanship first. Castiglia's body had been removed by the time the FBI arrived. Having just experienced his own refrigerator, Beck understood why.

There were photos of the crumpled, stained sheets turned back. He imagined Cara naked on the other side of the bed. He looked at the bedside table on her side. It was empty except for a reading lamp. The contrast nudged him. He looked for photos of the bedside table on Castiglia's side, which he remembered was cluttered. He found three different photos of the table—one by Cara, one he took, and the final photo taken sometime later by the FBI. He examined them closely. There it was—as clear as day. The water glass was missing in the FBI photo. By the time the agents had arrived, someone had taken it.

Beck looked back at his own photo to assure himself. *Yep.* The glass was still there when he was in the room early that morning. It was removed between the time he was there and when the US marshals and FBI arrived to document the death scene.

"Red, something's going on here." He turned toward his chair. "What do you think? Who would have moved it and why?"

Oliver had entered the room using a key he had in his pocket. Cara had told him she left Castiglia's room key at the front desk for Oliver. He must have removed it. *What about the glass is so important as to tamper with evidence?*

Fingerprints, thought Beck. The CPAC had Kelly's, but he'd bet the farm the water glass had someone else's. *The killer's, perhaps? Oliver's? And what does that mean? Could Oliver have poisoned Castiglia?* It was possible. He certainly had access. *But what was his motive?*

Beck turned to Red. "Poison was found in the CPAP machine. That implicates Kelly. Could they both have killed Castiglia? But if they were working together, why was Kelly taking the fall? Why would Kelly be willing to take the fall for Oliver?

"Red? Any answers?"

Could the two of them have an agreement on this? Or is Kelly being blindsided? Only after Beck had threatened to quit did Kelly admit it was really Oliver who hired Cara. Obviously, Oliver had pressured Kelly to keep his name out of it. Now Beck could see why.

He turned back to Red to continue their one-sided conversation. "Why the need for poison in Castiglia's drinking glass as well as his CPAP machine? Or was there?"

Beck remembered the water he was having tested. The results should be ready by now. "Red, I think I may have the answer."

He punched the lab's number into his cell. Yes, they said, the results were ready two days ago. "Sorry," the technician said. "We should have called but we've got a real backup right now."

Beck was on his way.

—⚏—

The technician explained what he had found in very technical terms. All Beck wanted to know was if there was any poison in the water that could kill someone. The short answer, the technician said, was no. But the well water certainly had its share of distinct properties, including chemicals to kill germs. In fact, he said, it appeared to have been treated in a water filtration plant.

"You sure you got this from a well on your farm?" the tech asked.

"Nothing that will harm anyone? Nothing in the water?" Beck asked.

"No."

"I can drink this?"

"Yep."

Beck didn't hear anything else after that. It was obvious what had happened. On his way back to his condo, he put it together. When Oliver entered Castiglia's room, he had taken the poisoned water in the glass, which Castiglia had obviously drunk, and poured what remained into the CPAP machine. This would make it appear Kelly had killed Castiglia. Oliver was framing Kelly.

He stepped into his condo and picked up the conversation again with Red. "Girl, it's all there. But what was Oliver's motive? He was trying to stop Castiglia from talking to me. That had to be it. And Castiglia, what was he going to tell me? He was going to talk about the secret society—the Circle—whatever it is. That has to be it, Red. Has to be.

"Castiglia was killed because he was going to tell me about this secret group. It was important enough he didn't care if he was seen in public with me. Actually, it appears he wanted to be seen. But why? Why flaunt that he was talking to a reporter? Why not just meet privately here in DC? For some reason, it was important to him that everyone know what he was doing. None of that makes sense. What motivated him to flaunt the fact he wanted to talk with me?"

Beck paced the floor. He sometimes thought he would wear a path in his oriental rug. "Red, was it arrogance? Did he think he was too powerful to be taken down? He didn't believe his life was in danger. Did he? Or maybe he thought no one knew who I was. Except, of course, both Oliver and Kelly did. They knew. Maybe when they saw me the night before, they figured they had no choice but to kill Castiglia."

Beck paced as he talked to Red. "That's it, girl. Maybe Castiglia didn't realize anyone knew who I was. No doubt he enjoyed the idea of talking right in front of them—about them—and they not realizing what he was doing. The ultimate chutzpah. He was a confident bastard. That's for sure.

"Or maybe it was just the opposite," Beck continued. "Maybe telling me was his insurance. Maybe he figured he was already in danger so his only safe route was an insurance policy. Me. That makes more sense. If I knew what he knew, they couldn't touch him without coming after me. And he knew, even in my unemployed state, I had access to the news media. My ultimate protection plan."

Beck continued pacing—his best method of thinking. "Red, now that I think about it, Castiglia was brilliant. No one there would recognize me except for Oliver and Kelly. So the others would see Castiglia talking to me at breakfast and not think much of it. Later, when this all came out publicly, they would realize who he was talking to. That would become the moment Castiglia became invincible. They wouldn't dare touch him, and he would have made a statement. He wasn't afraid of them. Just the opposite. They would now fear him. The man truly was brilliant to come up with such a scheme. But they got to him first."

Beck grabbed another six-month-old Corona Light from his fridge and returned to his pacing. He spilled some beer on his rug as he waved his arm talking out loud to himself. "Red, that means Oliver knows all about the Circle. And Kelly. Is he a member too? He must be. All those heavyweights at the resort. They all have to know. They left right away after Castiglia died to avoid embarrassing questions and to save their asses before the cops got there and started questioning people. That has to be it. They were leaving early to hide any links to the Circle. I need to figure out what the Circle is all about."

Beck stretched his arms and immediately regretted it. Pain shot through his ribs.

"Red. I need to call Curtiss and tell him Oliver's framing Kelly."

He dialed the lawyer's number, then stopped. He thought about Curtiss berating Oliver in the conference room. Curtiss seemed awfully eager to close the case and let Kelly plead guilty. *Can he be working with Oliver on this?*

He turned to Red. "Red, could Curtiss have been chastising Oliver because I found out too much? Is that why he's so eager to plead a case we're nowhere near solving?"

For the first time in more than an hour, Beck sat down on his couch and rubbed his temples. "But I don't know anything." He realized he was stuck and needed to change course. His theories were, well, just theories. And he wasn't sure which one was correct, or where the holes might be in his logic.

Maybe it was time for him to pull a Castiglia move and threaten to expose the Circle—whatever it was. Lead them on to think he knew more than he really did. That ploy had worked with numerous sources on previous stories. Maybe the members would then tell him more or do something stupid that exposed them and set the ball rolling.

He dialed again. A secretary kept him waiting so long he could have smoked an entire cigar while on hold. Finally, Curtiss came on the line. Beck explained an organization known as the Circle might be behind Castiglia's death and he had determined Oliver was responsible for setting up Kelly.

"Good work," Curtiss said. "I'll definitely keep it under wraps. Thanks for letting me know. What are you going to do next?"

"I'm not sure. I need to find out more about the Circle."

"Okay. Keep me in the loop."

Beck closed his cell phone. No, it wasn't about what he was going to do next—it was what Curtiss was going to do next. If he was right, Beck might have told Curtiss just enough to set him up.

"He knows," said Curtiss as he turned to Jackson Oliver sitting across the wide wooden desk from him. "Rikki knows about the Circle."

"I should finish him off," Oliver said.

"What?"

"I'll have some guys make him disappear."

"Are you nuts? He's a newspaper reporter."

"*Was* a newspaper reporter. You know that better than anyone, since you defended him."

"Doesn't matter. He's got contacts, connections. He's got investigative skills. He was one of the most dangerous reporters the *Post-Examiner* ever had. You just don't casually pick on a guy like that. He has information hidden away no one knows about—unless, of course, he turns up missing or dead. I can guarantee you if something happens to him, a lot of official Washington will be joyous—initially. But I bet that would change quickly. His fellow journalists around town would circle the wagons and be all over this. Who knows what might come out then?"

"You know that for a fact?"

"I know Beck Rikki and his ilk. Don't underestimate this guy."

"I thought the idea was to manipulate him since we discovered his connection to Castiglia."

Oliver obviously wasn't going to back down.

"I see how well you did with that," Curtiss said.

"We got him to place the story in the newspaper discrediting Castiglia." Oliver made a dismissive gesture, as if it was nothing to plant a damaging report about the deceased chief justice in the national news media.

"Yes, but he was never supposed to get this far, learn this much about the Renaissance Circle. You've made him a threat to the entire organization. It's a damned good thing I planted myself in the middle of Kelly's lawsuit so I can monitor the situation and clean up your mess." Curtiss was now fuming. Oliver was as much a threat to the group as Rikki.

"But he doesn't suspect you," said Oliver. "Take advantage of that. As long as he trusts you and keeps you in the loop—we have no worries."

"For the time being." Curtiss picked up his phone and punched in the number for his secretary. "Betty, call an emergency meeting of the partners for two this afternoon."

"Several partners are on client travel, Mr. Curtiss," she said.

"Well then, everyone who is in town."

He hung up and looked over at Oliver. "We need to bring everyone up to speed. If Rikki turns out to be a threat to our plan to shift political power, we need to agree on a plan of action. We can't change America without the right people in place."

"What would you propose?"

"Maybe you're right. Maybe taking him out is the only answer. But if we're going to do that, we need to figure how that would affect the Circle, too. Like I said, I know this guy. There would be a need for a lot of damage control."

Oliver smiled as if he had scored a major victory.

Curtiss knew better. He was just placating Oliver. He now had to deal with problems on two separate fronts—Oliver and Rikki.

He dismissed Oliver with the flip of his hand and looked down at some paperwork on his desk. He then sat back in his chair, scratching his chin, and considered the situation.

Oliver could no longer be trusted. *Who knows what he might do next?* And then he thought about Rikki. *Is he really a danger? If Rikki were to suddenly disappear, just how much damage could he really do from the grave?*

21

Beck paced vigorously in his living room again—ideas exploding—about to wear a new design into his oriental rug. He was missing something, struggling to figure out how Castiglia fit the Washington mold.

To the average tourist, Washington was the Mall with its magnificent monuments and museums. It was sugarcoated, high school history of the Founding Fathers played out in statues, bridges, rotundas, memorials, and great, Romanesque edifices.

For most federal employees who worked the daily grind of governing, Washington was an office cubicle lined with family photos, an adequate pension plan, and national politics just down the hall. But there was a segment of Washington at the upper echelon where the town was a battlefield—not of ideas but rather involving a life-and-death struggle for pure power. Here, they took their political science seriously. This was the area where Beck had played as a journalist.

Behind the bluster and facade of the city was a trail of death, deception and even mayhem. A bomb takes out a diplomat and his assistant. A dead president's former mistress—sister-in-law to a newspaper editor—is found murdered on the canal path in Georgetown. A Russian businessman is found dead in a hotel room near the White House. A car jumps a sidewalk and kills a Democratic National Committee campaign official just before a presidential election. A sitting senator's name shows up in a famous madam's telephone book. The famous madam later shows up dead.

Beck had visited the Spy Museum years ago and learned something he hadn't known. There were more foreign spies in Washington than in any other city in the world. His condo neighbor down the hall could be a spy for all he knew. The odds were relatively good.

Beck knew they played for keeps here. He had studied Washington's dirty linen, hanging it out to dry from time to time on the front page of the *Post-Examiner*.

His experience taught him Washington was the place where idealism came to die. Newly elected members of Congress would arrive in town inspired and in awe only to become thwarted by a deadlocked political jungle. To gain any influence, they had to get reelected. To accomplish that, they had to turn on the money spigot. Watching all of that money flow from lobbyists into their campaign coffers made them thirst for a little of that action themselves.

Greed had overtaken the city. It didn't matter if you were a Democrat, Republican or Independent. Everyone was on the take. Beck had seen it too often. He made a career out of writing about it.

Every conceivable business group had a lobbyist in Washington to protect its interests. To accomplish that, they flooded congressional offices with money by attending political campaign fundraising breakfasts, lunches and cocktail parties.

Washington's definition of an idealist was a lobbyist who owned more than three congressmen.

And if an incumbent was defeated at the polls, it got even better. Emeritus members of Congress would join the ranks of lobbyists and make millions wooing their former colleagues who still clung to power. It was the one issue a divided Congress could agree on.

Time and again, the city was exposed by journalists like Beck, and yet everyone yawned—the universal reaction. Honest indignation was no longer part of the city's DNA—or the nation's.

Beck struggled with the idea that Castiglia didn't fit this pattern. Unlike everyone else in the Naked City, he had no worries about having to raise millions for reelection. His was a lifetime appointment—in his case, *lifetime* being the optimum word.

Connect the dots. Always connect the dots. What was the chief justice really up to? Why did he want to use a reporter? That was the right word. He wanted to *use* Beck for his own purposes. Beck wasn't blind to that. He was part of the system—often the squeaky wheel, but still part of the gears of the Washington machinery.

Castiglia didn't bother to hide his conflicts, and, for the most part, they were minor—free trips, free meals, free upgraded hotel suites. The chief justice was known as a man of integrity with a big appetite. He knew exactly what the law allowed him to partake of, and he took full advantage.

Like or dislike his political leanings, from everything Beck had learned about him, he was a decent man. Yes, he loved the good life. He loved his pasta. But his record showed his judicial philosophy had never wavered.

Beck stopped pacing for a moment and looked up at Red. Then he looked to the ceiling and closed his eyes for a long time. *What am I missing? Castiglia, the ultimate enigma.*

Maybe he needed a different perspective—to look at Castiglia differently. *But how?* Beck glanced down at Red again and renewed his pacing.

Castiglia appeared immune to financial seduction. They obviously tried to woo him with wine and women. *But was a jurist of his stature, his brainpower, his ego, really susceptible? Did getting laid change anything?* The court, Beck had to admit, had a different culture than the rest of Washington, but that didn't necessarily change human nature. Did it?

"Red, maybe that's it. It's not about the money. It's not about power. Hell, Castiglia couldn't get any more powerful. He was on the same level as the president of the United States.

"Castiglia thought he was bulletproof, until for some reason he wasn't. So he arranged to meet with me. Red, if whomever he was afraid of were aware I knew what he knew, harming him would serve no purpose. So, they had to get to him before he talked to me."

He stopped pacing and sat on his couch thinking about that possibility. He ran his hands through his mass of hair. He'd been so focused on Castiglia that he hadn't noticed how badly he needed a haircut. He looked back toward Red for inspiration. His personal grooming would have to wait.

Someone out there knew the truth. *But who?*

His options were limited. His frustration wasn't.

He'd pay another call on Mr. Kelly. Maybe he needed to play some Washington hardball himself.

22

Curtiss walked into the conference room, eased into his chair at the head of the expansive mahogany table and looked up. Nearly all of his partners were present—twenty-seven in all, including Frederic Franklin Howell, the last living named partner at James Howell & Gordon. The most senior partners sat at the table in no particular order, with Howell in his wheelchair at the corner of the table next to Curtiss. Junior partners fidgeted in chairs along the walls.

The older partners tended to wear their suit jackets while the younger ones were less formal in their striped shirts, fancy suspenders and bright-colored ties. A half dozen who couldn't find seats milled around in the back speaking softly.

Curtiss didn't ask for a meeting often, so when his call sounded for an urgent session of the Renaissance Circle, every member made an effort to show.

All of the partners, even junior partners in James Howell & Gordon, were members of the Circle. He had seen to that. It was the secret to seniority and financial success at the firm—and one of the reasons he, as managing partner, had kept the firm's boutique status. It didn't need to merge with a larger law firm to bring in more revenue. Renaissance Circle members outside the firm funneled plenty of work to James Howell & Gordon. The group that recently met in Texas was proof of that.

Those deemed inappropriate for the Circle never made partner at the firm. Kevin Kelly had been a special exception. He was hired to keep an eye on Castiglia. Curtiss bought Kelly's connection to the chief justice, not the young lawyer's limited legal talent.

Curtiss reflected on how this all started. About six months ago he received a call from a Texas businessman expressing concern about Castiglia. The oil baron had gone hunting with the chief justice on his ranch outside of Austin. That evening, after too many glasses of Chianti, Castiglia had railed against how the Renaissance Circle had handled some sticky political situations. Castiglia called the actions un-American. After the call, Curtiss knew they had a problem and would need to keep an eye on the chief justice. And who better to do that than the justice's fawning former law clerk?

Curtiss was proud he had built James Howell & Gordon into one of the most powerful behind-the-scenes political operations in Washington. Thanks to the wide variety of legal specialty practices in the firm, the partners' tentacles reached everywhere in the nation's capital, extending into all of the dusty corners of the Capitol building and nearly every agency and department. They even reached into the Washington news media, thanks to his ties to the *Post-Examiner*. While Curtiss couldn't control what the newspaper wrote, he could persuade the editors to drop an offending paragraph or slightly shift the direction of a story.

It was all done under the guise of avoiding legal problems for the paper, but in many cases that was a lie. Curtiss preferred to couch it as a necessary convenience. He frequently clashed with the newspaper's in-house counsel, Robey Hedelt, who often saw no reason to cut targeted paragraphs in some controversial stories. Curtiss would always caution her that under his watch the *Post-Examiner* had never lost a libel case. And he had the publisher's ear, frequently inviting her and the paper's top editors to the firm's corporate box to watch the Redskins struggle through yet another miserable football season.

Curtiss realized the real advantage of having the newspaper as his client was being privy to explosive stories before they were published—not nitpicking at paragraphs. More than once after reviewing a controversial piece, he was able to pick up the phone and warn a client or colleague about a harmful story that was imminent.

That is how he got to know Beck Rikki and how he had managed to persuade Jackson Oliver to leave the Justice Department and become a partner.

Rikki, he knew, was looking at Oliver's questionable financial affairs in the Caribbean. Sooner or later, Rikki would pounce on Oliver.

Curtiss looked around the room, waiting for a few stragglers to take their seats. The only partners missing were those in the middle of litigation in some courtroom or in other parts of the country on business; and, of course, Kelly, who he made sure wasn't invited.

Curtiss was happy he'd nudged Kelly into hiring Rikki. He would use Kelly's proximity to keep a close eye on the reporter. It really wasn't much different than when he had read Rikki's stories before publication at the newspaper.

He rose from his seat at the head of the table. "Thanks for coming on such short notice. We have a problem."

He launched into his tale about how Beck was investigating Castiglia's death and how the old judge had apparently wanted to leak information to the reporter about the Renaissance Circle.

"We don't think Castiglia got a chance to talk to Mr. Rikki in detail, but we can't be sure. We do know Castiglia died before he was supposed to have an extended conversation with him. I'm told he was going to have breakfast with Rikki during our recent quarterly meeting in Texas. Why Castiglia thought that was a good idea, I don't know. It was almost like he was thumbing his nose at us. So we still need to diligently monitor the situation. If there is a problem, we may have to deal with Mr. Rikki."

"And how would we go about that?" asked one partner.

"We have an in-house enforcer," Curtis replied.

"Who is?"

"For obvious reasons, we keep that information confidential."

"Could such an action be traced back to Renaissance?" asked another partner. "We've built a good thing here. We don't need a threat like this Mr. Rikki fellow. We have too much at stake."

Heads nodded around the room.

"The Circle is set up as a confidential think tank for just that reason. Our sole purpose is to protect the republic and uphold democracy. Only the executive committee knows who everyone is. I'm general counsel and I'm not even privy to all of the information. It's safer that way. No, there should be no way to trace any action back to any member of the Circle."

Curtiss had just lied. While it was true he wasn't a voting member of the Renaissance Circle's executive committee, he did sit in on all of their meetings and knew everything the officers of the organization knew.

"Then why are we here?" asked another partner.

"We're trying to figure out what Castiglia was up to. He had expressed dissatisfaction with some of our actions. So, I thought I'd start with those most in the know—partners of this firm. We all cover different parts of the city. Have you heard anything about our late judicial colleague? We may not know yet what we're looking for. Castiglia was extraordinarily intelligent and, from his legal opinions and dissents, we know he was quite crafty. This Rikki connection might have been just a ruse, for all we know. Maybe we are looking in the wrong direction. Ask yourselves, why would Chief Justice Nino Castiglia want to expose the Circle?"

Curtiss looked at the partners around the table. "Anyone? Any ideas?"

There was a low murmur as members looked at each other and shook their heads. Curtiss stood for nearly a minute in hopes of some inkling, some suggestion.

"Come on. Someone must have an idea."

Still, there was silence in the room. Curtiss was growing agitated. "Surely someone has heard some rumbling, some rumor. No matter how suspect it might be, I'd like to hear it."

He scanned the room for an expression of concern. He saw nothing.

"Any suspicions? Anyone?"

He wondered if the partners were too intimidated, thinking they would look silly positing an outrageous theory or nibble of gossip, or whether there really was no information in this room of legal luminaries.

"Okay then," he said. "I want everyone to go into their respective corners of this town and discreetly inquire about the justice's last months on this earth. Was he particularly upset about something? What did he have on his mind?

Those of you who are regulars at the court, ask around among the clerks."

Seeing nothing, he moved on. "The second order of business is getting our new nominee, former president William Croom—Bill to many of us—to replace Castiglia. I'd like some insights on how that is going."

"It's looking better every day in the Senate," said a senior partner.

"I agree," said another. "Word on the committee is they have the votes. They need a few more in the Senate for confirmation. It's not a done deal yet, but we're closing in."

Other partners took turns reciting what they had heard in their particular political corridors. All of their reports were positive.

After more than an hour of discussion, Curtiss made one final plea for help on the Castiglia matter. The return of blank faces said it all.

"Then this meeting is adjourned."

—⁂—

Curtiss walked into his office and closed the door. Before he sat down, he picked up his phone and dialed a number he knew by heart but hadn't used in more than a year. It rang three times before it was answered.

"Yes."

"Sorry to bother you, Mr. President. We have a bit of a problem."

"One moment."

Curtiss heard muffled rumbling in the background. He waited more than a minute before it died down.

"Sorry, Charles. I was in the middle of a briefing. What's the matter?"

Curtiss explained the situation with Oliver. "I thought you should know, sir."

"I appreciate the heads-up. I will take care of this. You stand down, okay?"

"Will do, Mr. President."

The phone went dead. Curtiss looked at the receiver and placed it back in its cradle. He knew the Renaissance Circle's secrets would remain safe. For now.

23

Kelly looked surprised when he opened his apartment door to find Beck standing there. Beck had not called ahead.

The young lawyer was disheveled, still in his T-shirt and sweats, as if he had been up all night. The weight of the charges against him appeared to be taking its toll. He welcomed Beck into his living room. *It's time*, Beck thought, *to rough him up a bit.*

"You haven't been totally honest with me," Beck said. "I told you in the beginning if you held back, I was out of here. I'm quitting your case."

"What are you talking about? You can't. You can't do that." Kelly's voice cracked. "Right now everyone thinks I killed Castiglia."

"As far as I know, you did. To do my investigation, I've got to believe you. Right now I don't. You lied about what really happened, even admitting you held back information. I don't work with people who aren't straight with me. I came by to tell you that man to man, which is more than I can say you've done."

Kelly looked at him with a blank stare. "I really need your help."

"Then talk. I want to know about this secret group—the Circle. That is the key to your case."

"I can't," Kelly said. "If it gets out, neither of our lives is worth a damn."

"Oh, come off it. Stop being melodramatic." Beck's throat tightened. *What is Kelly talking about?* "You have no choice. Spend the rest of your life in prison—and that's likely to be a long time—or take your chances and come clean. You know what they do to guys like you in prison."

Kelly folded his arms and looked at the ceiling. Beck thought he saw tears run down his cheeks. *What must it be like to be under such pressure, knowing whatever he did right now could affect—even determine—the rest of his life?* Not that Beck felt sympathy for Kelly. He wanted the information. If he was going to break this case, he needed to know.

"Come on," Beck said. "I'm your ally here. We both want the same thing. We're in this together."

Kelly turned to him. "It's called the Renaissance Circle. It's a group of high-powered businessmen, rich assholes and politicians working together to change the world to their liking. It's all think tank stuff. I don't know anything else about it, except that Castiglia was a member and had expressed concern about it."

"What kind of concern?"

"We talked during a layover in St. Louis about six months ago. He was haunted about the way the Circle went about solving their problems. They'd discuss some issue and then a few months later something catastrophic would transpire and their problem vanished. It was as if they had some magical power or snapped their fingers and willed it away. Castiglia said it was more than a coincidence and he was alarmed."

"About what exactly?"

"You ever hear of Congresswoman Lisa Tucci?"

"Remind me."

"From Kansas. She ran on that tired old slogan 'Conservative with a Conscience.' She joined the Circle early and ran afoul of some of the leadership. She was found dead in her car at the bottom of the C&O Canal in Georgetown after going missing. Drowned. Or so they said. Three months before she died, Castiglia was telling me how she came to him expressing misgivings about the direction of the group."

"Did he tell you what those concerns were?"

"Something about a virus inside the federal government, trying to shift the culture of American politics."

"This is Washington, for crying out loud. Everybody claims they want to do that." Beck felt like he was getting nowhere. "How? How did they want to change the culture of DC?"

"I don't know. I never got any further than that."

"You weren't even curious?" Acid rose in his throat. He swallowed hard. Kelly was holding back. *Can he really know so little?* It didn't seem logical.

"Of course I was. But it became clear I was not to ask the justice too many questions about it. Discussing it made him uncomfortable. It was as if he didn't want to say too much or say the wrong thing."

"Why did Tucci go to Castiglia in the first place?"

"The chief justice may have been a far-right conservative—no doubt about that—but he was also a man of the law. He was an intellectual. He couldn't understand the meanness of politics today. His opinions were often acerbic, but there wasn't a vicious bone in his body.

"It was all about the law. I think he took that stance because he didn't want to consider the human consequences of some of his rulings. He especially abhorred death penalty appeals. He wanted to know nothing about the individual about to die. He followed the law to the letter. He thought he had no leeway.

"His mind was the only muscle he ever exercised—and you could tell this just by looking at him," Kelly said. A grin slowly grew across his face, and his eyes glazed as if he were remembering his mentor. "For him the Constitution was the Bible. He truly believed in public dissent and then, at the end of the day, in splitting a bottle of your favorite chianti with your intellectual opponent. He loved the clash of ideas. In a way, it dehumanized the law for him. He didn't have to deal with the real human situation, only the ideal."

"How did Castiglia get involved with Renaissance?"

"It was during my clerkship with him at the court. He told me some business people held a meeting in the bunker at the old Renaissance Resort in the mountains of Tennessee. Maybe they were inspired by the old congressional hideaway buried inside the mountain there. I don't know. But what came out of it was a complex behind-the-scenes political operation to fix things."

"Fix what things?"

"I assume he thought it would do great things to promote his stringent constitutional vision. But then the Circle seemed to veer off course. He told me it was starting to look like every other political interest group promoting its own self-absorbed agenda. The high-minded objectives it started out with—as he said they had originally been explained to him—seemed to vanish. In their place, odd coincidences began to occur a bit too often for his comfort."

"Tucci?"

"Exactly. And remember when Secretary of Labor Dallas McWilliams was struck with cancer a few years back?"

"And?"

"He was diagnosed just before he was to sit down with some of the biggest labor unions and negotiate new rules on mine safety. It would have cost the mine owners big time. He died six weeks later."

"I remember his death. It was tragic, but so what?"

"A nurse at George Washington University hospital where he died used to live in the building next door. We went out a few times. She told me it was odd no one was able to go into McWilliams's room without special protective gear. It seems McWilliams's system was overrun with a radioactive isotope. He was placed in an isolation unit. It was all hushed up, but she said it was obvious he was poisoned."

"Why?"

"The Circle opposed what the labor department was doing. Said it would give too much power to the left-wing nuts in the Democratic Party."

"So this Renaissance Circle has no real ideology. They kill a right-wing congresswoman and a left-wing cabinet secretary. That makes no sense."

"I didn't say I understood it."

"And killing Castiglia fits in? He was a right-winger."

"Not really. You're talking about his legal philosophy. He was a constitutionalist, not an ideologue."

But he looked like he fit the pattern, thought Beck. *Or maybe they killed him because he was about to go public.*

"Was Castiglia ever fearful for his own safety?" Beck asked.

"He never said anything to me about it."

"Why did he want to talk with me?"

"He wouldn't say—although when I asked, he mumbled something about the Circle, which I couldn't quite make out. He brushed me off."

"Did anyone else know about my meeting?" Beck asked.

"I think I mentioned it to—oh my god." Kelly buried his head in his hands. "I told Jackson Oliver. Do you think?"

"That you signed Castiglia's death warrant?"

"Oh my god." Kelly grabbed the back of a chair, his fingers dug in so deep Beck thought he might punch holes in the fabric.

"No. I don't think you did. I believe you're being set up."

"What?" Kelly's head snapped back, eyes flashing.

"The poison in Castiglia's breathing machine—the CPAP," said Beck. "It wasn't there after he died. Somebody added it later."

Kelly's jaw dropped.

"There was a drinking glass on his bedside table when I first entered the room that morning with Trowbridge," Beck said. "The photos the FBI turned over to Curtiss show no drinking glass on the table. It was removed before the FBI and the US marshals got there."

"So you think the glass was filled with poison."

"The water in the CPAP machine contained no poison before the FBI arrived." Beck studied Kelly's face, looking for any clue. There was none.

"Before the FBI arrived? How do you know that?"

"Let's just say I have a very good source. That's why I know you're being framed for Castiglia's death."

"But why me?"

"From what you've told me, I suspect this Renaissance Circle needs a patsy.

Someone volunteered you for the job. It seems obvious Renaissance doesn't want the evidence pointing its way. You're a convenient fall guy."

Kelly's shoulders slumped. "That sounds so, so . . . diminishing. This is my life. And I'm nothing more than someone's convenient dupe?"

"Fraid so. It's Washington. Someone has to take the fall."

Kelly looked like he was about to curl up in a fetal position in the corner.

"Could it have been Oliver?" Kelly asked, his eyes desperately searching for an answer.

"Maybe."

"But Oliver tried to help me when the FBI arrested me," Kelly continued. "He recommended Charles Curtiss as my lawyer. He said he was the best partner for the case."

"He did?" Beck got an uneasy feeling. He was officially starting to wonder if Curtiss could also be a part of this.

There was still one more issue bothering Beck. Kelly's answer to his next question would determine if he continued to help the young lawyer.

"When we first met, you told me all about Castiglia's conflicts of interest. Why would someone who says he loves the guy like a father do that? Especially tell a writer like me?"

Kelly grimaced and rubbed his hands together. "It was Oliver's idea. He said he didn't want Castiglia turned into a martyr. He said it would make it more difficult for President Harvey to appoint a successor. And now I get why, since Harvey, a Republican, is nominating a Democrat, former president Croom. I heard it on the news this morning. Oliver, with all of his political connections, must have known this was coming."

"And you went along."

Kelly bowed his head. "I'm new to the firm. I knew deep down the only reason they hired a kid like me was because of my relationship with the chief justice. I figured if I didn't go along, I wouldn't be around much longer. I've got a pregnant girlfriend and bills to pay. You know, be the good soldier. I loved the chief. At this point, I figured, what harm could I do?"

"Why don't you ask his family?"

Kelly stood and walked to the window with his back to Beck. *Typical lawyer,* thought Beck. *No loyalty, just expedience.*

"So why did Oliver care who the president nominated to replace Castiglia? Seems a bit premature, don't you think?"

Kelly turned to face him. "You don't understand. That appears to be all part of the plan."

24

Beck's mind whirled as he sat behind the wheel of his beloved Volvo convertible, waiting for the light on Pennsylvania Avenue. After months of sitting idle in his condo building's garage, his aging C70 rag top started right up, with nary a blue cough from the exhaust pipe.

Finally, he made a left onto Seventh Street on his way to Geneva's condo.

If Oliver was behind the murder and cared so much about who President Harvey appointed to be Castiglia's successor, then replacing Castiglia was what this was all about. *But was that the original intention, or was it because Castiglia was about to go public about the Circle?* At first Beck had thought it was the latter; now he wasn't so sure. Kelly was right. Make Castiglia look bad and whomever President Harvey chose to replace him would look better. The confirmation process would go smoother.

But why worry about that? Unless the president's choice is controversial. A Republican nominating a Democrat, by definition, would be an uphill battle, especially with the divisive mood dominating Capitol Hill.

Beck pulled into a space on the first level of Geneva's parking garage, turned off the transmission and sat silent in his car. *How clever,* he thought. *Could the Renaissance Circle have forced the president's hand and made him nominate their man? If that's the case, they even cleared the runway for the nomination.*

How devious. How smart. How well planned. *These Renaissance guys are good.*

He opened the door to Geneva's condo. There she stood, naked at the kitchen counter, pouring herself something to drink. His nerves tingled. No matter their differences, he could never escape her physical appeal. *Am I in lust or love?* At the moment, he didn't care.

He walked up and wrapped his arms around her, ignoring the pain in his sides. She turned in his arms and they kissed. He took her by the hand and led her to the bedroom.

—⁓—

Just one person disliked Jackson Oliver more than Beck—Vice President Daniel Fahy. Before scoring the veep job, Fahy had been one of Beck's best sources.

Now it took two days to get a message through, but Beck knew Fahy would see him. Beck was the one person in Washington who had enough ammunition on Fahy to bury him.

Beck grimaced. His role as a journalist was to expose politicians and hold their feet to the fire, yet he knew all types of incriminating information about them he could never publish. At times he felt he was doing just the opposite of what he had been trained for. But he understood the compromises necessary to get a story published.

Beck entered the Old Executive Office Building. He was still in awe of his surroundings—the ornate plaster designs, ceilings and moldings. It was built at a time when governments emphasized their majestic bearings, but today it felt old. The wood and the marble were dull. The air was stale. It lacked the pristine elegance of the White House next door. Beck figured some subcommittee chairman on the Hill was probably holding up an office facelift. Wouldn't be the first time.

Beck soon sat in a chair in front of a large desk, in what he assumed was Fahy's private office. The door flew open and a stern-faced Secret Service agent entered the room without a word and held the door like a robot, staring straight ahead and not at Beck. The vice president strode in. They shook hands and Fahy sat behind the desk while the agent slipped out, closing the door behind him.

Before Fahy became vice president, they had met from time to time outside the city in a shabby Virginia diner frequented by immigrant construction workers. Fahy had chosen the location because they would go unrecognized. So, meeting here—where visitor logs would often disappear—felt appropriate.

"You've come up in the world," said Beck, gesturing around the room.

Fahy smiled. "Not exactly the old café, is it?"

They both laughed.

Beck knew he was sitting in front of maybe the most powerful man in America. Not the world, he suspected. That would be the president. But Fahy was a smooth backroom operator. Beck suspected he handled things when the president needed six degrees of separation.

"I have a problem with an old friend of yours," Beck said.

"Oh?"

"Jackson Oliver."

Fahy stiffened.

"What's he been up to?"

"Seems he framed one of his younger colleagues, a Mr. Kevin Kelly, to take the fall for Justice Castiglia's death."

Fahy leaned back in his chair, limbs crossed, hands tightly clutching each arm. "Really? So who killed Castiglia?"

"I was wondering how you would feel if a certain story appeared in the newspaper outlining Oliver's guilt."

Fahy leaned forward, placing his elbows on his desk. The silence was awkward, but Beck had nowhere to go at the moment.

"You know there's no love lost between us."

"I kinda figured that after he blocked your efforts at Justice for so many years."

"Yet, if he hadn't, who knows? I may not be sitting here."

"True. Yet, I assume there is some lingering resentment."

"In this town, despite our reputation in recent years, to be successful you learn to work with your friends and your enemies."

"Is he an enemy?"

"I'm friends with everyone. Didn't you know that?" Fahy flashed a sinful smile.

"So, you wouldn't object if a story appeared stating what I just outlined."

"I don't pretend to control the press. What you do is your business."

"But it affects yours."

"On a daily basis. But we live with public scrutiny."

Beck grew annoyed at the verbal volleyball. It was like Fahy felt he was being recorded and was choosing his words carefully.

"Are we being recorded?"

Fahy shook his head. The question seemed to catch him off guard. "Of course not. Why would you ask?"

"Then let's cut to the chase. I need a credible source to talk to a certain journalist and plant a story. Someone who knows how to leave no trace. Someone who is not connected to me or directly to you, but who is very, very credible. Know anyone who is eligible for this beauty contest?"

"You mean gullible? I know all types of people."

"The story needs a credible source. An impeccable source. And I need that source to say certain things."

"I understand. What do you need?"

Beck knew he'd just crossed an ethical boundary from which he could never return.

As he stepped out of the Old Executive Office Building and into the sunlight, he punched a number into his cell phone. Four rings later, Kerry Rabidan answered.

"Kerry, I've got a story for you," Beck said. He told her he had a government source willing to confirm everything. Was she interested?

"I'm listening. But why are you being nice to me? Why don't you give this to our friends at the *Post-Examiner?*"

"Look, what you did to me was business. I get that. What my newspaper did to me was personal. You and I both understand when it's only business."

"Beck, I'm glad you see it that way."

—∽∽—

Three days later a *New-Times* headline blared the story that Castiglia wasn't murdered but died of an accidental drug overdose. His family had deliberately remained silent, allowing Kelly to be falsely accused, according to an anonymous government official. They knew Kelly would eventually be exonerated, her story said, but refused to come forward to safeguard the chief justice's reputation. Castiglia, Rabidan wrote, was addicted to opioids and had been obtaining illegal supplies since the drugs were prescribed to him three years ago for back pain.

Rabidan quoted a reliable source inside the Justice Department saying the chief justice's family blamed Kelly for mistakenly giving the unsuspecting jurist a toxic mixture of prescription medication and alcohol.

Castiglia's daughter responded angrily. She noted there was no truth to any allegations the family had engaged in any cover-up of her father's death. That would be immoral, she said. He father would have never stood for such behavior. In fact, she said, the family wanted the truth to come out no matter where it led. Her response was noted near the end of the piece.

The story went viral and made the morning news feed across America.

Beck called his old rival to offer his congratulations and suggested they meet for a drink that afternoon at the Reliable Source, the National Press Club bar. She agreed.

Three hours later she entered the bar. Beck had not arrived. She ordered a drink and looked around at some of the original editorial cartoons on the dark paneled walls. She waited about fifteen minutes before texting him. He texted back immediately, apologizing for being late and said he was on his way. As she hung up a well-dressed man approached her.

"Kerry Rabidan?"

"Yes."

"I read your story."

"You did? Like it?"

"Loved it. It kept me employed."

"How's that?" Kerry was about to whip out her notebook when he reached into his pocket.

"Ms. Rabidan, you've been served." He handed her a subpoena, turned and left the bar.

She opened it. The family of Chief Justice Nino Castiglia was suing her for libel for claiming they were guilty of covering up his real cause of his death. Her heart raced.

But I have a source, she told herself. Beck gave her a solid source, a government official who went on background, who would speak only if he remained anonymous. She flipped through her notebook and found his telephone number. She called. The phone had been disconnected.

What is going on? Then she recalled her conversation with Beck. *"You and I both understand when it's only business."*

She picked up her drink, chugged it and ordered another.

It was four in the afternoon, but Steve Giegerich was in the middle of some very kinky and vigorous sex with a former Victoria's Secret model he'd been trying to get in the sack for months. He was relishing the moment when he heard the special ringtone on his phone—the one he reserved for his most important callers.

He groaned in protest. "Shit." He rolled over, blindly searching for the jangling phone. He picked up. His partner swung her arm around his waist, trying unsuccessfully to pull him back into bed.

"It's Beck."

"Jesus," Giegerich said. "Can't this wait?" Beck told him the *News-Express* story got it all wrong. He wanted to know if Giegerich wanted the real story. Giegerich jumped out of bed and grabbed a notebook. His frustrated partner would remain so.

That weekend, the *Post-Examiner* carried a front-page story about the Castiglia family libel lawsuit filed against Rabidan and how the coroner's report showed no morphine or opioids in Castiglia's system. Instead, he had been killed by a strong sedative used in executions to stop one's breathing. It was murder—not an accident.

The drug was administered not through the CPAP machine, as originally reported nationwide, but was in a water glass on the bedside table, which had disappeared before the FBI closed off the room as a crime scene, according to a source on the scene.

Oliver Jackson, it said, was seen entering the room before the FBI or US marshals arrived. It explained he had a room key he had received from a prostitute who spent time with Castiglia the night before. Oliver hired the prostitute for Castiglia, the story read.

Beck finished reading. There was nothing about the FBI investigating Oliver or even questioning him. He thought about it for moment and then smiled. Fahy was letting Oliver twist in the wind.

After all, it was only business.

—⁓—

Oliver had refused to talk with Giegerich. He never talked to reporters. But after reading the *Post-Examiner* story, he wasn't sure his "no comment" was the right decision. He needed to put his own spin on this before it got out of hand. He was now a suspect in Castiglia's murder. His attempt to frame Kelly was falling apart.

How did the newspaper get the story? How did they know about the water glass? He'd removed it before investigators arrived. *Who would have known about it except for the prostitute? Trowbridge? No. He's loyal to the cause. No one else had been in the room. Had they?*

Except Beck.

Beck was at the resort. Could he be the source? But Justice Castiglia's overnight companion made more sense, he thought. *Gotta be the Texas hooker.* He had to get to her and ensure her silence, one way or the other. It was his only defense.

He needed help. He'd call a man who'd handled sticky situations for him in the past, who would clean up this entire mess and make it disappear. Oliver knew him only by his last name—Gardener. It wasn't his real name, but it still suited him. He was good at sowing seeds of destruction wherever he went.

25

Sunday was Fahy's only day to sleep in, so he was none too pleased to hear his private cell ringing on his nightstand.

"It's McCauley," said newly confirmed FBI Director Patrick McCauley.

"Yeah?"

"Disturbing news. You asked me to monitor Jackson Oliver and we just picked up a call to Grand Cayman in the Caribbean."

"I know where it is."

"Yeah, well, he was talking to an assassin they call the Gardener."

"Isn't that the one they picked up in Cayman for murder last year?"

"The same."

"How the hell is Oliver tied to an assassin?" the vice president asked.

"From what I can tell from their conversation, they've had a relationship for some time. We're just learning of it now."

"Wasn't he in prison?"

"His case is pending. Some big-time Miami lawyers are defending him. Apparently, drug money is paying his legal bills; he's got some powerful friends. They got him out on bail and they've been dragging out the legal process."

"Yeah, but he's up for murder. That's enough to incarcerate him before trial." *Half-baked island justice*, thought Fahy. "Unbelievable. I thought that case would be done long ago."

"That's not why I called. We have a bigger problem."

"Oh?"

"Oliver just ordered a hit on the prostitute who was with Castiglia the night he died."

Fahy was stunned. He gripped his phone tighter. His mind tried to catch up with what he just heard. "You're shitting me." Fahy knew Oliver was sleazy, but had no idea he was capable of murder.

"We have a recording. Clear as day," McCauley said. "Oliver's sending him to El Paso, Texas."

"What can you do to stop it? Can you pick up this assassin?"

"That's another problem. This Gardener character disappeared right after the phone call. By the time our man got to the residence where he was under house arrest, he was gone. Into the wind. The only good thing about it, when they find him—"

"You mean if—"

"When they find him, he goes to jail. No more house arrest."

"That's a big help. In the meantime, we could have a dead eyewitness on our hands." Fahy rubbed his brow. This was bad news. "What's the soonest this assassin can get to El Paso?"

"I figure a couple of days."

"Then get her out of there."

"Can't find her. Already talked with the regional office down there. Maybe she suspects something."

"Jesus. Can't you guys do anything right? We've got the suspected assassin of a Supreme Court justice hiring another assassin, and you're telling me you're helpless?"

Maybe Fahy had made a bad move recommending McCauley to direct the FBI. This was a Keystone Kops routine. *With all of the resources of the feds, they can't find and protect a prostitute in an isolated town like El Paso?*

"You still there?" asked McCauley.

"Yes, yes. I'm just thinking about everything you've said. So, in the meantime, pick up Oliver."

"Got a little problem there too," said McCauley.

"What else am I not going to like?"

"We didn't get a warrant to tap Oliver's phone. You wanted to keep this between us, remember? Can't arrest the guy on tainted evidence. We'd also be revealing some of our methods."

"Shit." Then Fahy remembered. "Hell. This is my fault. I should have never told you to bug the guy's phone."

"Actually, if we'd waited for a warrant, we'd never have uncovered this information until it was too late. We at least have a chance to save the woman's life," McCauley said.

"If we can find her," said Fahy. "Bring Oliver in for questioning. You can use that *Post-Examiner* story as your excuse. That should be enough to hold him for at least a few days and try to rattle him. I'll do some checking around too."

"Can do."

"And find Gardener and the woman. Jesus. Don't spare anything. Find them fast. The whole case against Oliver is based on her testimony—if we can stop him from murdering our prime witness."

Fahy took a breath. He needed to calm down and think this through. A plan began to emerge in his head.

"I can see how this could all work out nicely in our favor," he told McCauley. "I've got an idea. Let me run this past you."

They talked for another ten minutes as Fahy outlined his thoughts. When he finally hung up, he wondered how this got so out of hand. If it wasn't contained, it could blow up in everyone's face.

26

Beck recognized the name flashing on the screen of his cellphone.

"We've run into an issue," Fahy told him. "The prostitute is in trouble. She's the only eyewitness against Oliver and he just hired a hit man to take her out. The only thing linking Oliver to Castiglia's death is the prostitute. If he manages to kill our most important eyewitness, we have no case."

"But you've got the water glass."

"We've got diddly. You know perfectly well a newspaper story isn't evidence."

Beck kept quiet about his photos, which could prove the glass was still in the room that morning just before Oliver entered. To reveal them would not only put him in Oliver's crosshairs but also at the center of the prosecution's case. He did not want to go there. As far as he knew, no one suspected him—not even Oliver.

"The newspaper sure doesn't have the glass," Fahy said. "I'm sure Oliver got rid of it long ago. So the most compelling piece of our case against Oliver is Denise Fiori's account."

"Shit," he said. "We need to warn her."

"I was hoping you could help with that. She's disappeared. We checked her apartment. She's gone."

"How would I know where she is?"

"Don't screw with me, Beck. You've been digging into this from the beginning. You're too good to let a loose end like that go. Look, all I ask is that you find her and get her out of harm's way. I'm not sure the government can at this point."

"Shit. I'll see what I can do."

"I'll work on it from my end as well," said Fahy.

Beck hung up. *It's obvious why they can't find her,* he thought. They were looking for the wrong woman—Denise Fiori instead of her identical sister, Cara Beverly. As far as Beck knew, he was the only one who knew the truth about them.

But why can't they find Denise? Maybe something had spooked her. *Could she have just gone on vacation?* If that were the case, she would likely leave a trail of credit card charges behind, which the FBI could easily track. *How could she disappear so thoroughly that the FBI can't find her?*

He did a quick computer search for her phone number. No listing. *Idiot,* he thought. If he could find her on the Internet, the FBI would have done so already. He checked for her sister. Nothing. Surely the FBI would have figured out Denise had moved to a new apartment and found that by now. The post office would have all of that information.

He thought about it. Denise was the one in immediate danger, not Cara. Oliver was going after the wrong sister. This seemed surreal. What a difference between their world and his.

My world. He looked around Geneva's penthouse. In fact, he was on top of the world right now, literally and figuratively.

Geneva hummed a tune, busy in the kitchen. Outside, the swimming pool and hot tub beckoned. *How did I ever get here?*

He snapped back to his conversation with Fahy. Everyone else thought Denise was the prostitute, and that put both sisters in danger. He knew where to find Cara. He could just call the FBI and let them pick her up. Yet this was the same FBI that had given the Justice Department enough so-called evidence to indict Kelly. The FBI couldn't be that inept. This had risen beyond the law-and-order level. It appeared politics in high places was somehow pulling the strings.

Could that be Oliver or maybe the FBI? Could they possibly be working together? Oliver, after all, was once a Justice Department official. There were so many unanswered questions. Beck couldn't trust either department right now.

Geneva grabbed a couple of beers out of the fridge, popped the caps and headed enticingly across the living room in his direction.

"Sweetheart," he said, "I need to get to El Paso in a hurry before Jackson Oliver's henchman gets there." He explained his call from Fahy, and Geneva got on her cell immediately. After a short conversation, she hung up.

"You're lucky. A jet was ready to leave Reagan National and the flight was canceled half an hour ago. The crew is still there and looking for work. They'll be ready to go when you arrive. Have a good time." She turned up her nose. Her sarcastic tone sounded almost hostile.

Beck stood, took the beers from her hands and set them down on the coffee table. He gave her a hug, both in gratitude and to try to assuage her fear of him pursuing another beautiful woman.

Yet Geneva hadn't hesitated to help him. *What gives?*

He felt a piercing stab in his side and his psyche. He couldn't deny his guilt about using her money, like he was indebted to her. At the same time, he could feel himself forgiving how she made her dirty millions. Her money made their lives easier. Maybe it could do some good. *But am I forgiving her out of convenience?* He'd deal with that later.

"What about the beer?" she asked, nodding to the two bottles now on the table.

"No time. I really need to go."

"I've never known you to turn down a beer."

Beck grabbed the bottle and downed it, kissed her goodbye, grabbed his briefcase and overnight bag from the bedroom, hit his Uber app on his cell and raced for the elevator. An Uber driver was waiting at the curb. He was in the air within thirty minutes. No security lines. Not even a backup of planes waiting on the tarmac. He was beginning to like his lifestyle and this kind of travel.

—ɯ—

Five hours later, he turned his rental car onto Denise's street and drove past her apartment building. He needed to check the neighborhood to see if the FBI or Oliver's people were close by. It was late afternoon and there wasn't a parking space to be had. Finally, a block away, he pulled into an empty spot. He climbed out of his car, scouting the area, and walked casually toward her building. He slowed when he saw two men in a parked car across the street near the building's entrance. They were drinking coffee in silence.

FBI? Oliver's men?

Beck maintained his pace in hopes he'd avoid drawing attention as he passed. He strode up the walk toward her building. Once inside, he nearly ran to her front door.

He knocked. No answer, so he banged. *Where is she?* He was about to give up when he saw a shadow through the door peephole.

"Denise," he said. "Please open up. You're in danger."

Silence again.

"I think some men outside want to kill you."

The door flung open. Denise's blonde locks were disheveled, but she was still stunningly beautiful standing barefoot in a plaid skirt and black T-shirt.

"What?"

"Let me in. We need to talk, and you need to get out of here quickly."

He stepped into her apartment. Before she could close the door behind him, he turned to her.

"There are two men outside watching your building. I think they're looking for you."

Denise shrank back. Her mouth quivered.

Beck stumbled over his words, talking too fast, trying to explain the dire situation. He explained Oliver thought she was Cara. "She's the only witness who can tie Oliver to Castiglia's murder. You're lucky I got here before they did."

"Oh, my god. I just got home. They could have seen me come in."

"They're out front, parked on your street. How did they not see you?" Beck asked.

"I came through the back parking deck. There was no place to park on the street. I must have driven right past them."

"Then they either saw you and will be here soon, or they've already knocked on your door and will be back. Either way, we need to get out of here."

Beck wondered why the FBI didn't monitor all of the entrances. It made him think they weren't the FBI at all.

"Let me grab a bag and pack something."

"Fast," said Beck.

He listened to her scramble back in her bedroom and checked out her living room. Nice paintings and posters of museum shows. Some of the photography was stunning. There was a tasteful backside of a sitting nude. She was blond. He looked closely. *Yes*, he thought, *it could be Denise.* There was no way to know for sure, but he sure liked what he saw. It left everything to the imagination, which made it very powerful.

Denise emerged with a bulging, carry-on bag.

"You?" Beck nodded at the large nude.

Denise hesitated. "Cara persuaded me to do it over a bottle of wine one night. I only agreed because the photographer was female. But when it was done, I thought it rather tasteful."

"It's beautiful," Beck said.

Denise blushed.

"Okay. Let's go," he said. "I'll drive around the block to the back and pick you up."

Denise nodded.

Beck retraced his steps to his car, past the two men, who paid him no attention. One was staring into his smartphone while the other glanced at Denise's building and talked on his cell. He wondered how often they checked her door.

Beck pulled out of his parking place and inspected his rear view mirror for the two men. He turned left at the first intersection, heading toward the back of Denise's building. He checked his mirror again. Nothing. Denise waited at the end of the building's parking deck ramp.

She put her bag in the backseat of Beck's rental and slid into the front with him. As she did, her skirt ran up her thigh. She tugged at it, but not before Beck got a good view and smiled. They made momentary eye contact. Her expression said, *Really? Grow up.*

Embarrassed, he turned his attention to his driving, erasing his smile. *Beautiful,* he thought. *Absolutely beautiful.*

"Where are we going?" she asked.

"We need to get to your sister quickly."

27

"This could all blow up in our faces if we aren't careful," Fahy said. He sat in the Oval Office across the same antique desk once used by John F. Kennedy.

President Harvey smacked his knee. "Damn. Everything was going so well. I should have figured it was too good to be true."

"I thought it best to tell you in private," Fahy said. "I can't trust email, not even a phone call."

"Appreciate that," Harvey replied. "This room is one of the few places where we have complete privacy; no leaks. Just how dangerous is Oliver to us?"

"There's the possibility, if he finds the woman, that nothing gets back to us. But we can't take that chance. Our plans are too big to be thwarted by some two-bit prostitute."

"Aren't you getting that wrong? Don't you mean Oliver? She's not responsible for any of this."

"You're right," Fahy said. "We don't even know if she's the source for that *Post-Examiner* story. It seems fairly obvious she would be the one—"

"But your friend Rikki was there at the resort too, wasn't he?"

"Exactly," said Fahy. "And he's tied at the hip to the *Post-Examiner*. He used to work there."

"You don't need to remind me," Harvey said.

"Sorry. Didn't mean to bring up a sore subject." Fahy was referring to Harvey's ex-wife, Geneva, and her affair with Rikki. And now they were living together in Harvey's condominium. Harvey had been fooling around with other women for years, but to have his wife be unfaithful must have stung his ego badly. "Rikki is out there looking for the prostitute now."

"You sent a former newspaper reporter to find her?"

"We need to keep our distance from this whole affair. We need deniability—arm's length from everything. We can't let this jeopardize our plans. Who better than a reporter—or, rather, former reporter?" Fahy said. "He has credibility with his journalist colleagues, if not the public. And if he ever releases the story, it's his story, from his point of view—a narrative that is far removed from us."

"Fake news," said Harvey. "You are one crafty bastard." He smiled and shook his head in admiration. "But if the FBI just picked her up, we wouldn't be tied to that." He looked at Fahy, questioning. "What aren't you telling me?"

"This is my fault. I asked the FBI to bug Oliver's phone without a warrant."

"You what?"

"I let my animosity toward Oliver get the best of me. So, if any of this ever leaks to the public, legally we have no way of knowing the prostitute is even in danger. That's another reason I sent Rikki looking for her."

"This is a damned shit-storm."

"I'm sorry. This is my fuck up. If Oliver's people find her first, maybe it's just case closed. It may not be justice, but our efforts are not threatened. Just another murder in west Texas."

Harvey was silent. Fahy could tell he was thinking the situation through.

"What about Rikki?" Harvey asked. He tapped his fingers on his desk.

"He's on our side on this one. Remember, he's the do-gooder. He's out to save the woman's life. He has no idea he's saving our political ass and the entire Renaissance Circle agenda in the process."

Harvey shook his head and grinned. "Let's take a walk."

They stepped into the Rose Garden where the scent of a well-groomed, heavily mulched garden masked the stench of Harvey's sputtering political revolution. They squinted in the afternoon sunshine.

"I can't emphasize enough to keep this buttoned up tight," Harvey said. "We're embarking on a revolution, one nearly as big as our break from England back in 1776. If word about any of our plans leaks, our efforts are in vain. Even if Oliver goes free and that poor prostitute is murdered, it's the price we pay to save democracy. Understood? It's not just the future of the United States—it's the future of the world as we know it."

"If we succeed, do you think people will look back someday and thank us?" Fahy asked.

"They'll never realize it," Harvey said. "We will get no credit for eliminating the extremes on both ends of the political spectrum. Imagine how much better off America will be once we eliminate the left-wing Democrats and right-wing Republicans. We will be able to govern again. But this must be a silent coup. So much of our history is a secret, and this will be no different.

"American history has always been confined to the winners' shadows, even though we assert that the next generation is ablaze in sunlight. The public sees so little of it and agrees on none of it. Hell, we can't even agree on the cause of the Civil War.

"But a hundred years from now, long after you and I are gone, if we play our cards right, the Renaissance Circle should still be viable, assuring our democracy is the strongest in the world with a government that actually functions."

"That's the key," said Fahy, "but it must remain behind, in the shadows."

"And we will deliver."

"It will take a lot to succeed," Fahy said.

Harvey turned to him. "Do you think we've bitten off more than we can chew? I mean, really. This town is a mess. Do you think a few dozen business and political leaders can turn this whole screwed-up system around?"

Fahy never questioned the president's plans. But he knew him to be a perceptive, forward-thinking politician. *What thoughtful man embarking on such a consequential, covert effort wouldn't reconsider it at least once or twice?*

"If you don't do it, who will?" Fahy asked. "Do we continue down this dysfunctional road that could destroy our democracy? Besides, this is a bipartisan effort. Croom's on board and at least half of the Renaissance's members are Democrats. That's why it will work. It has to work. Which is why we have the best—Beck Rikki—working for us."

"And he doesn't even know it. You're good at that. I knew there was a reason I kept you around." Harvey grinned and winked. Then he slapped Fahy on the back. They strolled among the roses. "I wonder sometimes who made us god. But then I say to myself, 'This really is for the best.' Just don't let this situation get out of hand. I trust you. I need you to handle it."

28

Beck pulled up to the bungalow where he had seen Denise pick up Cara. He parked by the curb and Denise hopped out, grabbing her bag. Denise had not dared call her sister for fear it might be traced.

Cara opened the door. Her mouth dropped, probably not only at seeing her sister show up unexpectedly but also because Beck was standing behind her.

"What the hell? What are you doing with him?" Cara nodded toward Beck.

"Jackson Oliver has sent someone to kill you," Denise blurted out.

Without missing a beat, Cara waved them into her home and shut the door and turned to Beck. "What's going on?"

"You're the sole witness who can put Oliver away. He's hired a hit man to kill you. There were men waiting outside Denise's apartment building."

"So, Oliver is tracking Denise not knowing he really wants me?"

Denise looked at her sister. "Yes. I'm caught in the middle."

Cara hugged her twin. "I'm sorry. I never thought using your identity would get you involved in such a mess."

"Look," Beck said, "we've got to figure out our situation. Sooner or later, Cara, they will find you. The FBI is not stupid. I'm surprised they haven't hunted Denise down yet. They're probably checking birth certificates right now."

"Well, that will take them a while," said Denise.

"Oh?"

"Our birth certificates show our father's last name. When our father left,

Cara took our mother's last name. And I took my adoptive parents' name."

"That should slow them down for a day or so," Beck said. "And Oliver's people might take a little longer. But remember, Oliver was a top Justice Department official and worked in the White House. He still has access to people in government who can help him find you."

"Damn it," Cara said, looking at Beck. He could almost see the wheels turning in her brain.

"Exactly," he said.

"Then what do we do?" asked Denise.

"I don't know," Beck said. He turned to Cara. "Do you have enough room for the three of us to spend the night?"

"I've got a guest room and Denise can share with me."

"Is there somewhere I can put my car?"

"There's an alley in the back that leads to a parking spot behind my house. No one will see your car there."

"Good. I'll move my car and bring in my bag. Back in a minute."

—◊◊—

Beck was true to his word, and when he re-entered the house Cara was making a pot of coffee. They sat at her kitchen table to discuss their options. While they talked, she found a frozen pizza and put it in the oven. The day was waning.

"So, Beck, what do we do?" Denise asked again.

"I think it's too dangerous to stay here. I can take you both to Washington. I can put you both up in my condo since you don't seem to mind sharing a bedroom."

"With you?"

"Of course not. I live with a lady friend in downtown DC. My condo is unoccupied across the river in Alexandria. No one will think to look for you there. You can hide there until we figure out what to do next."

"How do we get there?"

"You let me take care of that. Can you be ready to go early tomorrow morning? I need only make a phone call."

Cara looked at him, her expression questioning. Beck could tell she was trying to figure out his angle.

Beck retreated into the living room and called Geneva to schedule a private plane.

"You want to do what? The prostitute? *And* her sister?" Geneva asked.

Jealous. Yes, she'd seen the topless pictures of Cara, but he'd explained who she was. Was it because Cara was beautiful? Geneva wasn't exactly lacking in that department.

"Yes. Cara Beverly and Denise Fiori," he replied.

"Why do you need to bring them to Washington?"

"I don't know what else to do with them. If I leave them here, they're in danger from Oliver's people. If I bring them to Washington, at least I can keep tabs on them. Hide them somewhere."

"How do you propose to do that?"

"I thought I'd put them up in my condo."

"What?"

"Well, I am staying with you." Now Beck was convinced Geneva was jealous. "It will only be until I can find them a safe place to stay. I need to hide them."

There was silence over the phone. "Jen?"

"Okay." She gave him a name and number to schedule the plane and her credit card number. He called. The private jet would be at the local airport, ready to go at ten in the morning.

He hung up. Beck thought about Geneva. Her attitude toward Cara and Denise was revealing. It was obvious his relationship with her had taken a hit. When he got back to Washington, he would need to deal with that.

He joined the sisters in the kitchen where he explained he'd made reservations for all of them. He thought it best to keep the exact nature of his plans to himself for now, although he wasn't sure why. Part of him wanted to leave now. *But where would we go? A hotel?* It was already dark, and if they were followed, it would be impossible to see. He could be putting them in more danger. He liked his chances better in daylight.

Cara mixed drinks for all of them. Beck was more of a beer and wine guy, but tonight he welcomed anything with alcohol. It wasn't long before he felt a buzz. The women were already there. The conversation was slurred and lively and they quickly began to laugh at almost anything. He wasn't sure if the sisters were incredibly witty or if the alcohol lowered the bar.

Finally, Cara showed him to her guest room. After using the bathroom, he closed the bedroom door, stripped and crawled into bed, falling asleep immediately.

That night he dreamed of having sex with Denise. At first, she was on top, but later they switched positions. They went at it forever. She was an extraordinary kisser and lover. When they were through, she took him by the hand and they showered together, and it was another sexy dream as they got all lathered up.

The next morning, he woke, pulled on his clothes and wobbled out of the bedroom. Both women were dressed in matching white robes sitting at the kitchen table drinking coffee. Denise's was a large men's robe. *Figures,* thought Beck. He thought about his dream and it brought a smile to his face, only to wince as he realized his head was throbbing.

"You got any aspirin?" he asked Cara.

"Sorry. I guess I made the drinks too strong last night," she said.

"Yeah. I'm more of a beer drinker. Should have been more careful."

Cara brought him three aspirin and a cup of coffee. Beck's head was unusually foggy this morning. He needed to sober up. They were far from being out of the woods.

He looked up at the kitchen clock on the wall. "Oh shit. We're late. We've got barely an hour to make the plane."

The sisters looked at each other, startled.

"We need to get moving."

The women rushed to Cara's room to dress. Beck left his steaming coffee on the table and made his own exit. They were all dressed and packed in ten minutes. Cara and Denise each carried a small suitcase and purse. Beck laughed to himself. Hell, they could take half the household if they wanted since they had a private plane all to themselves. Now he realized one of the advantages of having not told them about their mode of transportation.

They piled into Beck's rental, and he headed down the alley and onto a side street. He turned onto the street in front of Cara's house, always checking his rearview mirror. As they drove away, a car immediately pulled out from a parking space not far from her house.

"Damn," Beck said.

"What?" asked Cara from the passenger seat.

"I think we're being followed," he said. Both sisters turned and looked out the rear window.

Beck turned at the next corner. A block later, a large white sedan turned at the same corner. Beck turned again. So did the sedan.

"We need to lose them. We can't let them know we're headed to the airport. We'd be too easy to catch."

"Take the next left," Cara commanded.

Beck followed her directions, making several turns through her neighborhood. She steered him through an alley. Then another.

"Stop here."

Beck pulled to the curb. They waited, watching the rear window. Soon, the sedan appeared a block away, and Beck gunned the engine.

"How do you think they found us?" asked Denise.

Cara didn't answer and instead gave Beck more directions. She turned to Beck.

"Give me your phone."

"What?"

"Give me your phone."

He looked at her, questioning, but then took one hand off the wheel and reached in his pocket.

Cara turned to her sister. "Give me your phone." Denise handed it over. Cara began to disconnect the batteries.

"Hey, what are you doing?" Beck said, seeing his phone in pieces.

"They're tracking us with GPS on one of our cell phones, stupid." When she was done, she had taken the batteries out of all three and dumped all of them into her purse. "Now turn here," she instructed. He did. "Now here," she repeated, sending him through a series of quick turns.

Beck was now on a four-lane highway. How he got here, he hadn't a clue. She had guided them around in what seemed like circles. Ten minutes later he saw a sign for the airport. "You're good," Beck said to Cara. She smiled at him.

He turned onto a road for the general aviation terminal and immediately slammed on the brakes. One hundred yards ahead the white sedan was parked across the middle of the road, blocking entry to the terminal. Beck could see a dark figure behind the wheel, and he remembered seeing two people in the car earlier through his rearview mirror. *How do they know about the plane?*

He spun the car around, laying a patch of rubber on the asphalt. It was a trick he had learned in high school when he raced his father's car on the backcountry roads of Virginia. They shot down the access road, heading back toward the highway. But while he was maneuvering, the two in the sedan had pulled a quick turn and were close behind.

When he hit the highway, Beck put the car in fifth gear and hit ninety in a matter of seconds. The speedometer crept up to ninety-three, then ninety-nine. He could hear a whirring sound in the engine. He had maxed out.

"Hand me the phone," he demanded of Cara. She did, but he immediately realized by its weight that it had no battery. "Battery. I need to make a call."

She fumbled trying to reload his battery.

Beck called the number of the private aviation firm and was put through to his pilot. He explained their situation and asked if they could meet elsewhere.

"There's a ranch, the Winslow Ranch, about twenty miles from where you are," the pilot said.

Beck hung up and kept driving and glancing at his rearview mirror. The car behind was creeping closer. He kept his foot to the floor. Soon they were on a slight decline and his speed picked up. He looked at his stick shift—an automatic stick, not a regular stick—and he saw the overdrive button. He couldn't believe it. He hit the switch, and the car accelerated. *Yes*, he thought. *We have a chance.*

The car sped up. He looked in the mirror again. The white car was keeping pace.

"What are we going to do?" asked Denise, twisted in the back seat and watching the car pursuing them.

"We're meeting a plane at the Winslow ranch."

"A plane? And at the Winslow? Not good. Not good," Cara said.

"What's the matter?"

"Winslow is full of feds and drug dealers."

"There's an airstrip there. A plane will touch down and pick us up."

"Exactly. That's where drug dealers land. The whole town knows about the place. It's too dangerous."

"We don't have much choice." Beck wondered about the plane he had rented and the crew.

The white car continued to gain on them. Beck kept his foot pressed to the floor.

Suddenly, he heard a loud sound and a jet swooshed over their head, not a hundred feet above them. It was so loud he thought either it had crashed or he would, but it lifted into the air seconds after passing them. The blowback from the engines shook the car. He hung onto the wheel to control the vibration and could feel an ache in his ribs. *Not now*, he thought.

Beck watched as the jet slowly circled back in a wide arc in the sky. This time it came right at them.

He kept his foot on the gas as the plane approached. It swooshed over at about fifty feet and kept going toward the white car. As soon as it did, he noticed the white car back off. Its occupants wanted nothing of what the jet had to offer.

"About a mile up the road, turn right," demanded Cara.

Beck kept his eye on the white sedan as he began to slow. At the intersection, he saw a sign for the ranch. He made the turn and sped up again.

"About a mile up here, you turn again," Cara said.

"They're still there," Denise said, turning from her perch in the rear seat.

Beck checked his mirror again. The jet had scared their pursuers into backing off, but not by much. He made another turn and another and soon came upon the entrance to the ranch. He turned in and followed the runway signs. He sped up to about fifty on the small road; the white car was just turning into the ranch. He saw the runway and a plane at the far end. He didn't stop at the terminal but drove right onto the runway. At the far end, he pulled to the shoulder.

He craned his neck to see the white car slamming onto the tarmac, tires squealing as it turned in their directions just a few hundred yards away.

"Out!" he yelled. The woman swung their doors open, and Beck popped the trunk. He looked down the runway. The car was now about two hundred yards away. "No time," he yelled. "Leave the bags."

Beck stopped, remembering his briefcase with his laptop. He grabbed it off the top of the luggage pile in the trunk but left his overnight bag and ran toward the plane. He remembered the car keys and tossed them over his shoulder.

The pilot seemed all too aware of what was happening. The steps descended and the engine continued to whine at a high pitch. The girls stumbled getting up the steps. First Cara and then Denise. Denise hesitated and Beck literally pushed her on the butt. His foot missed the first step, sending him stumbling, but he managed to claw his way up the small stairs while hanging onto his briefcase. One of the crew retracted the steps, signaling to another in the cockpit to get moving.

Before they were seated, the plane surged. The rush slammed him against one of the executive chairs in the passenger section. The twins were already seated.

"Fasten your seatbelts," yelled one of the pilots, who didn't take the time to close the door to the cockpit. They tore down the runway as two men jumped out of their car and looked up. Beck could only imagine what they were saying.

—⁓—

Beck was pressed into his chair, his briefcase on the floor. His eyes closed. The steep angle of the plane as it rose kept him snuggly in his seat. Even if he wanted to, he couldn't move. He glanced over at the girls. Denise covered her face as she cried. Cara looked resolute, shaking her head.

Beck closed his eyes again. *How did they track us to the airport? Could they have traced my rental car? Could they have known about the plane?* This group had to be tied into government databases. They could have recognized Geneva's name on the plane reservation. But that would mean they were tracking him. *How did they know I was even here? If they knew our destination was the airport all along, why not just wait for us there? Too public?* It made more sense for the trackers to grab the three of them on some quiet side street.

All of this meant one thing. They knew the flight plan the pilot filed. Someone was likely going to be waiting for them when they landed in Washington.

The plane leveled and Beck looked up at the cockpit. The captain rose from his seat and came back to the cabin. He wore a crisp, white, short-sleeve shirt with official-looking epaulets and sat in a swivel chair across from Beck. There was a table between them.

"Captain Vernon Harris," the pilot said, shaking Beck's hand. "Haven't done that for a long time." He was smiling. "You wouldn't believe some of the flights we've had in and out of that strip. So, what's your story?"

"These ladies here. They're government witnesses and some not-so-nice men don't want them testifying in court," Beck said.

"Figured it was something like that. Lots of government witnesses go through that airstrip. They had to lengthen it a while ago just so jets like this one could take off and land there. Used to be just prop planes."

"We have a problem," Beck said. Denise and Cara eyed him, following every word of the conversation. Beck figured there was no point in hiding any of this from them now. "I think the people who are after us—there will be more of them waiting when we land at Reagan National."

"Ah, that's no big deal," said the pilot. "I can take care of that. You might have noticed our little fly-by. We have experience in these types of situations."

"How did you know it was us?"

"Nobody else driving that fast with a car right behind 'em," said the captain, smiling.

Beck wondered what kind of pilot this guy was.

The pilot returned to the cockpit. This time he shut the door behind him. Beck closed his eyes. After a restless night of dreaming about Denise and a rough morning, he could use some rest.

Denise and Cara found some small bottles of wine and began self-medicating.

—m—

Beck awoke with Denise's face close to his and her hands around his waist. *Am I in heaven, or what?*

"The pilot needs you to buckle up," she said, her beautiful eyes looking into his. "We're landing." She buckled his seatbelt, then bent over to cross the aisle to take her seat, but not until he got a nice view of the back of her long legs in her tight skirt.

He needed to clear the cobwebs, wake up and get serious.

Beck looked out the window and saw countryside. They were landing at an airport he did not recognize. When they were on the ground, the plane taxied over to a small building and the pilot cut the engines. The cockpit door swung open and the co-pilot entered the cabin and flipped a latch, releasing the exit door, which also served as stairs to the tarmac.

The captain stepped out of the cockpit. "Welcome to Stafford County, Virginia," he said.

"Where?" asked Beck.

"You're about thirty-five miles south of Washington. Interstate 95 is just beyond the end of the runway over there," he pointed, "and over there's a rental car waiting just for you." The captain pointed through the window at a blue Ford and black Chevy.

"Take your pick. Whichever one you don't choose, we'll take to our hotel. I don't think you'll find anyone here to greet you. We made a last-minute change in our flight plan. Anyone who might be tracking your progress would be unable to react in time to deal with that. They're probably a good forty-five minutes to an hour away."

Beck helped the ladies climb down from the plane and thanked the pilot and co-pilot for their assistance. It was at that point, standing on the tarmac, that he realized he had only his briefcase and the women had only their purses. He felt violated, knowing some goons would rifle through their stuff back in Texas.

They piled into the Ford. A key was under the mat.

29

After weaving through rush hour traffic, Beck opened the door to his condo. He had considered dropping off the rental car and thought better of it for now, so he left it in his parking garage.

He showed them the bathroom and the bedroom. They would have to share the bed. He would leave Cara and Denise here until he could figure out what to do.

He led them through the living room and to his balcony. Cara walked into the kitchen and opened the refrigerator. It was bare, and she gave him that look.

"I'm staying with my lady friend. That's why I thought this might work for you for the time being."

"We'll need some food and supplies," said Denise. "Is there a grocery and pharmacy nearby?"

Beck hadn't thought that far ahead. He called Geneva to let her know he would be a while. He told her he was going to run to the store and stock his refrigerator for his guests. Geneva sounded none too pleased. When he hung up, he told the girls he was heading out to buy groceries.

"Do you mind if we tag along?" asked Denise. "You have no idea what we eat, and I checked your bathroom. We need soap and some other stuff."

Beck felt embarrassed. He hadn't lived here for more than six months, and he didn't know if there was even toilet paper in the place.

They took the elevator to the parking garage and piled into his Volvo convertible.

Less than an hour later they were back in his kitchen with six bags of groceries and toiletries.

Cara announced she wanted to take a shower while Denise declared she was going to take a nap. Beck eyed his humidor. It had been a long time, so he decided to have a cigar before heading back to Geneva's. He grabbed a just-purchased beer from the fridge. It wasn't as cold as he liked it, but he wanted one badly. He popped the top and foam sprayed all over his sleeve, chest and face. *Shit!*

He grabbed a paper towel and wiped his mouth and mustache and then pulled off his shirt and walked down the hall to his laundry room and tossed it in his washing machine. He was about to head to his bedroom when he saw the closed door and heard the shower running. Oops, he had company. *Damn, what a nuisance,* he thought. Shirtless, he headed for the balcony. Now he really needed a beer and cigar.

Twenty minutes later Cara called for Beck from the living room. *Now what?* He crossed the threshold into the room to find her standing there in his bathrobe and holding a set of bra and panties.

"I found these in one of your drawers," she said. "Mind if I borrow them?"

Beck's jaw dropped. He was used to seeing Geneva in various states of undress, but not another woman.

"Since I don't have anything to change into, I was wondering if you would mind," she said, holding the garments out as if they were a sacrifice to the gods. "The panties are my size. The bra looks like it would be a little tight on me, but I don't mind showing off a little extra cleavage."

"Ahhh—" Beck didn't get a chance to finish his sentence. A key turned in his front door lock and Geneva strode into the room. She gasped at seeing Beck standing half dressed and face-to-face with Cara.

"Beck?" She looked straight at him, then at Cara and then at Beck again.

"Sorry. She just got out of the shower," he said.

"Really."

"Geneva, I—"

Geneva strode up to Cara and snatched her underwear from Cara's hand. "I can't believe you, Beck." She glared at him, her eyes filled with rage.

She yanked open the front door and slammed it behind her.

"Damn," Beck said. He ran to the door and into the hallway where Geneva waited for the elevator.

"Look, be reasonable," Beck said.

"Reasonable?"

"She just got out of the shower. She left her clothes behind when we escaped Texas. We were being chased. She and her sister are hiding out here. I was just getting ready to come over to your place. Look, I told you I was bringing them here."

"You were just getting ready to come to our condo dressed like that?"

"I spilled beer on my shirt, and I'm waiting for Denise to finish her nap so I can go in my room and get a clean shirt."

"Sure you are."

"Geneva. Come on. Nothing happened. Cara is the prostitute I was telling you about. She doesn't care if she's clothed or naked. Sorta like you."

"You're comparing me to a prostitute?"

"That's not what I meant. You know that. She was just asking if she could wear some of your clothes until she could wash hers or buy some new ones."

Geneva glared daggers. And if she had one in her hand right now, he had no doubt she'd use it on him.

She glanced away at his front door, her key still in her hand. Her answer was immediate. She stormed back into his condo. Cara was standing with her hands on her hips, still in the living room, with a grin on her face, apparently trying not to laugh. Geneva ignored her and walked back to the bedroom with Beck on her heels. There she discovered Denise, naked, asleep on his bed with a single sheet covering her.

She opened the closet door and took out two of her suits and a pair of slacks. She pulled the remainder of her underwear from the bottom drawer of his dresser.

"Tell your friends they'll have to get their own clothes. And from what I can see, they wouldn't fit in mine any way."

She strode down the hall toward his front door. This time Beck did nothing to stop her. He heard the door slam and his brain began to hurt. He sat on the edge of his bed, head in hands. He felt Denise stir on the mattress behind him. He turned to look. She'd slept through it all.

Cara appeared in the bedroom doorway, her eyebrows raised.

"Guess that was the girlfriend, huh?"

Beck looked up at her. She was still in his bathrobe showing lots of cleavage and leg. "At least put some clothes on."

He stormed back to the kitchen and grabbed the beer he'd left on the counter, chugged the entire can, and then opened a second. He grabbed a bottle of scotch and a glass and headed for the balcony.

He relit his cigar and tried to make sense out of what had just happened.

Cara reappeared, this time wearing one of Beck's shirts.

"Sorry. I guess I caused you some problems with the girlfriend."

"Ya think? Is it your habit to always walk around half naked in front of strange men?"

"Oh, come on, Beck. I haven't any clothes to wear. I found some women's clothes in the drawer. I was polite enough to ask. Both Denise and I showered and didn't want to put dirty clothes back on. Denise went to bed, but I couldn't sleep. That's all it is. I just started the washing machine. Look, I'll make it up to you. Dial *Jenoa*, or *Geneva*, or whatever her name is. I'll talk to her and explain."

Beck thought about it. Not a good idea. But then, at this point, what could it hurt? He dialed and handed the phone to Cara.

After several seconds, she said, "Geneva? This is Cara Beverly. We just met—sorta. I was holding your undies . . . Yes, that was me. Look, I wanted to explain. I'd just gotten out of the shower and . . . No, I don't . . . No . . . I have no designs . . . yes . . . okay." Beck wondered what hell Geneva was giving her. Then, without saying a thing, Cara handed Beck the phone.

"Yes," said Beck into his cell.

"You can find some other place to sleep tonight."

"Geneva—" Beck stared blankly at the phone like he was about to ask a question.

"Sorry. I guess I wasn't much help." Cara said.

"Thanks for nothing."

—◊—

A half hour later Cara poured him another scotch. Cara watched Beck take a couple of big gulps and wipe his mustache with his bare arm. She handed him back his half-smoked cigar. Beck took another hefty draw, leaned back on the balcony chair, propped his feet on the table, and blew out a soft stream of pale smoke.

Cara liked his confidence and his concern about Geneva. She could tell he had strong feelings for her. Cara hadn't known that feeling from a lover for a number of years. Men paid for her affections. Yet she knew she got something in return and used men in her own way—not to build a loving and lasting relationship.

Cara refilled her glass and raised it in a toast. They clinked their tumblers in mutual discomfort. Two hours later they were both slurring their words and only the stub of Beck's cigar remained in the ashtray on a side table. Cara stood up and beckoned him. "Come on, buster. I'm going to put you to bed."

"I can't sleep here. Jeez."

"You're not driving anywhere."

She pulled him to his feet and held him tight so he wouldn't fall. He wrapped his arms around her and attempted to walk. They stumbled, but she managed to recover, pushing him into the living room. She attempted to lower him onto the couch. As they faced each other and looked into each other's eyes, he clumsily moved in and kissed her. Cara did not resist. The kiss lasted a long time. They fell onto the couch together—Cara on top.

He had passed out.

He won't remember any of this in the morning, she thought.

She stood unsteadily, unbuckled his jeans, and pulled them off, leaving him there in his boxers. She left his pants on the coffee table and looked at him. "God," she said, watching his slumbering soul. She swept his brown locks off his forehead and watched his chest expand and contract, listening to the quiet rush of air gently nudged from his lungs. "Geneva, you're a stupid woman. Beck, you're a good man. You saved our lives and this is the thanks you get. I'm sorry. Men like you don't come along very often."

30

The next morning on the front page of the *Post-Examiner*, the headline said it all: *Jackson Oliver Charged in Justice's Death.* Dan Fahy read it while sipping his morning coffee alone at the vice president's mansion. He couldn't help but smile. Federal prosecutors had finally gotten their shit together and gone after the son-of-a-bitch.

He thought about the years he had slaved at the Justice Department while Oliver played politics at the White House, only later to return to Justice and become his tormentor. While there, he sat on so many of Fahy's government corruption cases—allowing politics to rule instead of the law—that Fahy had finally lost count. *How many politically sensitive cases has Oliver killed? How many dirty politicians went free because of him?* Fahy had been relegated to going behind Oliver's back sometimes to try to advance a case. He had met Rikki that way last year when he leaked him a story.

Yet, in almost every instance, Oliver had managed to thwart him. This time, Fahy had the SOB by the balls. The vice president had personally lobbied the Justice Department. He had pressed them to move forward after the *Post-Examiner* story explained that Castiglia's water glass had been poisoned. But he needed to get his hands on the newspaper's evidence.

He didn't have to explain to FBI Director Patrick McCauley how politically sensitive the case was. McCauley owed him his career, which assured Fahy his influence would not be disclosed. When federal agents interviewed the prostitute in their El Paso office a day after the justice's death, they made it clear she should not mention her involvement in the case to anyone. Not family, friends, anyone. Especially not someone like Beck Rikki.

Fahy picked up the FBI report on the table and reread it. During the interview, she told agents she had given Oliver the key to Castiglia's room when she left sometime after midnight. She got down to her car in the parking lot and realized she had forgotten her keys. So she headed back into the resort to find them. When she stepped off the elevator, she saw Oliver leaving Castiglia's room. And he spotted her.

She explained to Oliver she must have left her keys in the room. Oliver insisted she remain in the hall while he looked for them. She thought it odd, since she could probably find them faster. She figured the chief justice was sleeping. Oliver found her keys on the floor by the bed, he told her.

Cara's statement made her the chief witness in the government's case against Oliver and cast serious doubt on Kevin Kelly's guilt. It had also prompted the FBI to examine Castiglia's sleep apnea machine sitting in a Texas police evidence locker. The newspaper was right, the FBI concluded. Poison was found only in the water chamber inside the machine. None was found in the hose connected to Castiglia's breathing mask. It was impossible for Castiglia to have been poisoned through the machine. It was an obvious plant, the FBI report concluded.

That jelled with the coroner's report. Since he had apparently been using the machine that night, the coroner swabbed Castiglia's nasal passages and found no evidence of poison. Traces, however, were found in his throat. Now it all made sense. Kelly had told the truth, the FBI concluded. He simply set up the machine next to the bed for Castiglia.

But how did the newspaper know that? How did it know to print that story? Cara had sworn she'd never talked to Rikki.

It was another sign Rikki was more adroit than Fahy had given him credit for. While he could sometimes manipulate the former reporter, Fahy could never really trust him to stop probing for the truth. Rikki always knew more than he let on, which made him an important tool for Fahy but also a dangerous one.

Fahy needed to be careful how he used Rikki and to monitor him more closely.

The FBI had told Fahy that Rikki was in the room when Castiglia's body was discovered, and the resort's owner, Michael Trowbridge, had left him there for a few minutes to secure the room while Trowbridge sought help. Obviously, Rikki found something while he was there. He was a reporter, for god's sake. It was in his blood to snoop.

Could he have tampered with evidence? He left no fingerprints. He wasn't that stupid. Yet, Fahy knew he could never let the FBI investigate Rikki. Any attempt to go there would put his own career in danger. Rikki knew too much about his cutting corners at the Justice Department.

He wasn't sure what Rikki's ultimate game was. He noted the byline on the first story—the story that got the newspaper sued by the judge's family. Kerry Rabidan. That was the woman who last year had destroyed Rikki's career. *A little payback?* Fahy wondered. If so, Mr. Rikki may not be the innocent he purports to be.

Interesting. In less than a year, the best two reporters in town had been neutralized. And they'd done it to each other. Fahy laughed. *Whoever said politicians are the* only *backstabbers in this town?*

The second story—the one in the *Post Examiner* that pointed the finger at Oliver—gave Fahy the idea to send Rikki after Cara. He would have her find out what Rikki knew.

It had been so easy. When he heard Oliver was going to try and track down Cara and shut her up, Fahy lied to Rikki, saying the FBI hadn't found her yet. They'd found her shortly after his call with the FBI director. *Reporters are just so gullible,* he thought. To think Rikki believed the FBI couldn't find her. Really? Instead, they would be there in plain view to protect Cara and Denise against Oliver's men. But Rikki wouldn't know that.

Rikki must be so driven by his passion to solve the mystery that he never stepped back for a moment to contemplate reality. That was fortunate for Fahy. Rikki continued to be blinded by his own naked ambition. Rikki wasn't just an ink-stained wretch. Ink was the lifeblood of his metabolism.

Fahy finished the report and picked up the newspaper article again. The attorney general had assured him that Cara's testimony would bury Oliver. Even without the missing glass, there was enough circumstantial evidence to send Oliver away for a long time.

He couldn't be happier. He wanted to meet this woman, Cara. From the selfies the FBI had shown him, she was quite a dish. And he had a good excuse. She still hadn't told the FBI how Rikki fingered Oliver. It was the one missing link that bothered Fahy.

31

Beck awoke to rays of the morning sun burning into his brain. He smelled bacon and heard it crackling on the stove. He was staring at the ceiling. *Where am I?* He felt a leather armrest sticking to his clammy scalp. *Oh. My couch.*

He tried to sit up to challenge the day, and his head roared at him to not bother. This was the second time in two days he'd awoken hungover. He wasn't normally a heavy drinker. Just two or three light beers in the evening. But ever since he met Cara and Denise, he felt like he'd become a raging alcoholic.

He tossed off his blanket. He didn't remember grabbing it last night. Hell, he didn't remember lying down on his couch. He swung his legs onto the rug and slowly rose, his head following three steps behind.

"Good morning," came a voice from across the room. One of the sister goddesses was cooking. It was subtle, but Denise's voice had a more sophisticated lilt.

He noticed they had many of the same mannerisms but different temperaments. Denise was more guileless. Obviously, she hadn't had Cara's rough upbringing. That was clear even to Beck Rikki, fumbling amateur psychologist.

"How are you feeling this morning?" Denise asked.

Beck warmed to the soft inflection of her voice.

"Cara told me about last night. I'm sorry we've caused you so much grief."

Shit! Geneva. The fog cleared. He remembered Geneva had walked in at that inopportune moment last night and then stormed out. He needed to square things with her.

"I really appreciate what you've done for us," Denise continued.

"Yeah, I need to figure out what's next. Try to fix my own personal life or save yours and your sister's."

Denise looked askance at him. She was attired in one of his dress shirts. It fit her exactly like the one Cara wore last night. It was just long enough to cover her ass and not much else.

Denise coughed. "I apologize for my state of undress." She motioned at his shirt. Beck thought he glimpsed a wicked smile, or maybe it was wishful thinking.

"Cara threw our clothes in the wash last night. I've got the dryer going now. I hope you don't mind. At least we will have something to wear today. You look like you could use something too."

He looked down and realized he was standing in his boxers and then quickly looked back at Denise. She was enjoying this.

"Cara is asleep," Denise said, "but I could get you some clothes from your closet."

Beck grabbed his trousers off the coffee table and pulled them on. He felt awkward and embarrassed and wondered why. Had it been Cara, it probably wouldn't have bothered him. Denise was different. Still, it all made him feel like a visitor in his own home.

"Coffee's on the counter. Breakfast is almost ready. Why don't you have a seat at the table?"

She motioned to the dining room as she brought over a large plate of bacon and scrambled eggs and set them in the middle. They sat across from each other. Beck thought the coffee tasted especially good this morning. He wondered what she had done to it.

They sat in silence for a few awkward moments before Denise spoke. "I appreciate what you've done. I'm not sure what we're doing here, though."

"Your sister is a big threat to Oliver. We need to get her in touch with the FBI or the Justice Department or somebody official. We need to get her some protection. I will bet she could be their most important witness."

"And me?"

"You're easily mistaken for your sister no matter what you do. That puts you in danger as well. I don't know what to do about that. Until your sister is no longer threatened, I think you need to stay out of sight too. I see no other way. Do you?"

"This all scares me. I lead a nice, quiet life back in Texas, and this is so far beyond the pale for me." Her eyes glistened.

Beck reached out and covered her hand with his.

"I'm no hero, but I'll do my best to keep you safe."

Denise rose from the table. Tears streamed down both cheeks. Beck stood and came around to hug her. She nearly fell into his arms and began to sob. He felt her tears against his bare chest.

"It will be all right," he said. "I promise."

He reached out and lifted her chin to look into her glistening eyes. He wiped the tears from her cheek and touched her mouth with his finger. She craned her neck up toward him and he bent down and kissed her on the lips. Lightly at first, and then their mouths opened and their tongues explored each other in a torrid union.

Finally, Denise pushed back and again they looked at each other. She grabbed his face in both hands and kissed him again and then pushed away without a word. She turned and walked down the hall to his bedroom.

Beck stood there motionless, watching his own shirt float behind her against the glide of her long, bare legs, hinting at so much more. And then she disappeared behind his closed bedroom door.

He stood in the middle of his own condo, and he could do nothing. He had just kissed another woman and realized he felt no guilt.

32

"We traced the private jet to a small municipal airport in Stafford, Virginia. From there they took a rental car, which as of today has never been turned in," said FBI Director Patrick McCauley. The director had arrived at the vice president's mansion on the grounds of the Naval Observatory on Massachusetts Avenue shortly after Fahy finished his breakfast. Fahy invited him into the sunroom to revisit the facts in the case.

"So, our number one witness is safe?" asked Fahy.

"They're in Rikki's condo over in Old Town. We're monitoring everything."

"Everything?"

"You may remember Rikki has been living in the Bahamas for the last six months with Ms. Kemper. We figured since he was now hanging out with the president's ex-wife, it might bode well to install a listening device or two in his place. He made it easy, being gone for so long."

"Legal?" Fahy asked.

"Let's just say it was a private job."

"You guys amaze me."

"We try to be on top of things."

Fahy grinned and tapped the glass-top table. He couldn't very well object to the illegal surveillance after he had asked the director to do the same to Oliver.

"I'd like to talk to this Cara Beverly lady," Fahy said. "That is her name, correct? Denise is the sister whose name she used?"

"That's right."

"Obviously, Cara's going to have to testify against Oliver, and I want to know what she knows."

"Is that a good idea? It could be seen as interfering in the investigation and prosecution."

"Then set up an interrogation with you and some Justice Department attorneys at the Old Executive Office Building, and I'll just happen to drop by."

"You really despise Oliver, don't you?"

"It's the old prosecutor in me. I want to make sure we have nailed this case down tight. We're dealing with circumstantial evidence, and that's not always a dropkick through the goal posts."

"Overwhelming circumstantial evidence," McCauley said.

"Yeah, well, you thought you had that with that Kelly kid, too. Remember? We need Cara's sworn statement, or the government has no case. Except for the FBI, Justice hasn't even interviewed her. And the FBI questioning wasn't under oath. Right now, I'm thinking Beck Rikki has done more for this case than the FBI. What the hell?"

"Not quite sure what the attorney general's strategy is. Not my call."

"Let's get Cara Beverly in here. I want to speak with her. In the meantime, I've got some chewing out to do at Justice."

"Ahh . . . one more thing." McCauley rubbed his hands together.

"Yes?"

"There was a big blowup last night at Rikki's condo. Seems Ms. Kemper doesn't like the idea of him hosting two beautiful women at his place. Apparently, she stormed out of there last night. She slammed the door so loudly, she almost burst the eardrums of one of my agents."

"A real split? Should I let the president know?"

"I wouldn't go there yet. We will monitor the situation."

"I know the president would very much like to get back together with Ms. Kemper."

"Like I said, we'll monitor. I'll let you know if there are any more developments."

"Okay. In the meantime, I'll think I'll reach out to this Cara Beverly woman. I want to talk with her."

33

Beck's cell chimed. The screen said it was Kevin Kelly.

"You see the morning paper?" Kelly asked.

"No, I haven't."

"They dropped all charges against me and charged Jackson Oliver."

"No shit. That's wonderful news. Congratulations."

"I wanted to thank you for everything you did for me."

"I really didn't do that much."

"It's going to be a bit strange at the firm, I guess."

"How so?"

"They took Oliver into custody," Kelly explained. "I'll be the one walking into the office without a cloud over my head but probably a target on my back. I may get blamed for this by some of the partners."

"That does sound a bit dicey, but you'll be okay," Beck assured him, though he wasn't so sure. If he were a betting man, Beck figured Kelly would be out of a job six months after Oliver's trial concluded—no matter what the verdict. He figured Kelly's Washington career was dead man walking.

They wrapped up their conversation, having nothing left in common to talk about except for a confident-sounding Kelly reminding him to send a final bill.

Before Beck could put his phone down, it vibrated and rang again in his hand. He lifted it to his ear.

"Did you find the woman?"

It was Dan Fahy.

"Yes."

"We believe the prostitute. Her name is Cara Beverly, and she's our key witness against Oliver. The Justice Department needs to interview her. We think her testimony is essential to convicting Oliver. Are you in town? Is she with you? Can you bring her by the Old Executive Office Building today?"

"Uh. Yeah." Beck wondered why the rush.

"You with the sister too?"

"Yeah." Beck frowned.

"Bring her too. Be at the main entrance in two hours. I'll have my people notify security."

The phone went dead before Beck could speak. He had wanted to ask Fahy about some protection for the women. After yesterday, he wasn't sure his condo was the right answer.

—⁓—

Beck played chauffeur driving along the George Washington Parkway toward the 14th Street Bridge. It was a gorgeous day, so he put the top down on his aging Volvo. Cara was in the front seat with him and Denise was in the back getting windblown. He found a space in a parking garage near his destination and left the top down. He learned long ago with a convertible to either keep the doors unlocked or put the top down if he didn't want vandals to destroy his ragtop. It was one of the few older classic versions that still had a canvas roof. His pride and joy.

As they stepped out of the car, he noticed Denise's hair was swept back in a sexy, slightly tangled look. She was stunning, like a *Vanity Fair* model. Beck had a hard time taking his eyes off her as they walked the block to the Old Executive Office Building.

When they identified themselves at the entrance, an attorney quickly appeared and escorted them to a small conference room.

"I'm Andrew Laye with Justice, one of the attorneys investigating this case. We would like to interview each of you individually."

"Me too?" asked Beck.

"Yes sir," said Laye.

Beck smiled. He was used to talking with legal blowhards who were full of themselves. This was the first time any attorney had ever called him "sir."

—⁓—

Laye and FBI Chief McCauley had finished interviewing Cara under oath behind closed doors. They asked the stenographer to step outside in the waiting area, where Denise and Beck sat reading old magazines. As soon as she closed the door behind her, Fahy entered the conference room through another door. He introduced himself and sat down at the table.

McCauley turned to Fahy. "We have her entire testimony under oath, and it all corroborates what we already know. With this in hand, we have a solid case."

"Ms. Beverly, our nation thanks you for volunteering to come forward to find Chief Justice Nino Castiglia's real murderer," Fahy said.

"Just trying to explain what I saw. Nothing more." Cara sat straight in her chair with her hands clasped in her lap.

"You've been extraordinarily helpful. With your testimony in court, we should easily get a conviction."

"I have to testify in court? Nobody said anything about that. This man is out to get me."

"That's what this is all about. Your testimony will put Oliver behind bars forever."

"Forever?"

"Yes. You will never have to worry about him again."

"I guess . . . if that's the case."

Fahy was irritated. *What is she thinking? Does she not realize the importance of her testimony?* He never considered this was anything but a slam-dunk. They now had her recorded statement under oath. But still, that wasn't as strong as her voluntarily taking the stand. Oliver's defense attorney would scream if she didn't testify. And if she was subpoenaed and forced to testify, he worried how credible she would come off to a jury. Fahy couldn't leave that to chance.

"Is there any doubt you would be willing to testify?" Fahy asked.

"Uh. I guess not. I just didn't understand."

Fahy continue to feel uneasy. She wasn't as strong a witness as he had hoped.

"The FBI asked you to keep an eye on Mr. Rikki. Did you learn anything about his investigation?"

"He's a very attractive man. I did discover that."

"Please. We're serious. If there is anything you can tell us about what he is up to. The FBI agents who interviewed you earlier asked you to watch him should he show up on your doorstep."

"Which he did."

"They specifically asked you to report back to us."

"Us? You? I did as I was told. I had nothing to report. Nothing at all. As far as I know, all he did was help my sister and me get out of Texas before that thug Oliver could get us. And it was a close call, let me tell you."

"You were never in any danger."

"What?" Cara looked surprised.

"Those weren't Oliver's men chasing you. They were the FBI."

"What the hell for? We could have gotten killed."

"That was for Mr. Rikki's benefit. We had to convince him he was the only one who could save you."

"Why?" Cara shook her head, obviously not understanding.

"Deniability. If the whole story ever gets out, it's his story. From his point of view. It doesn't lead to the government, only to Jackson Oliver and you and your sister. Since you and your sister are innocent, you have nothing to worry about."

"Why would the government care about deniability?"

"We have our reasons. Look at it from our point of view. Mr. Rikki has his story he can tell, and his is the only story that exists for public consumption. I can't go into details, but this is for your own good. I assure you, you were never in any danger. We've been protecting you all along."

Fahy worried he might be telling her too much, but it was obvious he needed to reassure her the government had always been in charge and all would be well.

"What happened to Oliver's man who was coming after us?"

"We're not sure. He never showed up. We had agents watching your sister's apartment and your house and they never saw anyone."

"Is he still out there wanting to kill us?" Cara fidgeted in her chair.

"If he is, you have no worries. Rest assured, we will protect you."

They broke up the meeting, and Fahy left. McCauley reminded Cara not to speak of her testimony to anyone and not to tell Beck that the only danger they were in during their escape was from his driving. Laye and McCauley showed her the door.

Laye immediately led Denise into the conference room. McCauley instructed the stenographer to return, and they began their interview under oath with Denise.

McCauley's purpose behind this interview was to ascertain Cara's truthfulness. Denise's testimony would be considered hearsay and not admissible in court. After half an hour, Denise corroborated what she knew of Cara's testimony. The parts she couldn't were insignificant. Best of all, the lawyers found no contradictions. Cara, they determined, was telling the truth.

They followed the same routine as before, asking the stenographer to step out and then Fahy stepped in. Laye and McCauley explained the situation. They were more than satisfied with both women's testimonies.

Fahy thanked her for being there and her willingness to testify, knowing her words would not be used at trial.

"Anything I can do to help," she said. "I'm sorry I didn't know the answers to all of your questions. As you might imagine, this has been very upsetting."

"I understand," Fahy said. "You're very kind to share what you know with us."

Fahy noticed immediately that Denise was a softer, more modest version of her twin. She was willing to help her government nail the dog Oliver. It was too bad the sisters' roles weren't reversed. If only Denise were his witness, life would be so much easier. He took an instant liking to her.

When they were done, Fahy again thanked her, holding her hand a few seconds longer than was appropriate. He then left through the side door.

Denise entered the waiting area after being interviewed. Laye and McCauley invited Beck in. They began as soon as the stenographer sat.

The interview lasted no more than fifteen minutes, with Beck relating their escape from west Texas. They thanked him for his cooperation.

McCauley stopped the stenographer and turned to Beck. "We believe we need to provide Cara and Denise with round-the-clock protection. Are they going to be staying with you at your condo?"

"Yeah, but I don't know for how long."

"We'd like to provide them with twenty-four-hour protection. After your departure from Texas, I think it's called for," said McCauley.

"Okay. They'll be at my place until we find something more suitable."

"We will send a protection detail over early this evening. Do we need to bring cots?"

"They're sharing my bedroom. All I've got is a couch in the living room."

"We'll handle it."

They shook hands, and Beck left the room, feeling relief. Denise and Cara would no longer have to rely on him. He needed time to figure out his own life and find Geneva.

When he stepped into the waiting area, the sisters were talking. He heard Fahy's name in the conversation.

"So what about Fahy?" he asked.

"Oh, nothing," said Cara. "Just a difference of opinion, that's all."

"Do you think there'll be enough room in my car for you and your differing opinions? Let's get out of here."

—⚭—

They walked the block back to Beck's car, and he sped out of the parking garage. Traffic seemed light for a midafternoon until Beck realized it was a Saturday. His life for the past few days had been one big blur.

He drove across the 14th Street Bridge, ignoring the speed limit, and turned onto the GW Parkway toward Old Town Alexandria. He picked up speed. Reagan National Airport loomed on the left and a large estuary of the Potomac River was to his immediate right. It was a perfect sunny day to have the top down.

A car passing him suddenly lurched into his lane, slamming into his Volvo on the driver's side. Beck gripped the steering wheel and fought to control the car.

"What the hell," he screamed at the massive black SUV. "Move over, you son of a bitch."

The car sped up slightly and then veered into his lane again, pushing the Volvo toward the raised curb.

The SUV's tinted windows were high above his road-hugging sports car, making it impossible for Beck to see anyone in the vehicle. The driver was either drunk or deliberately trying to push him off the road. Beck gripped the steering wheel even tighter, trying to keep his Volvo from turning wildly. Muscling the wheel made his injured ribs catch fire.

Cara grasped the top of the roll bar above the windshield and screamed. Denise had nothing to hold onto in the back seat. Beck glimpsed her in his rearview mirror, desperately trying to reach forward to grab ahold of Cara's headrest. The surge of the car was apparently making it impossible.

The SUV hit them again, scraping metal to metal and jerking the Volvo to the right. Beck pulled the wheel hard, pain searing through his side. He was sandwiched between the SUV and the curb.

Beck slammed on the brakes, hoping the SUV would zip past him. Instead, it mirrored his movement.

Beck's side mirror dangled precariously, banging against the driver's door. He used all of his strength to hold the steering wheel steady. He jammed on the gas, but as he sped up, the SUV moved in unison. He accelerated again and again heard steel scrape against steel. The front side fender of the SUV was right at his door.

Beck felt the car hit the raised curb with an awful thud. He heard his tire explode. Then the Volvo lurched upward and was airborne. His foot was still pressing the accelerator and the engine screamed a high-pitched whine as it revved wildly. The tires gripped nothing but air. The car sailed past a lone tree and then slammed headfirst into the water. Something smacked his face, forcing his body back in the seat. The airbags had erupted. Water flew everywhere, and so did the screams.

He opened his eyes and felt cool water around his legs. His car was now level, sinking slowly into the water. The airbags had collapsed. Cara was screaming and jerking on her seatbelt. The car began to tilt to his side. The engine died. Steam hissed from the hood, forming an impenetrable cloud in front of him. Exploding bubbles rose from the murky water like rapid gunfire and surrounded him.

Water rose to his chest. He couldn't move. He was still strapped into his seat. He grabbed for the shoulder belt but couldn't find it. *Is it on the right or left?* He couldn't remember. He frantically reached to his left. Wrong side.

He grabbed the strap across his chest and followed it down to his right. The water was engulfing him. He took a breath and he was underwater. Then an arm hit him. It was Cara's. She was free. Beck had unlocked Cara's seatbelt, not his own. He desperately grabbed his seatbelt harness, following it down to the catch and finding the button.

Beck moved his legs to escape, but they were entangled under the steering wheel. He thrashed violently, unable to breathe. The car lurched. It had hit the bottom in the shallow water. His right foot was caught and he pulled, ripping his pants. His knee was out from under the steering wheel. Beck pressed with all of his might and catapulted himself upward.

He burst through the surface, his lungs on fire, gasping for air. His arms thrashed against the murky water. He sank under the surface and inhaled the awful stench. He whipped his arms and hands against the water again and resurfaced. He coughed out the putrid substance and vomited.

He paddled in place, his adrenaline-infused arms and legs churning with panic, keeping his head barely above water. Finally, he felt a log and other debris beneath his feet and stood. He could breathe again, but not without detonating pain in his sides.

At first he thought his body was on fire. But there was only water and the smell of gasoline and oil as a gleaming, blue film spread over the water's surface. There was no fire beyond the inferno from his broken ribs.

Now he could barely move his arms in rhythm to stay afloat. He looked around but did not see Denise or Cara. He turned, trying to get his bearings, just as he heard a scream to his right. It was one of the women. He saw her about twenty feet behind him. She was holding her sister, who appeared unconscious. Beck finally made it over to her and, with no energy to mutter a word, wrapped his arm around the unconscious woman's chest and began dragging her to the shoreline as the sister followed.

Before they could get to the bank, two firemen in full gear came sloshing through the water in their direction.

Beck slipped under the water, and everything went black.

34

Beck awoke in a hospital, hooked up to several tubes. The room was full of voices. He struggled to see. There appeared to be doctors, nurses and several men in suits. He recognized no one.

"Mr. Rikki? Mr. Rikki? Can you hear me?" said a woman in a white doctor's coat.

Beck looked toward her voice. Her face was not in focus. He stared in her direction.

"Mr. Rikki? Mr. Rikki."

"Yes," he whispered.

"You were in an accident."

The woman's features began to form. Instinctively, he tried to reach out to her. A sharp pain pierced his body. He yelled and reflexively closed his eyes.

A hand touched his forearm lightly, trying to comfort him, and he made out a smile on the woman's face.

"Mr. Rikki, I'm Doctor Van Der Jagt."

Beck grimaced in pain.

"You've been in an accident. Do you remember?"

Beck nodded, slowly.

"There are some men from the government here who would like to speak to you. Are you able to speak?"

Beck nodded again.

Immediately, a man in a suit stepped in front of the doctor. "I'm Agent

Howard, Drew Howard. FBI."

"Where are Denise and Cara?" Beck whispered.

The agent looked at the doctor. Both turned back to Beck.

"It was a very tragic accident," Doctor Van Der Jagt said. "We can talk about it later. Where do you feel pain?"

"Fuck pain. Where are Denise and Cara?"

The agent looked at the doctor again. The doctor shook her head. "Mr. Rikki," said Howard, "Cara is going to be okay. She is pretty banged up, but she'll be okay."

"And Denise, what about Denise?"

The agent again looked at the doctor. Doctor Van Der Jagt raised an eyebrow in resignation. Agent Howard turned and spoke again. "I'm sorry, Mr. Rikki, she didn't make it. She was killed instantly, thrown from the car on impact."

Beck groaned. "Not Denise. No, not Denise."

"Mr. Rikki," said Howard.

"Leave me alone."

"We need to talk."

"Leave me alone."

The agent shook his head at the doctor, who signaled a nurse. The nurse opened the plastic line that was dripping a sedative into Beck's arm.

He fell asleep.

Beck awoke hours later to an empty room. It took him several minutes to realize where he was. Then he remembered doctors, nurses and law enforcement all gathered around his bed earlier. The rest flooded his mind. *Denise. Why Denise?* A beautiful, kind woman. Now she was gone.

Beck found the call button and pressed for the nurse.

"Can I speak to Cara Beverly?" he asked, barely above a whisper.

"I'll check," said the nurse. She left the room. A few moments later, she returned. "She'd like to see you."

"Can you unhook me from all of these?" He glanced back at the machines monitoring his vitals and pumping liquids into his body. "I think I can walk."

The nursed checked Beck's chart on the computer and began fiddling with the tubes behind him.

"I can't unhook you from the IV, but I can make you mobile," she said. She left the room and almost immediately returned with a wheelchair. She helped Beck into the chair and hooked a pole to the back and hung his IV bag. A uniformed guard held the door open as the nurse wheeled him into the hall.

Guard?

The nurse pressed open the door to Cara's room and wheeled Beck in. After positioning him next to the bed, she left and closed the door behind her. Cara was in bed with bruises across her face and a bandage on her head. She had a black eye.

She looked at him, moving her head slowly.

"I'm sorry," he said.

She was silent. *Does she recognize me?* Beck wondered if she was in shock or had a concussion. *Any chance of brain damage? Oh Jesus. What have I done?*

"I just can't believe she's gone. Why her? Why not me?" asked Cara.

This was a side of Cara he hadn't seen. In their days together, she'd shown only how tough she was. Now she was a grieving, vulnerable woman.

"What happened?" she asked.

"All I know is someone ran us off the road. I don't know who, but the FBI was in my room earlier trying to find answers."

"You okay?"

"Sore. Really sore. Did the FBI visit you?" Beck asked.

"I don't know. If they did, I was asleep. Do they think it was Oliver?"

"Dunno. I assume. Whoever it was didn't stick around. And I know it was deliberate. I couldn't keep the car on the road."

"Oliver finally found us here."

"Yeah, or at least his people did. Right now we both have armed guards in the hall outside our rooms." Beck made an involuntary motion toward her door and felt a painful jab in his side. He grimaced.

"That cinches it, doesn't it?" Cara said.

"Yeah. I guess it does."

"We're still in danger. The feds assured us they were going to protect us." Cara looked at the sheets covering her. She appeared to be taking stock of her situation.

"The FBI was going to give you and your sister protection this evening. Or was it last night? I don't even know what day it is right now. Anyway, you have protection now."

"A lot of good that does my sister."

"Yeah." Beck noticed her left arm was in a cast. She noticed him staring.

"They said the airbag might have done this to me," she said, tilting her head toward her arm.

"At least you had your seatbelt on."

"If only Denise—" Cara began to cry. She couldn't lift either arm, so her tears streamed unrestrained.

Beck sat awkwardly beside her bed, not knowing what to say or do.

"I'm sorry," he repeated, his voice barely audible and cracking. He wasn't sure she heard him. *This was my fault.* He encouraged them to come to Washington. He took them to see the FBI and Justice officials. He was driving home when they were attacked. If only he had been able to hang onto the wheel longer. *If only . . .*

35

Beck was released later that afternoon. He learned he had been hospitalized overnight; while he was sore, amazingly the doctor told him he had not broken anything, only exacerbated his previous rib injury. He was all strains and sprains but nothing that would last long—except for the possible damage to his psyche. The doctors encouraged him to see a mental health therapist.

An agent gave Beck a ride to his condo. When they arrived, he asked the agent if he planned to stay. He told Beck he was neither a witness nor essential to the case, and that no one thought he was in danger.

Great, thought Beck. *Somehow, I needed a guard before they interviewed me just before my release. Someone just tried to kill Cara, killed her sister instead, and I'm nothing more than collateral damage.*

After the agent left, Beck shuffled toward his bedroom. It was the first time since he had returned to Washington he felt he could walk freely in his own home. But when he stepped in the room, it felt strange. He looked at the girls' few belongings, and the last seventy-two hours flooded his brain.

Either Cara or Denise had forgotten her cell phone and a set of keys. A pair of earrings were on the dresser. Denise's, he remembered. Dangling black pearls. She had looked so good in them. Then he thought about their one kiss. Magical.

He shook his head and stepped to the closet. There were no other signs they had even been here. No purses. No clothes. They had washed and worn the same clothes they wore the day they arrived. Any other possessions were now at the bottom of that estuary along with his prized classic convertible.

Beck spied two of his dirty shirts on the floor—the ones the girls had worn. He picked them up and could smell their scent. Slowly, he pulled the dirty sheets and pillowcases off his bed, careful not to inflame his ribs. He tossed them along with his shirts in the washing machine. He grabbed an extra set of sheets from his linen closet and made his bed.

Beck picked up the cell phone from his dresser and tried to turn it on. Dead. No wonder one of the sisters had left it. And the keys too. No need for them or a dead phone. One of them must have left her charging cord on the tarmac back in Texas.

First a car chase and now someone had purposely run him off the road, trying to kill him. And his girlfriend had disappeared, mad as hell at him.

Where is Geneva? He hadn't heard from her. Certainly she would contact him when she learned of his mishap, no matter how angry she was. He walked into his kitchen, looking for a phone charger, and found one in the cabinet beneath his silverware drawer. He plugged in the phone and made a pot of hazelnut coffee. He grabbed the morning paper the FBI agent had brought and stepped out onto his balcony to read while he waited for the phone to charge. But first, he would call Geneva.

Her phone rang several times before rolling over to voicemail. He left her a message to call, saying he had been in an accident but was okay. Surely that would get her attention.

He returned to the kitchen fifteen minutes later and turned on the sister's cell phone. It pinged as it accepted old texts and emails that had been waiting since the battery died.

He thumbed through text messages until he stumbled upon nude selfies of Cara and the chief justice. Apparently, she'd decided to take some using her own phone. Beck had seen similar ones from the federal prosecutor, who had turned over photos from Castiglia's phone to Kelly's lawyer. At least he knew who belonged to this phone.

Curious, Beck flicked his finger and dozens of pictures raced by in a blur.

He tapped the phone's screen to stop scrolling. There were nudes of her smiling with several men. In some, she was actually engaged in a sex act.

Beck felt dirty but continued to scroll. There was a US senator, the late labor secretary, a famous union organizer, and several of the businessmen he recognized from the dinner in Texas. *She sure gets around.* And she sure liked to photograph her clients.

Even the rich and powerful have weaknesses, Beck figured. *So driven, so desperate to succeed, so entitled.* They acted as if they were immune to rules of society. It was all about a sense of privilege. There certainly was plenty of that in Washington.

He wondered about Cara. *Sure, she's a prostitute, but that doesn't define her. Or does it? Is her profession humiliating or empowering?* Whichever it was would determine a lot about who she was.

He thought about Geneva. Her lifestyle troubled him. At first it was a turn on, but after a while, seeing Geneva naked all of the time became just the opposite. She was a nudist—in private, but still a nudist. He'd learned from her it had nothing to do with sex. It seemed to empower her in some way. She was doing exactly as she wished and didn't really care what Beck thought about it. More than once she had said there was absolutely nothing wrong with the naked body. "We all have one" was one of her favorite lines.

Is Cara any different? So she slept with a lot of men. It wasn't like Beck hadn't slept with his share of women over his lifetime. *But she does it for money.* Beck almost broke out laughing at the thought. He should be so lucky. The best he'd done was a few cheap gifts from the women he'd bedded. He remembered the doctor he had once dated. The most he received from her was a few quarters for a parking meter.

Beck wanted to think he was progressive, but he admitted he really wasn't, at least when it came to prostitution. Even growing up with his crazy flower-child parents, he still experienced their monogamous relationship and love. He was tolerant and accepting of a lot of things. And even if some viewed prostitution as a victimless crime, it still disturbed him. It was different from nudism, and it did define Cara's relationship with others. *Shit,* thought Beck.

Guess I'm a prude.

He felt like a voyeur looking through her photos. But he couldn't stop. He pulled up her photo app. More photos of Cara with men. He examined a couple, recognizing a mogul and politician whose names he couldn't recall. But most of the faces were familiar.

And then he stopped scrolling.

He looked at himself in a photo. *Naked?* Cara was naked beside him.

How? He couldn't believe it. *I never . . .*

He examined the photo. They were on a bed. Her hand was shielding his privates from the camera. One of her breasts pressed against his bare chest as she kissed him on the cheek. His eyes closed as if he were enjoying this. Then he recognized the iron bed. He'd slept in it at Cara's house. He remembered the dream he had about sleeping and showering with one of the sisters. *Could it have not been a dream?*

He swiped the photo. There was a second one of them together. He quickly thumbed through seven more. Nine photos in all of him naked in bed with Cara—the mole under her breast fully visible. Each picture showed him with his eyes closed as Cara pressed her body against his.

These were all staged while he slept. Then he remembered the hangover the next morning. Cara had mixed his drink the night before. She'd drugged him. Probably that date-rape drug. That made her business even more despicable.

So what was the motive? Blackmail? He deleted the photos of him, one by one. He scrolled back through to ensure they were all gone. He had no desire to become part of her permanent collection, or vulnerable to her motives.

36

Denise Fiori's funeral was a large affair that overflowed the aging Spanish-style Baptist Church in El Paso.

Six days after her death, the preacher's eulogy talked lovingly about her volunteer work, her professional awards in the business community and her selfless deeds for her church. She had even gone on several church mission trips to help build homes in Central America.

What a contrast with her twin's homemade pornography, Beck thought. He wondered if anyone here knew what her sister—now in mourning in the front pew—actually did for a living.

Next to Cara sat an older woman in a black suit with flowing white hair and a black veil covering her face. He couldn't make out her features from his seat in the back. She draped her left arm around Cara's shoulder. *An aunt, perhaps? Maybe another cousin.* He'd met a couple of the cousins last night during visitation at the funeral home—a homely male and another hot female—and yet another, an older female, was seated in the front pew on the other side of Cara. Beck assumed the man seated next to the older woman was her husband or boyfriend. *What's with this family's DNA?*

A couple of times, Cara slumped against the older woman's shoulder. Cara was taking this hard. Beck felt responsible. If he just hadn't brought them to Washington. He struggled to remain objective and not get caught up in the emotions of the moment. But each time he looked up at Cara, it got more difficult.

It appeared the entire local chamber of commerce was in attendance. And an entire row of women sat in the front pew across the aisle from Cara. A cadre of Denise's girlfriends, perhaps.

Beck looked for familiar faces but saw none.

The service painted the image of a conventional woman who was active in the community. *But was that all?* Maybe, like her sister, she had a hidden life. *What did Denise tell me?* Yeah, she said she enjoyed her quiet life. She was a private person. As he looked through the crowd, her life seemed much more active than she had let on. It appeared she knew everyone in town. Yet, she had downplayed her accomplishments. He liked her modesty.

Beck skipped the reception afterward, going straight to the airport to rebook his reservation for an earlier flight home. He'd had enough of El Paso and his depressing feelings. He just wanted a couple of drinks and to fall asleep on the flight. He accomplished both.

37

"Ms. Beverly is here."

"Perfect. I'll be right over." The vice president put down the phone.

He braced himself. Cara Beverly had been through a lot. Despite privacy laws, the doctors had kept the FBI informed of her condition and said she would eventually be okay, at least physically. But, they cautioned, they were not sure of her mental state. She'd suffered a terrible loss and was taking it hard.

FBI Director McCauley told Fahy that Cara seemed more reluctant about testifying against Jackson Oliver. Her memory, or at least her confidence, he feared, may have been shaken by the accident. Fahy knew that without her the case against Jackson Oliver would fall apart. He needed to handle this delicately.

Fahy rose from his desk and headed to the Old Executive Office Building. Immediately, an aide and his Secret Service detail fell in behind him. The walk through tunnels, hallways and stairs took about eight minutes. When he arrived at his outer office, he looked over his shoulder at his detail, and they all stepped back, taking stations in the outside hallway.

Cara sat in the outside office with his secretary.

"Good morning, Ms. Beverly," he said.

She looked at him and nodded but said nothing.

"It's good to see you on the mend. You're looking well. I'm so sorry about your sister."

He led her into his private office. She seemed smaller than he remembered, and her arm was in a sling with no cast. He could tell she was wearing a lot of makeup to hide bruises on her face, yet she seemed just as beautiful as when they had first met.

Following the accident, Fahy arranged for the government to fly Cara and the body of her sister home to El Paso, using the excuse that she was a government witness. McCauley had arranged for four plainclothes FBI agents to accompany Cara—everywhere. "Don't let her out of your sight, not for a minute," he'd ordered.

Now he had to ensure she would testify against Jackson Oliver in open court.

"Thank you for everything you've done for me," she said.

"I know it's been tough on you. I appreciate you returning to discuss the Jackson Oliver situation," he said.

"I don't think I'm the right person for this," Cara replied.

"Of course you are. You'll be great. You just tell the jury and the judge what you know. That's all we're asking. The Justice Department prosecutors will work with you on your testimony so you'll be completely prepared."

"But I'm not."

Fahy moved to the visitor's chair next to her. He gently clasped her hand in both of his. He noticed how soft her skin was and looked directly into her eyes. They were pale blue, the same as the water lapping the beach of a Caribbean island. His pulse quickened. It had been so long since he had been with a woman. He willed himself to concentrate.

"I know this is difficult," he said. "But we're not only tracking down the killer of Chief Justice Castiglia. This man orchestrated your sister's murder and tried to kill you too." Fahy watched her face react to his words. It was as if she had just realized who was responsible for her sister's death.

"We need your help to put Oliver away. You're the only link we have between Oliver and Justice Castiglia's death. That's why we need your testimony. You can put your sister's killer away forever."

"I can't," she said.

Fahy sagged. He thought she had been coming around when he mentioned her sister's murder.

"Of course you can. We'll help you in every way possible."

"Look, I appreciate you putting me up in a hotel, giving me armed guards and helping me with all of my recent travel, but I'm not the right girl."

"Why do you say that?"

"Because I'm not Cara."

Fahy's mouth dropped. He let her hand slip from his.

"I'm Denise."

Fahy just sat there. Staring. "You're serious."

"I know. It sounds crazy."

"That's an understatement. You've let everyone believe you're Cara—the doctors, the FBI, your friends back in El Paso. Everyone has been mourning the wrong sister."

"I've been struggling. Everyone started calling me Cara at the hospital. Then it all just snowballed. It took me nearly a day after the accident before I could talk. It consumed me until I even began to believe it for a while. But I'm getting better since the funeral. I'm trying to pull my life together again. I'm Denise."

"It just seems so unbelievable."

"I have a lot of explaining to do to friends and family when I return to Texas."

Fahy was struggling to wrap his head around this. He liked Denise, if she really was Denise.

"I need to put my old life back together as much as possible. That's why I agreed to meet with you today. You've been very kind and I owe you an explanation before I return to Texas for good. For everything you've done for me, you at least deserved that much."

That sure sounded like her. The rhythm and cadence of her voice. The words. They lacked Cara's hardened edge. *This is Denise, and that changes everything.*

Fahy saw his entire case disappear in a blond flash. That slime-bag Oliver would slip through again. He'd accomplished exactly what he'd set out to do: eliminate the one witness who could destroy him.

"Look," Fahy said, "I need your help." He reached for her hand again, and again a tingle went up his spine at her warmth. "Without you, the man who killed your sister will go free. That hasn't changed, even if you aren't Cara."

Fahy felt desperate. He was making it up on the fly. "Would you be willing to help us anyway?"

"I'm not sure what good I could do."

"You can still testify against Oliver."

"But I don't know anything. I mean, yes, I could tell people about what I heard from my sister, but that's not much."

Fahy saw an opening. "We have a situation where we know he's guilty, but we can't prove it in court without a witness. Do you agree he killed Chief Justice Castiglia and your sister?"

"Yes. I believe that." She grabbed a tissue from the box on his desk and dabbed her nose.

"The evidence is overwhelming. Would you be willing to say that in court?"

"But I don't know that."

"But you just said you did. You believe he is a murderer. If I could just get you to say that in court, it would go a long way toward putting this dangerous man in prison for life. He would no longer be a threat to you, which you must understand he still is. He killed your sister. Remember that. He killed Cara. There is nothing to stop him from coming after you again—especially if he's a free man and believes you're Cara. If for no other reason, help us to stop him from coming after you again."

Denise sat silently, looking down at their hands intertwined on her lap. Fahy placed his other hand over hers and lightly stroked them.

She looked up. "Mr. Fahy, uh, Mr. Vice President—"

"Dan. Please call me Dan."

"You're right. I guess I'm in danger. I hadn't really thought of that."

"You can do this. You can work with the prosecutors to go over the evidence and then tell them about the glass in the hotel room."

Denise eased her hands from his grasp and tugged at her tight skirt. She placed both hands on the arms of her chair and shifted her posture, never looking at him.

Fahy said nothing. She pulled a strand of hair that had fallen across her face back behind her ear and turned to him. Her hair fell down again, accentuating the lovely curve of her jaw and chin. *God, she's gorgeous,* Fahy thought.

"If I do this, who will know about it?"

"Only the two of us."

"The prosecutors won't?"

"Not if you do your homework. I can arrange for you to visit the resort so you know the exact layout. We can tell the prosecutors you just want to familiarize yourself with the crime scene again.

"I can show you the crime scene photos taken by the FBI and the photos your sister took with the chief justice's phone. You can read your sister's transcript to know exactly how she testified already. You must be consistent with everything. You must memorize every word. It will take work, but the prosecutors will help you."

"I thought you said only you and I will know the truth," Denise said. "If the prosecutors are coaching me, they will too."

"That's easy to overcome. You and I will work together first. I'll get all of the evidence, and you can memorize it before you even talk about your testimony with the prosecutors. If there's something you don't know, just tell them you forgot and need to look over your transcript again.

"Look, the prosecutors want to convict Oliver. They'll coach you as well. They do that for every case they take to court. They'll even suggest how to answer certain questions during cross-examination from Oliver's lawyers. If you flub something during their coaching sessions, they will just write it off as a case of nerves. Witnesses are always nervous before they go to court. Federal prosecutors are your advocates. They want to win. Trust me."

"I guess that will work," she said.

Fahy felt relief. The odds were against them, but maybe they could actually pull this off.

"We'll make a great team," he said, "and I'll be there with you every step of the way."

37

Beck had slept in and was just reading the *Post-Examiner* when the phone rang.

"Beck?"

"Geneva." Beck dropped his newspaper on the floor.

"How are you?"

That's a funny question. She's avoided me for a week and suddenly she's concerned about my wellbeing?

"Sorry. I'm not doing well. I was in a car accident and one of the women I was trying to help was killed. I'm struggling to recover."

"I know."

"You know?"

"I have friends who told me about it."

"Well at least you could return my phone calls. And by the way, I didn't have an affair with either of those women you saw in my condo that night when you stormed off."

"I know that too."

"Your behavior was over the top. It screamed you don't trust me."

"No, it didn't."

"Well, what then?"

"I've known Cara for several years."

He couldn't believe what he was hearing. "You what?"

"We met several years ago. So when I saw her there with you, I flipped out."

"Why?"

"She and I had a brief fling. It started with a one-night stand."

Beck's head spun.

"It was short, a couple of months, and very intense," she said. "It was right after I'd learned Harv had had a series of affairs with congressional staffers. I was angry. I was determined to hurt him the same as he hurt me."

Beck tried to take it all in. His girlfriend had a lesbian affair with a prostitute. This was too much. "Knowing you, I just find that hard to believe."

"It's true."

"Tell me the whole story."

"I'm embarrassed. I'm also sorry for the way I've treated you."

"You're also stalling."

Beck heard her take a deep breath.

"It was three years ago. I was at an all-day conference Harv asked me to attend in his absence. It was an off-the-record political powwow with a group of powerful people upset with how Washington wasn't working. They were seeking solutions. At first I thought it was just one of those political think-tank meetings, but then it became pretty obvious they were criticizing both parties, especially the fringes of both, and blaming them for Washington's impotence. They were serious. It was all non-partisan. I realized it was different from other groups. They were determined to make big changes in Washington. It was called Renaissance something."

Beck was stunned. Suddenly, he could barely hear, like he was swimming underwater. *Did she just say she was at the birth of the Renaissance Circle?*

"Cara was there, clinging to the arm of some Texas oilman," Geneva said. "Well, they held a cocktail party and afterward we sat at the hotel bar. Just the two of us. I was feeling blue about my marriage, and I opened up to her. One thing led to another and we ended up getting a room for the night. It lasted a couple of months, as I said."

Beck was struggling with the image of Geneva and Cara in bed. She was the sexiest lover he'd ever had. He couldn't imagine her with a woman.

Everything in his life was starting to fall apart.

"That doesn't explain everything," he said. "This is just too coincidental. I was a reporter for too long. I don't believe in coincidence."

"You're right. The call you received from Castiglia? I arranged it. Harv called me long ago, asking about you. He said Castiglia needed someone to tell his story to. He asked me if you would be interested. I told him you would."

Beck was speechless. *All of this started with my girlfriend?* "Why didn't you tell me?"

"Harv asked me to keep it quiet. He said it was important to Castiglia. I also thought it would be good for you. You seemed unsettled. I could tell you were itching to get back in the reporting game. So I decided to grant Harv's wish. I thought you needed this. I thought I was doing you a favor."

"Yeah, well, that got Castiglia killed."

Beck heard Geneva breaking down. At this point he didn't care. She hadn't been honest with him about so many things—her money, now this. *What am I supposed to believe?*

Beck wasn't going to apologize for what he had just said. He believed it. Had he known President Harvey had initiated this whole thing, he might not have accepted Castiglia's invitation. *Oh hell, who am I kidding? Of course I would have.* He was just mad at Geneva. She had thrown their personal life into a paper shredder.

The phone was quiet, but he still heard her breathing.

"Beck?"

He didn't answer.

"Beck, I'm coming back to DC."

"Why did you leave in the first place?"

"Isn't it obvious?"

38

Fahy was good as his word and gathered copies of all of the photographic evidence and transcripts from the FBI. For two days, Denise visited his hideaway office and went over everything before he had her talk with prosecutors. She became upset only once when she saw the nude selfies of her sister with Castiglia. Fahy instinctively put his arm around her and held her for a moment, trying to reassure her. She buried her head in his chest and clung to him for a moment.

Later, he explained to the prosecutors that she was emotionally shattered and her memory fragile. They were to treat her gently. *That*, he thought, *will protect her against any missteps that could reveal her identity*.

The prosecutors suggested she revisit the resort to refresh her memory. The room had long ago been cleaned after the FBI and US marshals relinquished possession, but Michael Trowbridge, the proprietor, kept the room empty out of respect for the chief justice. The trip was arranged to allow her to get a lay of the land—where the dining room was for the party the night before; how her sister got from the party to the chief justice's room and from the room to the hotel lobby. She even examined the parking lot, although where Cara had parked had no bearing on the case.

Beck was seated in the back of the courtroom when US District Court Judge Savage banged his gavel. Because it was a high-profile case, the Justice

Department fast-tracked the trial. Several federal judges volunteered to clear their dockets to hear the case of their fallen colleague.

It began in a federal courtroom in Washington early on a Monday morning. Cara's arm was finally out of its cast and her bruises had long disappeared. The jury was seated by late afternoon and Judge Savage announced opening statements would begin the following morning as he gaveled Monday's session to a close.

Beck had been in this courtroom before, and when Judge Savage banged his gavel and glanced his way, Beck thought he saw a glint of recognition.

The judge spent the first few minutes the next morning explaining to the jury what was about to happen. Then the case started in full, with Oliver's attorney, Charles Curtiss, and the federal prosecutors making their opening remarks.

Curtiss, thought Beck. Interesting choice. *First he represents the man Oliver set up and now he's representing Oliver.* A little too cute, perhaps. Beck wondered if Kevin Kelly had complained of a conflict of interest. *Or is there even one? Wouldn't that be Oliver's call?* After all, they weren't prosecuting Oliver for framing Kelly.

If nothing else, Curtiss's presence at the defendant's table confirmed Beck's suspicion that the cunning lawyer was somehow deeply involved in all of this.

The EMTs were called to testify. Michael Trowbridge was called to the stand. Even the snotty front desk clerk who had given Beck the stink-eye was sworn in. Beck wondered why he had never been subpoenaed. *Why am I not a witness?* The only thing Beck could figure was Trowbridge's testimony would be enough. Perhaps Beck would have been overkill. He felt relieved.

He thought back to the time he was questioned at the Old Executive Office Building. The inquiry was perfunctory. Still, they went through the motions. It made him wonder. *Do I know something they don't want me to share in court? Could I be holding the key to this mystery and not know it?*

By midafternoon, the prosecutors called Cara to the stand. After she was sworn in and accepted by the defense as a witness, she was asked to walk through the events of her night with the late justice.

At one point she recognized Beck sitting in the back of the courtroom. They made brief eye contact and then she returned her focus to the attorneys. She explained the circumstances of the night of the party in the main dining room and her evening before and after with the chief justice. She said she had been seated across the table from Castiglia. Beck remembered it differently. *They were sitting next to each other.*

Then she explained about seeing Oliver leave Castiglia's hotel room after she had returned to pick up her misplaced keys. When he saw her approach, she said, she noticed him slipping a small bottle into his pocket. She had thought nothing of it at the time. It could have been anything—even his own medicine. Only later, after learning of Justice Castiglia's death, did she grow suspicious.

She also testified about seeing the drinking glass on the bedside table and told the jury it was still there when she left. Once she had finished telling her story, the prosecutor continued his questioning.

"Now, Miss Beverly," he said, "the defense is going to say you have a grudge against Mr. Oliver. You blame him for your sister's recent death in an auto accident."

"I admit that I do," she said, "but my feelings about him have never changed."

"Do you have any evidence the accident you and your sister were in was caused by Mr. Oliver?"

"None."

"And does your feeling that Mr. Oliver may have caused your sister's death affect your testimony in any way about the murder of Chief Justice Nino Castiglia?"

"Absolutely not. I saw what I saw. I may not have any evidence that he killed my sister, but I can testify to what I saw when I was with Judge Castiglia."

Clever, thought Beck. *A preemptive move.*

After another twenty minutes, it was the defense's turn to question Cara.

"Now, Miss Beverly," Curtiss said, "you state the death of your twin sister has no bearing on your testimony against Mr. Oliver."

"That's true."

Slowly, methodically, the defense attorneys tried to attack her testimony and credibility, but Cara wouldn't fold. *Nothing new there*, thought Beck. *Unlike her sister, she's a tough cookie.* But something bothered him about the testimony. She had gotten the seating wrong at the dinner party, and there was something else he couldn't quite place.

He listened intensely as Curtiss appeared to be wrapping up his questioning. Beck closed his eyes, trying to concentrate. Cara's voice brought back memories, but they were memories of Denise. She sounded just like Denise. The actual words were more Cara, but the tone, the rhythm, was pure Denise. He remembered that morning in his condo when they had kissed.

That made no sense. It was as if Denise's death affected Cara so much that she'd assumed her sister's mannerisms, her lilting speech pattern.

Finally, Curtiss finished his questioning and the judge asked if the federal government had any follow-up. It didn't. Beck watched Cara step down from the stand, tug at her tight skirt and then leave through a side door. The judge adjourned for the day.

The prosecutors were lighthearted, shaking hands. They appeared happy with the day's events. The defense table, not so. Curtiss and two other defense attorneys were discussing something intensely. They were not happy.

And Beck was disturbed by what he had just witnessed in the courtroom.

39

"Congratulations," bellowed President Michael Harvey. Giving a hearty laugh, he welcomed his new chief justice, William Everest Croom, into the Oval Office. He slapped him on the back and gave him a firm handshake.

"We did it. Damn it. We did it," Harvey said, motioning for Croom to take a seat on one of the couches facing each other. Harvey sat across from him, a silver coffee service on the glass-top coffee table between them. The president and former president now sat as equals again—each head of one of the three branches of government.

"Care for any?" Harvey motioned to the coffee as he poured a cup for himself.

"Too late in the day for me, but thanks," Croom replied. "I take my hat off to you. I can't believe you pulled this off. And it all appeared so seamless."

"Don't kid yourself. We traded a lot away to get you on the bench. I gotta give my man Dan Fahy a lot of credit," said Harvey. "He called in a lot of favors. He made it look easy. The public has no idea how much arm-twisting went into this one. Who would have thought in these times a Republican could appoint a Democrat to the high court?"

"It did help that I knew everyone in the Senate. We're a couple of troglodytes, you know. A Democrat and Republican who actually like each other. Doesn't happen much anymore."

"Okay, so our sell-by dates may have expired long ago, but we proved congressional bipartisanship may still have a long shelf life. Bill, mark today as the true beginning of our silent revolution—our silent coup. We can do this." Harvey sipped his coffee and set his cup down.

"I sure hope you're right," Croom said. "Yet, I still don't like the circumstances that led up to this. I can't believe one of my own political appointees actually killed Nino. Nino was a good guy, even if I didn't agree with his politics and extremist jurisprudence."

"He was. But we have to play the hand we're dealt. "

"I suppose." Croom let out a sigh and shook his head.

"Our next step is to start pushing Congress back to the middle where it belongs." Harvey poured himself more coffee and then stopped, looking at the cup.

"We've got a big agenda. It will take decades. I hope you will be around on the court for another twenty years. Me? I've got seven years at best. So I need to rely on you and the Renaissance Circle to carry on without me."

Harvey picked up his cup and walked over to his desk. He reached in a drawer, pulled out a bottle of bourbon, and poured a shot in his coffee.

"Well, now, you didn't tell me the type of coffee you were serving," Croom grinned.

"Reconsider?"

"I think I will." Croom poured himself a cup from the silver service and Harvey walked over and handed him the bottle. The new chief justice took a sip. "Now that's some of the best coffee I've ever tasted." Croom gazed around the Oval Office, his eyes darting from wall to wall.

"What?" Harvey asked. "Don't like my interior design?"

"You know, you get used to this office. You feel it's yours. But you're only a short-term tenant. It's strange to come in here and see how you've changed it."

Harvey looked at his friend. "I understand. Just so you know, you're welcome here anytime, old friend."

"Old is right. We'd better get moving now while we still can."

They both laughed.

"Speaking of time, you can answer a legal question for me," Harvey said.

"The first one for the new chief justice. How much time do you think Oliver will get?"

"Well, thanks to your friend Charles Curtiss presenting such a weak defense, I'd guess life. I can guarantee his appeals will go nowhere." Croom offered an exaggerated wink. "I'm surprised Oliver didn't press Curtiss to be more aggressive. Oliver's a sharp guy— at least he was when he worked in my administration."

"It's hard to attack a woman on the stand and not turn off the jury," Harvey said. "Curtiss handled that just right."

"For us, maybe," Croom interrupted. "Oliver may soon regret handing over his entire defense to Curtiss."

"He didn't have much choice, now did he?"

Croom raised his cup. "To us and the future of America. Cheers."

"Cheers," Harvey replied.

Both men smiled, knowingly.

Harvey set down his cup. "And once again Beck Rikki is in the middle of everything. I'm worried about him. He can be dangerous. I wonder—I wonder if he knows when he's being manipulated and if he just plays along."

"He seems like a smart guy. I think he's decided it's a fair trade."

"Strange bedfellows," said Harvey, as he poured another shot of bourbon into his cup.

"Strange indeed," said Croom.

40

There was no Secret Service around that Beck could see. Vice President Fahy welcomed Beck and closed the door to his Old Executive Office Building office. The jury had handed down its guilty verdict two hours ago.

"So, what's so important we had to meet today?" Fahy asked.

"That was not Cara on the stand. That was Denise," Beck said.

"What do you mean? Denise is dead." Fahy's response sounded hollow.

"There's been some mix-up. Somehow Denise is alive. Not Cara. I could tell from the way she talked. And some of her testimony was wrong."

"Are you sure?"

"I'm sure. Did you notice her tug at her skirt after testifying? That is pure Denise."

"But what about Oliver? Don't you think he's guilty?" Fahy's jaw tightened.

"Well, yeah, but—"

"Then what's the problem?" Fahy asked.

"She didn't see anything. She lied on the stand."

"How do you know?"

Beck couldn't tell if Fahy was concerned or challenging him. "She wasn't sitting across from Castiglia at the dinner party as she testified in court. She sat right next to him."

"Oh, come on. Anyone could make that mistake."

"Hardly. The chief justice couldn't keep his hands off her the entire night. I was there; I saw it."

"Maybe she was embarrassed and didn't want to say anything about it in court." Fahy leaned back in his chair and propped his feet up on the desk.

"Get real. She spent the night with him. She identified nude photos of herself and Castiglia under oath," Beck said. "What difference would it make if she said she sat next to him during a dinner party, being groped half the evening?"

"Can you prove she's Denise?"

"Well, no." Beck's voice trailed off.

"Then what's your point?"

"I'm sure she's not Cara."

"Okay. Let's say you're right." Fahy lifted his shoes off of his desk and sat up. "If you go to the judge with this, after a jury has just unanimously convicted Oliver, you'd better be damn sure. No judge is going to undo a jury's conviction without compelling evidence. How could you prove any of this?"

"There's only one way. Cara has a mole under her left breast. Denise doesn't."

"Oh, so you, a former reporter with a tarnished reputation, are going to ask a federal judge to have her strip-searched. That will go over well. No evidence, just a hunch, and the court is going to roll over and order a key witness to take off her blouse? I don't think so. And how can you be so sure you're right?"

Beck felt the air go out of his argument. "I can't."

"Exactly," Fahy said. "And what if you're wrong? She would have one helluva civil suit against you, and who knows what the judge would throw at you. Now think about it. Is Oliver guilty or not?"

"But if she's not who she says she is—"

"Guilty or not?"

Fahy was right. Beck, like everyone else, knew Oliver was guilty. And it sure wouldn't bother Beck if his old nemesis went to prison, especially after Oliver tried framing that kid lawyer, Kevin Kelly.

Maybe it wasn't Denise on the stand, he thought. Cara could have just forgotten where she was sitting that night. Her cell phone photos proved she had slept with any number of powerful men. Maybe Castiglia was just one in a long line of high-profile but forgettable lays.

"It still bothers me," he said.

"The court system isn't perfect, but we get it right 99 percent of the time," Fahy said. "Welcome to the slippery slope of life. It's messy. Sometimes the ends *do* justify the means. Sometimes not. We must hope the final outcome is right and ethical and—even if, as you suggest, a little black magic was necessary to pull it off—it doesn't make it wrong."

"I get it now," Beck said. "I get why you didn't want me to testify in court. I might have contradicted Denise. You couldn't take that chance. And Oliver's attorneys are afraid of me. They don't know how much I know, so they figure to keep me out of the courtroom."

Fahy grinned.

"Can I trust you?" Beck huffed.

"Look," Fahy said, "you and I have a special bond."

Beck couldn't argue with that. Their relationship was one giant stalemate. Neither could make a move on the other.

"I'll make you a deal. I'll keep my mouth shut about Denise if you explain what in the hell the Renaissance Circle is all about."

Fahy looked as if Beck had just asked for his first child. "You know about that?"

"Obviously. But not enough that I don't need to ask the question. Is the Renaissance Circle tied to Castiglia's death?"

"If I tell you, you are sworn to secrecy. This is totally off the record."

"Sure," Beck said. "Off the record."

"The Renaissance Circle was formed by a bunch of business executives and politicians from around the US who don't like the deadlock here in Washington. They blame the political extremes on both sides—Republican and Democrat—for tying the government up in knots and making it dysfunctional. So they decided to do something about them."

"And that is?"

"Get rid of them."

"That's the most ridiculous thing I've ever heard. You can't just wipe out the far left and far right."

"Can't you?" Fahy rose and walked to the other side of his desk to lean against it. "Where did the political middle go over the past thirty years? Who wiped them out?"

Beck had never really considered such a thing. "And killing Castiglia was part of that?"

"I don't think so. I don't think his death was planned. I think it was a last-minute, rash decision."

"And then I walked into the picture." Beck was beginning to see Fahy's logic.

"Yes. Castiglia's plan to meet with you must have scared someone," Fahy said. "It appears to me the Renaissance Circle feared Castiglia might go public by talking to you and destroy their efforts. They realized too late that inviting Castiglia to be a member—no matter what you thought of his court rulings—turned out to be a mistake. He was a man of integrity. He loved the Constitution. When he was invited to join a few years back, I suspect Castiglia thought the Renaissance Circle was a gentlemen's club where you could network and intellectually decipher today's politics. At some point he uncovered the meaning behind the organization. Being a man of honor, I'm sure he felt he had no alternative but to expose their plans. But who could he trust? When he looked around the room, he realized most of the people he considered friends were now—in his mind—trying to undermine our democracy. So he thought of the Fourth Estate and you. And when you showed up, Oliver was alarmed and, from what I've been able to put together, took matters into his own hands."

"Wow. Killing a Supreme Court justice for his politics. That's unbelievable."

Fahy walked to a window and looked out into the sunlight. "Not for his politics," he said, still with his back to Beck. "For his integrity and his willingness to expose the Renaissance Circle. You must understand, the Circle has been working on moving Washington to the middle for years. It's a slow process. The public has been unaware, and the Circle wants to keep it that way. It doesn't murder people. It works through the political process. Oliver was an aberration."

Fahy turned to Beck. "Now we have an agreement. You can say nothing about any of this. I expect you to honor that pledge."

Beck realized Fahy had outmaneuvered him. He hadn't expected the Renaissance Circle to be anything like Fahy described it. Now he understood the Circle was a conspiracy. And his off-the-record pledge wouldn't let him tell anyone.

Fahy knew just how to manipulate him. He must have realized Beck would eventually figure out the truth, so he locked him into keeping a secret instead. Just like the prosecutors in the courtroom on the first day of Denise's testimony.

"But this is a crime," Beck protested. "I can't stay silent about murder."

"No, it's not. The Renaissance Circle was not implicated. It was Oliver—a lone wolf. And thanks to Denise's testimony, he's been convicted and justice will be served."

Beck wasn't so sure. He wondered how much Fahy really knew about the Circle. *Is he aware of the previous political "accidents" that resulted in the deaths of those who opposed the organization?*

—⁂—

Beck didn't bother to close Fahy's door when he left.

As he walked down the hall, his cell phone vibrated. It was his former editor Nancy. He let it go to voicemail. He did not trust the privacy of a phone call with his old editor while he was still inside this building. Something about the place gave him the creeps. Enemy territory.

He summoned an Uber, headed for Alexandria and called Nancy from the back seat.

"Just wanted you to know," she said, "Baker won't be hiring Rabidan after all."

"Oh. What happened?"

"Seems she's tied up in a major libel lawsuit with Castiglia's family about her story saying they deliberately tried to cover up facts about his death."

"That's too bad. I know what that feels like," Beck said.

"Do you? You didn't have anything to do with this, now did you, Beck?"

"Of course I did. I gave Giegerich the correct facts for *your* story so the *Post-Examiner* came out smelling like a rose."

"You know what I'm talking about. You wouldn't feed her a bad story to torpedo her career and her chance of getting your old job here at the *Post-Examiner*, now would you? Maybe a little payback for what she did to you?"

"Now why would I do that? Beck asked. "I can't help it if she got sloppy. Don't blame me for her shoddy work."

"Beck—"

"Gotta go, Nancy. I just got home." Beck killed the call.

Fahy wasn't the only one who got his revenge.

41

Beck heard the strange ringtone while he was in his kitchen and ventured back to the bedroom. Cara's phone was ringing and vibrating on top of his dresser. He picked it up and looked at the screen. It said the W Hotel.

"Yeah?"

"Beck?"

"Hello, Denise." He knew he had nothing to lose in revealing his hand.

"This is Cara. How can you be so cruel?"

"Sure it is. And I'm Justice Nino Castiglia back from the dead. Seems we both finally have something in common."

"That's not funny."

"Neither is perjury." The phone fell silent. Beck looked at it to ensure the battery hadn't gone dead again.

"How did you find out?"

"I have my ways."

"What are you going to do about it?"

"Nothing, at the moment."

"What are you doing with my sister's phone?"

"What are you doing calling it?"

"The phone company told me to double-check before cancelling her service. I thought it would be at the bottom of that lake with your car. I'm trying to clean up her affairs. I'd like to have it, if you don't mind. It may have some personal items, like names of people I need to notify."

"It sure does," said Beck.

"Oh?"

"Your sister has quite a photo collection."

"Oh?"

"It's not family friendly."

"Oh."

"Yeah. Your sister liked keeping trophies of her conquests. You sure you want to see them?"

"Yes. Like I said, it may have phone numbers of friends I need to notify."

"Very well. I guess it's better in your hands than mine."

"Maybe we should talk in person," she said.

"Ya think?"

—⚡—

Denise led Beck into her large, beautifully appointed hotel suite without a word. *The government appears to be treating its star witness well,* he thought. They sat facing each other on a small couch. She offered him coffee. He declined.

He thought about embracing her the way they had that morning in his condo. But it didn't feel right. He had grieved for her enough. Now, for whatever reason, he felt different.

She smiled that beautiful smile. He leaned in, but she did not react. *Curious.*

He was close enough to notice her hair smelled of jasmine. When they embraced before, she had been using another shampoo. He remembered it well. It had a mango scent. The memory, like the scent, lingered.

"I'm glad to see you're okay. Have things changed between us?" he asked.

"Of course not," she said, looking at him curiously. "My phone?"

He handed it to her. "Sorry, but I had to open it to find out who it belonged to. I figured out it was Cara's, especially after I found my picture on there."

"Your picture?"

"Your sister set me up, just like all of her other clients. Her phone is full of Castiglia-style selfies. There's a long line of political celebrities and me. I assume she wanted mine in case she ever needed blackmail material."

"I can't believe that. You helped us. She had her faults, but she wouldn't do that."

"It's all there, with the exception of my photos. I deleted them."

"You did?"

There was something about her tone, like she was disappointed he had erased his photos. That didn't seem like the old Denise.

The old Denise. Of course. He realized what had been bothering him. It was so diabolically twisted. *Why did it take me this long to see it?*

Denise looked at him curiously. Beck smiled. He could tell she was worried he may have just figured it out.

"You haven't told me everything," Beck said. "What about your little charade? You have a lot to explain, or I can tell the truth to a certain federal judge, my pals in the media, and of course the vice president. Somehow, I don't think you'll end up in a suite as nice as this one."

—⁓—

On the Uber ride back to his condo Beck realized there was one question he had failed to ask: Who was behind his mugging in El Paso? Yet, after their conversation, he understood he had known the answer all along.

Oliver's men hadn't followed him there, as he previously believed. Had he thought it through, he would have realized that was impossible. He would have spotted anyone following him on that long, lonely stretch from the resort along the miles of desert highway on his drive to El Paso.

Denise and her evil twin were responsible. It seemed obvious now that after Denise slammed the door in his face the first time he met her, she contacted her sister, who took immediate action.

Or maybe Denise wasn't alone when she answered the door at her apartment that day. Perhaps Cara was there too and then followed him. He remembered sitting in his car outside of Denise's apartment for a few minutes, taking in their brief encounter and trying to figure out his next move. That may have given Cara enough time to react. She, no doubt, had the connections to call on a couple of thugs to follow him and send him a message of tough love, facedown on a city sidewalk. His side ached just thinking about it. He smiled. This was the first time in this reporter's life he actually could blame the messenger.

The story was falling into place. Their conversation in the hotel made him realize she was a woman filled with more ambiguities and complexities than he had given her credit for. And then he realized why she didn't resist when he threatened her—why she was so willing to tell him the entire story. Now he knew everything.

But it cost him dearly.

42

Fahy showed Denise to a chair and sat across from her in his hideaway office.

"I appreciate you coming by before leaving for Texas. I wanted to thank you for what you did in the courtroom and assure you everything will be okay. What you did was extraordinarily important for the country. Had you not testified the way you did, a killer would have gone loose."

"You mean, had I not lied."

"Okay. I didn't want to be so indelicate."

"It's all right. The son of a bitch had it coming. He killed my sister. She would have wanted me to do this."

What a coup, he thought. He was finally rid of Oliver. Federal prosecutors had told him privately that Judge Savage was going to sentence Oliver to life. To ensure Oliver accepted his sentencing without a fight, President Harvey sent word to him he would receive a pardon after a modest number of months behind bars.

Fahy knew that would never happen, but by the time Oliver caught on, he would be all but forgotten. He would then have to struggle through normal channels seeking an appeal. That would take forever and lead nowhere. And if it ever did travel up the chain to the top, well, they had a friend on the Supreme Court.

Just to be sure, Fahy had McCauley plant an informant in Oliver's holding cell after the verdict to explain to him what would happen in prison if he were to open his mouth about the Renaissance Circle.

Fahy grinned at the thought. Oliver was out of the way forever. He deserved it. For a moment, he tuned out Denise, but the word "Renaissance" leaped out at him.

"It meant a lot to her and she was angry at Oliver for what he did," Denise said.

"Really? She was a supporter?"

"You didn't know? She was the first female member."

Fahy flinched. "I had no idea. I simply thought she was a high-priced hooker."

"Not exactly. My sister was one tough cookie. Sure, she slept with the chief justice, and she slept around with some powerful businessmen. She said she got a real kick out of it. If men could sleep around, she once told me, then why couldn't she?"

"She told me she began to understand the power she had over men several years ago after she slept with a middle-aged business tycoon. He practically begged her not to leave and offered her a new car. It was that simple. She understood the advantages of sleeping with very rich and very married men. And she had her fun. They gave her jewelry, furs and clothes. But as she slept with more men, she began to understand her favorite gift was information. Gossip, she discovered—whether it was a stock tip or the inside word on some political deal—meant power to her. She could use it to manipulate prominent men to do just about anything she wanted.

"Like you, I first thought she just slept around," Denise continued. "But over time I began to realize how she operated and I actually admired her work ethic, even if I didn't like her choice of careers. Gradually, she began to wield more power in the organization. Men she never slept with would sometimes come to her for advice.

"She asked me a few years ago for help with her finances. I was surprised at how well she had done. She had some very fat bank accounts and needed financial advice on how to manage them. I was glad I could help. I put her into some very lucrative investments.

"And then they actually hired her to organize the Renaissance meetings. That gave her more access to their secretive executive committee."

"I don't know that much about the Renaissance Circle," Fahy said. "Who's on the executive committee?"

"Cara never said. Some pretty powerful people. I could tell by the way she talked about it. At one time I thought it even included the president. But now I realize I was mistaken. I didn't know enough about the organization to understand what my sister was mixed up in. I sort of get it now."

"President Harvey?" Fahy asked. "That would be the day. He certainly knows them well. He's using them to advance his political agenda. That's what we all do. We ally with outside organizations. Hell, the truth is we manipulate people."

Denise looked at Fahy and smiled. "I guess my sister did too. She knew who pulled the strings in the organization, and she was well paid for her services."

"And well paid for the services she provided individual members too, I assume," said Fahy.

Denise eyed him with a slight look of annoyance, as if she was the only one permitted to say such things about her sister. "Yes, that too. It didn't hurt that she slept with the right men. Why do you think she took the selfie with Castiglia? She has a complete file of photos with other powerful men."

"In bed with her?"

"Yes. She made sure they knew she had an entire collection of photos so no one could touch her. The hint of blackmail was all she needed."

"Did she have photos of Oliver?"

"I don't know. She never mentioned him. But I do think it came down to him or her. She was the unofficial enforcer for the group. Until Castiglia, the group had only been involved in trying to sway elections or political dirty tricks. Nothing lethal she ever told me about. Oliver went rogue. I would bet the Renaissance members gave her carte blanche to deal with him."

"But his people killed her before she could kill him?"

"Yes." Denise choked back a sob. She teared up and turned to Fahy. At that moment, they reached out for each other, and she sobbed softly in his arms.

"I'm sorry about your sister," Fahy said, gently massaging the back of her neck as she cried on his shoulder.

"What you've done is very brave and you alone are responsible for bringing justice to your sister's murderer. You should be proud of what you've accomplished."

Denise pushed back from their embrace and looked up at Fahy, their arms still interlocked. "None of this would have happened," she said, "if Oliver hadn't recognized Mr. Rikki and seen him talking briefly with Castiglia when he arrived that Friday night long ago. All I can think is that Oliver panicked and because of that, my sister is dead."

She began to sob again but this time less violently. Her crying soon subsided and Fahy led her to the couch. They sat together. He was curious about what she had previously said. "Cara was an enforcer for the Circle?"

Denise grabbed a tissue from the end table and softly blew her nose. "You would have never guessed, would you? A woman. But think about it. If you're going to operate behind the scenes the way the Circle did—does—what better way to get things done than to have a woman do it? Who would suspect?"

"Until Oliver came along."

"Which is why I eventually saw your point and had to help you put my sister's killer away."

43

Beck didn't drink martinis, but today he was already on his second. Geneva had called to say she would probably be late arriving. He wondered where she had been and what had become of their relationship.

He leaned back in her hot tub, sipping on his half-filled glass, appreciating the sun's colorful prisms cascading through the alcohol and his brain. He thought about his life and how things had gotten so incredibly off-kilter as he got closer to the truth about Chief Justice Castiglia's death.

As he sipped, he slid further into the tub, careful not to spill his drink. He began to feel at peace as the water roiled and drowned out the noise of the city around him. His sunglasses were the darkest pair he owned, yet they were no match for the broiling, orange fireball that reddened his face. *Or is that the alcohol?* Either way, he was bound to get burned.

Beck never heard Geneva arrive. But suddenly she appeared before him, a shapely shadow backlit by the sun. He said nothing, just shielded his eyes with his free hand. She pulled her hair back and tied it with something, exposing a hint of soft curves on both sides of her rib cage. A ray of sun flared between her thighs and disappeared.

It's almost an invitation, Beck thought.

Her shadow climbed into the pool and she sat opposite him, spreading her left arm wide in a familiar gesture of hugging the side of the tub so she wouldn't slip. He thought about what he wanted out of their relationship. Right now, he wasn't sure. He took a gulp of his martini and set the empty glass down on the ledge. With his other hand, he turned off the jets. Suddenly, there was silence. Just him and her shadow.

"So," he said.

"So," she replied.

"Well, that's a helluva conversation starter."

They both laughed.

"You first," he said.

"No, you."

"I'm half in the bag."

"Angry with me?"

"Something like that."

"I deserve that. I'm sorry I deceived you," she said.

"It wasn't the first time."

"You have me there."

"What is so difficult about a little trust in our relationship?" Beck thought it funny. Before he met Geneva, he was the two-month dating phenom. Now he was the one talking about trust.

"I don't know. It's just the way it's always been."

"That's a non-starter."

"No. I don't mean with us. I mean me."

"Oh. The old line 'It's not you, it's me.' Are you breaking up with me?"

"Oh, stop it. You're the only man I've ever known to trust me—"

"Shows how gullible I am."

"Stop. I should do better in returning the favor. Of trust, I mean. Before you, sharing was difficult. It's so easy to slip back into my old ways. This town's backstabbing culture prevented me from believing in anyone."

Can I trust her? He pondered his desire to sleep with Denise. Now, at least, he was relieved Denise never gave him that chance. He knew deep down he would have taken it. Instead, Denise was now like a statue to a dead relationship high atop a pedestal he would always admire. It was safer that way. She was now dead to him. But he still struggled, thinking about what might have been.

Geneva slid awkwardly over to his side of the tub and took his hand away from the jet controls and placed his arm around her shoulder. He let it lie there, limp, his forearm balanced on her shoulder, his fingers dangling passively above the water.

"So, did Oliver really kill the chief justice?" Geneva asked.

"Nope."

"Who did?"

"You."

44

Fahy looked at Denise with longing. They were locked in an awkward arm's-length embrace. He had been comforting her. He wanted more. He slid his arm free and reached for her hand and clasped it gently. Surprisingly, she gripped him tightly, her thumb rubbing his skin. Then he put his arm around her and she reached out for him and buried her face in his shoulder again.

She looked up at him. Her eyes still filled with a glassy reflection, but now her mouth was open, almost saying something. Without a word, he leaned in. She followed his cue and they kissed. Lightly at first, then with an unfamiliar ferocity. He pulled back, unsure.

"Don't let go," she murmured.

His hands roamed cautiously, rubbing her ribs and slowing moving down her back. She gripped his neck and pressed him tighter to her. Their kiss never broke.

Finally, she grabbed his hand and placed it on her right breast. She whispered his name and almost inaudibly said, "I want to be with you."

His groin leaped to attention. He couldn't believe this was happening. This beautiful creature wanted him. He pressed her breast softly through the fabric of her clothing.

"Come with me." He took her hand and led her out of the office, past two guards seated in the hallway, past another office to an unmarked door. Inside, he showed her his windowless hideaway, outfitted with a queen-size bed, walk-in closet, and bathroom with shower. Though it was relatively small, he found it was more comfortable than the vice presidential mansion, which was more history museum than home.

"One moment." Fahy quickly stepped out of the room.

A guard was seated in a chair across the hall.

"Jason, I'll be awhile."

The guard nodded and said nothing.

He returned almost immediately. "I told the staff I would not be available for a while."

Denise smiled and wrapped her arms around his neck. She kissed him passionately, her tongue darting, exploring his mouth. He had forgotten the thrill of a woman, especially one who was pursuing him. It awakened something inside. He embraced her and caressed her body. She began to remove his shirt and he tugged at her blouse.

"Please," she said and stepped back.

Fahy looked at her, questioning. She turned and stepped to the door and locked it. Then she turned off the lights. They stood in the dark, their only light a horizontal seam seeping beneath the closed bathroom door. Her shadow slinked in front of him and he felt her hands reaching for his belt buckle. As she did, he instinctively reached up to touch her soft flesh. In moments they were both on the bed, fumbling in their first awkward moments together. Their lust endured for more than an hour until they both collapsed, exhausted, and fell asleep.

—⚬—

Fahy awoke. A small glimmer of light from the bathroom door and the light from his digital clock on the bedside table outlined shadows on the ceiling.

His head hurt. He stared at the ceiling, remembering incredibly athletic sex. He had opened two bottles of champagne from his small private fridge, and they had done it in every possible position on every available surface in the bedroom. The alcohol blurred his memory, but he knew it had been some of the greatest sex ever.

What he could recall brought an incredibly wide smile. Denise must have learned a few tricks from her sister. After all, Cara was the pro and would have known every move that pleased a man. But they were still sisters, and sisters talked. If this afternoon was any indication, Denise was a very good listener.

He quickly glanced over at the silhouette of her naked torso. *What a body,* he thought. He felt ready for more.

His cellphone buzzed, and he turned to the nightstand. He pressed a button to stop the commotion. He didn't want to wake Denise. It appeared to be just another email. He noticed his morning security briefing was missing from the screen. *Odd,* he thought. Usually, by now the briefing was ready and sitting in his inbox. He studied his phone and realized it wasn't morning at all. It was still the same day. It was only seven thirty in the evening. He'd slept just a few hours.

He set down the phone and flipped on the small reading lamp and turned to look at the woman lying naked next to him. She was sleeping on her back and the sheets were crumpled down below her bikini line, exposing her voluptuous breasts and taut stomach.

Fahy remembered how he reveled in her flesh. His gaze followed her shoulder to her arm, which stretched across her stomach to her hand clutching the bed sheet as if she were deliberately covering herself—as if she were being modest. *Not after today,* he thought.

He wondered about asking Denise out on a date. *But how can a vice president finagle a date with any semblance of privacy?* He would have to keep it private. If word got out, it would expose their connection. Yet, he could envision himself in a long-term relationship with this woman.

He heard the soft ding from his cell phone notifying him he had a text. Fahy scrolled down through several texts. Nothing important. Then he came to a photo sent more than an hour ago. It was of him. *What is this?* The photo showed him naked in bed with the beautiful blonde who now slept next to him. In the photo she was vigorously pleasuring him with one hand while taking a selfie with the other.

After all of the champagne they consumed, he had forgotten about her taking the photo. Now, his memory was stirred; he remembered she had taken several. One he recalled was of him licking champagne from her bellybutton. *Oh shit.*

He scrolled through the other photos and winced. An agonizing sense of dread overcame him. His head was clearing quickly, and the pictures reminded him of what Denise had told him about how Cara was the enforcer for the Renaissance Circle. But something didn't ring true. *What was it?* He retraced her story in his mind. *Of course*, he thought. *It's beginning to make sense.*

Cara never worked for Oliver. Not if what Denise told him last night was true. If anything, Oliver would have worked for Cara. As Denise described it, Cara had the clout with the Renaissance Circle. That meant Cara had lied about being hired by Oliver. Oliver had worked for her.

Oliver was Cara's stooge, set up to take the fall. Cara wanted to cast suspicion on Oliver to deflect attention away from herself. Oliver didn't murder Castiglia. Cara had.

A jabbing pain hit Fahy's stomach. Like a magician, Cara's sleight of hand misdirected her audience, making everyone see one thing, when in reality something else was taking place right in front of them.

He'd been duped. The Circle had sanctioned murder as part of its effort to remake the political system. He needed to tell President Harvey. They were relying on an organization far more sinister than they had bargained for to promote their political agenda. He could feel himself being sucked into a conspiracy—a black hole from which there was no escape.

Now it seemed obvious. Cara was in Castiglia's room and could have poisoned the chief justice at any time. Oliver, the fall guy, knew he couldn't possibly take on the Renaissance Circle, so in desperation he tried to manipulate the evidence and cast blame on Kevin Kelly.

Fahy had been blinded by his own obsession to seek revenge and put Oliver behind bars. Cara must have known about his history with Oliver and played on his animosity.

Fahy turned to the photos on his cell phone. He remembered from last night's conversation that selfies were Cara's not-so-subtle form of blackmail, to keep the powerful men in her life under her control.

Well, at least Denise doesn't operate that way, the vice president reassured himself.

Fahy jerked up into a sitting position. He looked at the flawless naked woman next to him. He examined her large breasts that slumped in smooth, soft mounds to either side of her chest. This time he did not look with lust but with the eye of a litigator searching for a clue. His gaze stopped. He leaned forward, sinking into the mattress while trying to focus on what he thought he was seeing.

Under her left breast. A small mole. A mole he knew did not belong to Denise—the woman he thought he was sleeping with—but to her twin sister Cara.

"No," he said under his breath. "It can't be."

Why didn't I see it earlier today? He thought for a moment. She had turned off the lights just before taking off her blouse. *Modesty,* he'd thought. But now he knew better. She didn't dare let him see her mole before she had gotten what she wanted from him.

She had almost bragged, giving him an instruction manual about how she would do it—or at least how her supposed dead sister would have done it. And he never caught on. He was so blinded by his lust that the thought never crossed his mind.

Cara had tricked him into believing she was her twin sister, Denise. Even in court. She had stumbled over facts she knew well during her testimony, enough to convince Rikki she was Denise. And the skirt tug. She had even deceived them with that. *How incredibly clever*, Fahy thought. *How devious.*

There had been no misidentification after the crash. Denise really was dead. Since then, Cara had stolen her sister's persona to accomplish . . . *what?* He closed his eyes in defeat. To manipulate him, of course. This was her long game. She tricked him into sleeping with her so she could take blackmail photos of him.

The Circle was going to do whatever it could to manipulate the American political landscape. This would ensure his full cooperation. *What have Harvey and I gotten ourselves into? Is Harvey her next target?* This was not a peaceful transition of

American political power. It was by whatever means necessary.

The Renaissance Circle's enforcer was sleeping right next to him, as confident as anyone could be. Her emailed photos were her signature blackmail. She had all but explained that to him last night. She had just guaranteed his future cooperation. He was another pawn on her political chessboard.

Fahy shook his head, partly in admiration but mostly in disgust with himself for letting her get the better of him.

Yes, it looked like he might have a relationship with her after all. But not the one he had envisioned.

He turned back to her, watching the soft, subtle, rhythmic movement of her chest rise and fall as she slept peacefully. She had a slight smile.

He lifted his cell phone and slowly read the email message under the last photo

Mr. Vice President. Remember what you told me earlier that we would make a great team? This will assure you I'll be with you every step of the way. —Cara

45

"Hello?"

"Charles, it's Frederic. Could you come by my office?"

"Certainly. Be there shortly." Charles Curtiss was tired. It had been a long day, but he rose from his desk to visit the oldest partner in the firm. Frederic Franklin Howell was the last living named partner at James Howell & Gordon. Howell showed up every day in his motorized wheelchair but did little legal work anymore. Mostly, he advised his partners on political nuances inside the beltway. Few could match his knowledge. Howell had ceded seniority to Curtiss when he decided to cut back his workload.

Curtiss donned his jacket, straightened his tie and left for the elevators, heading two floors below toward the tax division. His heart pounded as he lumbered to the other end of the building.

Tentatively, Curtiss stepped into Howell's outer office. He wasn't invited here often. The senior partner's personal secretary, a slender woman of about sixty, with spiked gray hair and stylish glasses, led him into the inner sanctum. The corner office had the scent of old money and the hint of power. The rich leather couch and chairs, the oriental rug, the perfectly groomed plants in their ornate urns, the richly paneled walls—all shouted clichés of prominence to Curtiss.

Howell sat behind his oversized desk, rumpled in his wheelchair, collar askew. He had shrunk. His shirt had not. Both had seen better days.

Curtiss stood there until Frederic motioned him to sit.

"Charles. Coffee? Something stiffer?"

It was late. He could use a drink. "Scotch, please," he said.

Howell motioned his secretary, who wobbled on her three-inch heels to a small bar in the corner where she filled two tumblers with ice, then poured liquor from an expensive crystal decanter. She handed one to Curtiss and placed the other on Howell's desk on a brass coaster and quickly disappeared, closing the office door behind her.

"I was thinking about the Renaissance meeting you called the other day," Howell said.

"Yes?" Curtiss felt a hint of excitement. *Has he found something?*

"I was at my doctor's yesterday. Chip Willis was the doctor to the stars in this town for many years. An elite clientele. Like him, all aging now. One of those stars was our friend, a certain Chief Justice Nino Castiglia."

"I see." Curtiss sat forward in his chair, almost spilling his drink.

"Yes. And while it's against medical ethics to talk about another patient, my doctor and I have been friends for so long, well, ethics be damned. We sometimes share information. I knew all about the prostate cancer lab results for that scumbag senator, David Bayard, before he did. I knew Senator Mike Patten was getting bypass surgery before he even told his wife."

"And Castiglia?"

"I'm getting to that. Sad. Very sad," said Howell. "He's dead now, so old Chipper didn't mind talking in detail over a few bourbons last night. Sad. So sad."

Curtiss sat motionless, his cold tumbler growing warmer by the minute, waiting for Howell to get to the point before his ice did.

"Poor guy," Howell said. "He was dying of pancreatic cancer. He might have had a year, more likely six months. At least that's what Chip told me. Nino's family took it pretty hard. He was on a lot of drugs trying to slow it down. Ease the pain. Castiglia's family tried to get him to stop doing so much traveling. He refused."

"I had no idea . . . So, he knew he was dying?"

"Sure he did. One of the smartest men I ever met. He was determined to live his remaining months in his own way. No different than he'd done his whole life."

Curtiss slumped back in his chair and took a gulp of scotch. "That explains his attempt to meet with that reporter in broad daylight in front of all of the Circle members. It's clear he felt he had nothing to lose."

"That's what I thought after ole Chipper told me about Nino's condition."

"Thanks for the information. I understand Nino's motivation now." Curtiss set his glass down on a carved glass table next to him and pressed on his chair's arms to stand up.

"There's more," said Howell.

Curtiss lowered himself slowly back into his chair. It creaked under his weight.

"The cancer spread to his brain. He had been showing signs of inappropriate behavior, Chipper said. It wasn't senility. But the cancer was affecting his critical thinking—hell, all of his thinking, really. Apparently that had been a problem for a couple of years and then he was finally diagnosed. Chip recommended the specialist he finally went to."

"I never heard anyone express any doubts about his mental faculties."

"Chip said Nino was able to cover it up with humor. Relied on his clerks to write his legal opinions and dissents for the past eighteen months."

"The chief justice told your friend Chip all of this?" Curtiss asked.

"Yep. He'd been Nino's doctor for more than twenty years. Got him through prostate cancer, two hernia operations and even a bout of impotence. They had a long history, and more than just a doctor-patient relationship. Chip was a pallbearer at his funeral."

"I see."

"That's why Chip knew about Nino's inappropriate behavior, like sleeping with prostitutes."

"I thought Castiglia had done that for years."

"Only in the last year or so."

"How did the doctor know that?"

"Because Chip diagnosed Nino with syphilis and hepatitis six months before he was murdered."

"You're kidding." Curtiss slumped back in his chair. He noticed his tumbler still half full. He reached for it and looked into the glass for answers, guzzled all but the ice, and felt the long burn going down.

"Chip wouldn't kid about a thing like that." Howell folded his hands together on his desk and leaned back in his wheelchair. "Castiglia knew he would die of cancer long before anything else got him, so he refused medication. I think that might be the only rational decision he made in his final months."

"What do you mean?" Curtiss was getting a glimmer of the larger picture.

"That cancer in his brain. Nino acting inappropriately. Chip said Nino showed no regret for sleeping with prostitutes. It wasn't part of his personality."

"He was consciously infecting these women?"

"That's the question, isn't it? Did he realize what he was doing? Had the part of his brain that fed his conscience been damaged by the cancer?"

That didn't make sense to Curtiss. "I always thought it was his conscience that egged him on to blow the whistle on the Renaissance Circle."

"Precisely. Was our boy infecting these women on purpose or had he become a mental mess? We'll never know now, will we?"

Curtiss hated ambiguity, but as a trial attorney he'd learned long ago to navigate around it. "Nino's carelessness, we'll call it, could create serious problems."

"Does it now?" Howell said. "You know things I don't. Well, I won't ask."

Curtiss read his cue. He pressed his meaty hands on the chair arms again to help raise his bulk. "You've been a great help. You've answered a lot of questions for me. I'm trying to imagine the fallout."

Howell shook his head, grabbing a cigar from an ornate humidor on top of his desk. "He was a good man. I sure hope none of this goes public. Not a great legacy to leave behind."

"Of course not," said Curtiss. "No need for that."

Legacy? Is that what Howell calls it? Curtiss would have to think about that one. It seemed more like some very serious consequences for the Renaissance Circle. Nino may have done more harm than he ever intended.

46

"Me?" Geneva challenged. "How can you say that? I never murdered anyone." She sat up, lifting her dark hair out of the hot tub, and shook her head, whipping her hair loose as the weight of the water helped it unravel, slinging droplets everywhere. Beck was in her direct line of fire and shielded his face.

His phone dinged with a text. It was sitting on the side of the hot tub near his empty glass. Geneva looked at him with an expression that said, *Don't you dare.* He casually turned away and grabbed it with his free hand, using his thumb to manipulate the device. There was a selfie of Cara—posing as Denise—and the vice president, both naked.

Only after Beck explained at the hotel he'd figured out her identity and threatened to expose her to Fahy did she relent and tell him the entire story. In exchange, Beck agreed to keep her secret. She had one more play, she told him. She needed a little more time.

She got her latest trophy. Beck grinned. It was just as Cara had scripted it.

"Who is it?" Geneva asked.

"A message from the vice president." He began typing a reply with his thumb.

"Since when did you and Fahy become such intimate friends?"

"We go way back," Beck said, turning to Geneva. His phone pinged with another text.

"Shouldn't you get that?"

"Nah. It's probably just another one of my many female admirers sending me more nude photos and begging me to save the world."

"I'm glad you can handle only one naked woman at a time."

"How many can you handle?" Beck shot back.

She looked at him blankly. She removed her sunglasses. Her eyes were red. Beck's heart winced.

"You never did have an affair with Cara," Beck said. His eyes burned into hers. He hated being lied to.

Weeks ago, when Geneva had first looked over his shoulder at Cara's naked selfies, she had taken an unusually long time to examine the photos. She even commented on Cara's mole. Geneva's curious reaction made it obvious she didn't know Cara. Beck was sure of that.

Beck turned away and picked up his phone again. This time he recognized a familiar photo—one of the selfies he had erased from Cara's phone.

I keep extra copies, she texted.

He smiled. Of course she did. He would have thought less of her had she not. Cara thought she could set him up just like all of the others. What she didn't realize was blackmail worked on only those with something to lose. He'd bungled a great career not so long ago and had been publicly humiliated. Now this Castiglia investigation had surfaced simmering tensions in his relationship with Geneva. He wondered if he was experiencing the beginning of the end or if they could repair the damage.

Fahy didn't appear to have that option. The photo of him with Cara could cause him irreparable political harm. Beck now had a copy of a compromising photo, too—for once getting the better of Fahy.

He remembered the conversation back at the W Hotel. Cara had explained she could tell from the way Fahy had looked at her that he was smitten. Most men were, she told Beck.

Beck had also pressed her on Jackson Oliver. What was the deal there?

Oliver had proven untrustworthy, she explained. He panicked when he came under suspicion and overreacted. The Renaissance Circle frowned upon disloyalty. That was the glue that would guarantee its future success. Once you joined, you were a lifer.

Cara had said that Oliver never figured out she poisoned Judge Castiglia, so he made his clumsy play to eliminate her, thinking she was about to finger him. Oliver had no idea who he was up against. His murder conviction, Cara explained, was simply a convenient way of getting rid of a problem.

Beck had cringed when Cara told him she was the real murderer. She said it matter-of-factly, as if daring him to do something about it.

Beck was sure it was Oliver and had even gotten his colleague Steve Giegerich to write a story accusing him in the *Post-Examiner*. *How could I have been so wrong?* He felt culpable for Oliver's imprisonment, even though a jury convicted him of murder. He remembered Fahy's warning a year earlier during a previous investigation: "Very infrequently, but still too often, justice is neither fair nor right."

After Cara confessed all to him, Beck understood he'd gotten several details wrong during his investigation. But humiliation worn privately was no humiliation at all, only personal torment. No one else need know—at least for now, until he could figure out what to do, if anything, about Cara.

Ultimately, this entire affair came down to trust. Things might have turned out differently had someone just trusted someone else. The chief justice might still be alive had he believed in the work of the Renaissance Circle. But in the end, he was undone by his smarts, his integrity, and his suspicion of wrongdoing.

Oliver might not be incarcerated for what would likely be the rest of his life had he trusted the Renaissance Circle and not panicked and tried to frame Kelly for the murder. That was one massive guilty conscious he was nursing.

Fahy was set up because he was too cunning. He seemed to never trust any circumstance around him. He was a man who relied totally on his honed instincts. He never understood the Renaissance Circle had a murderous side. But his radar must have picked up something along the way that set off alarms. Of course, that would have been hard to detect because Fahy was the master of the poker face.

And finally there was Cara, the biggest offender of all. She trusted no one and had a rich portfolio and an entire photo album to prove it.

Beck looked at his personal life. It was no different. Geneva hadn't trusted him enough to confide in him. So now he was returning the favor. *What a shitty way to carry on a relationship. What a way to live.* He was lost in his thoughts when Geneva broke the spell.

"How can you ever accuse me of killing anyone?"

"Sorry. I was distracted by my fan mail."

"Stop it. Get serious for a moment." She gave him a soft playful punch in the shoulder. "What do you mean by saying I killed Chief Justice Castiglia? I did no such thing. Jackson Oliver did. A jury convicted him."

"No. He was as confused as everyone else. Even I thought he was guilty. Oliver stole the glass from Castiglia's room and I couldn't figure out for the longest time why he would do that if he hadn't killed Castiglia."

"Then why? Why steal the glass?"

"Orders."

"Who ordered him to steal the glass?"

"The same person who ordered Cara to kill the chief justice."

"And that was?"

"You."

"How can you say that?" She squinted at him and the dimples around her mouth disappeared.

"Cara left the chief justice dead early in the morning," said Beck. "She stuck around a while, I assume, to ensure he was dead. She made it appear he died of natural causes. But who would the authorities first suspect if he hadn't?"

"Cara."

"Exactly. So she had to make sure she covered her trail. It took her more than three hours to drive home, and sometime during that trip she remembered the glass filled with poison was still on the bedside table. Apparently, she left the chief justice a lot later than she let on. Probably around four or five in the morning, I'd say. It makes sense for how things went down. Cell phone service was nonexistent for most of her drive home. So, it was hours before she could call Oliver and tell him to remove the glass."

"She instructed Oliver?"

"Yeah. She may have woken him up, or he may not have realized the importance of moving quickly. Maybe he didn't know about my early-morning breakfast with the chief justice. Whatever it was, he didn't get to the room in time. Before he had a chance, Trowbridge and I had already found Castiglia's body."

"But how did the poison get in Castiglia's CPAP machine?"

"I saw Oliver sneak in Castiglia's hotel room after Trowbridge and I left. Like Cara said, he had his own key. He might have gotten it from Cara. He might not have. It doesn't really matter. But what I do know is he must have panicked, thinking here was a chance to frame Kelly and keep the focus off of the Renaissance Circle. So he poured some of the poison in the machine. Probably emptied the rest in the bathroom sink and walked out with the glass before anyone noticed.

"Remember, I saw Oliver enter the room with his own key, but I never saw him remove the glass. I assumed he did since it later turned up missing. But it's all circumstantial. I doubt what I know would ever be admissible in a courtroom."

"All of this makes my head hurt. How did you figure this out?"

"I couldn't put it all together until you told me about your affair with Cara and that Harv had called you and asked if I would be willing to talk with the chief justice." Beck picked up his empty martini glass and stared at it, deciphering his disappointment. He could use another right now.

"The chief justice didn't know me," he continued. "Probably didn't know who I was. Oh, he might have recognized my byline from the newspaper over the years, but I'd never met him. Why would he call me out of the blue without someone having first dropped my name? They needed a person they knew would be almost certain to investigate Castiglia's allegations. Obviously, the chief justice didn't trust his own government and friends to investigate the Circle. Too many of them were members. And how did he get my unlisted number? Someone in your husband's administration would have given it to him."

"Okay. So Harv called me. But I didn't order anyone killed."

"Oh, you might not have actually issued the order, but you passed it on to Cara from your ex-husband, the president of the United States. That phone call Cara made to you from my condo after you stormed out only confirmed it. That's when you passed on your ex-husband's instructions to Cara to set up Fahy."

Beck was enjoying this. It had taken hours of wear and tear on his oriental rug talking to Red to pull the sequence of events together.

"I'd called you when Denise, Cara and I got to my condo. I told you we were back in Virginia, and I was running to the store for groceries. My condo hadn't been lived in for months and needed a resupply. It was then that you tried to phone Cara with your ex-husband's instructions, but her phone was dead. You didn't know that in the rush to escape El Paso she left most of her luggage on the tarmac back in Texas. Her cell phone charger must have been in her suitcase.

"In your hurry to get to my condo before I got home from the store, you must have parked on the street. Had you parked in my building's garage, you would have seen my car and known I'd already returned. When you burst through my door, that look of shock on your face was real. But it was not your shock at seeing Cara standing their nearly naked in my living room. It was your shock at seeing me. I wasn't supposed to be there yet. In your mind I should have still been at the store. You'd figured it all wrong. All three of us—Cara, Denise and I—went to the store and got the shopping done much faster than I would have had I gone alone. You were counting on that.

"Cara is pretty damned cunning. She'd never met you despite your claim to the opposite. But she knew something was up. Maybe President Harvey had told her about his ex assisting him to enlist me. I don't know. So, after you stormed out, and realizing her phone was dead, Cara used the excuse of patching things up between us to use my phone to reach you. That's when you gave her instructions to blackmail Fahy. He was the one loose end that worried the president."

"But I didn't. I swear I didn't blackmail Fahy," Geneva said. "I gave Cara a code. It was strange. I was to tell her to 'approach the dragon slayer.' That's all I told her. Honest. I didn't know it meant to blackmail Vice President Fahy. Harv used me just like he uses everyone."

Her statement struck close to home. Beck felt he was being manipulated at times during this entire sordid affair. Yet, in the end, he was pretty sure he had sorted it all out.

"Obviously Harv couldn't reach Cara either," she said. "So he called me and offered a carrot if I would help him. He said if I would pass on the code to her, he would settle on this condo. It would be mine, free and clear. I would be free of him forever."

She fell silent for a moment and looked at Beck. "Why would I want to set up the vice president?"

Really? She doesn't get it. "Because, believe it or not, Fahy was the only innocent in all of this. Besides Castiglia, he was the only one who had any suspicions about the Renaissance Circle. Your ex—the president of the United States—was worried Fahy would find out he had actually ordered the hit on Justice Castiglia with the Renaissance Circle's blessing."

Geneva pulled herself up straight in the tub. "Harv had him killed?"

"Yep."

"Oh my god, and I played a part in the cover-up. Honestly, I didn't understand what he was up to."

Beck eyed her suspiciously. *Can I believe anything she says?* He picked up his cell phone and pressed a button. He held the nude picture of Fahy and Cara in front of her. She gazed at it only briefly and then shifted her guilty glance sideways.

"Ask yourself this," Beck said. "Why would the president want to ensure Daniel Fahy's silence? He wouldn't need to blackmail his own vice president had your ex not personally ordered the hit on Castiglia. That also explains Cara's last-minute scheme to pretend to be her dead sister. She could tell Fahy was attracted to her when they were talking about her testifying at Oliver's trial. So she switched gears and created an elaborate story out of whole cloth and successfully impersonated Denise for weeks. She knew Fahy would never hop in bed with a prostitute, but he might with her equally attractive twin sister. Cara exploited his emotions and set him up for blackmail—this picture." Beck waved the phone in his hand.

"If Fahy has any ambitions of succeeding your ex-husband in office, the photos could kill his chances. He will now have to play along with whatever Cara wants."

"But that still doesn't mean I ordered the murder of Justice Castiglia." Geneva could not hide her confusion.

"Think about it. Your ex-husband set up Castiglia by asking you if I might be willing to meet with the chief justice to explore something that was bothering him. I assume at some point earlier Castiglia had contacted President Harvey with his concerns about the organization. Your ex-husband was alarmed to hear the justice had serious doubts about the group that was the foundation of his secret agenda. Castiglia had no idea of President Harvey's involvement, and Harvey had to keep it that way. It gave him the upper hand. So, the president feigned concern. He then called you to see if it was okay if Castiglia called me. And then he called Castiglia back, suggesting the chief justice seek me out. A journalist, I'm sure he explained, would be more than willing to expose the organization.

"That also put distance—at least in Castiglia's mind—between President Harvey and the Renaissance Circle. Castiglia thought Harvey's assistance was proof he, too, had suspicions about the Circle and could therefore be trusted. That gave the chief justice the confidence he needed to call me. What Castiglia didn't realize was he was being played. In fact, your ex-husband was testing Castiglia to see which way he would go. Didn't your husband call you back to see if I was meeting with Castiglia?"

"Uh. Yes, he did."

"You see? When Castiglia actually agreed to meet with me, Harvey confirmed his worst suspicion: the chief justice was going public. Harvey couldn't risk the Renaissance Circle being exposed so he had to eliminate the threat."

"Oh my god." Geneva shook her head, looking down at the water. He thought she was choking. She looked up at the colorful sky and closed her eyes. Beck thought he saw a tear, but he was determined to keep his cool and not let her emotions affect him. He wasn't finished yet, but they might be.

She looked back at him, squinting in the sun, which would soon disappear behind the Pennsylvania Avenue cityscape. "What is so important about this Renaissance Circle that they have to hide its existence?"

"Your ex-husband apparently thought he could use it to move Washington's power game in a new direction. The Circle's purpose is to build the political center and lay waste to the far left and far right. He blamed the polarizing wings of both parties for putting Washington into a state of perpetual political stalemate and uproar. He figured if the extremist wings of both parties were eliminated—over time—he could make Washington function again without a lot of rancor."

"And one of their methods was murder?"

"Correct."

"Why don't you go public with all of this?"

"I have no evidence. Everything is circumstantial. I can't prove Oliver is innocent or that Cara did it. I can't prove orders came from the president. Hell, I can't even prove the Renaissance Circle exists. Cara was very smart in how she handled this. She wasn't even worried about telling me the whole story. She understood there isn't a collaborator or document to prove any of this."

"Unbelievable. If you can't write a story about it, how about a book?"

"Who'd believe it?"

"A novel, then?"

"That's possible."

"You could call it *Naked Truth*," she said and laughed. She lowered her eyes as if to confirm their own lack of cover under the water. "Maybe something like truth masquerading as fiction."

Beck looked askance at her, at a few wet strands matted to her face and neck, at droplets of hot water running down her long, slender neck to her beautifully tanned, bare shoulders. He liked what he saw. "Truth is," he said, "we all want simple answers. It's not easy to accept the truth about anything we can't see."

"Alternative facts." Geneva smiled at him and reached for his hand under the water.

"In this case, an alternative universe."

Beck caressed the back of her hand with his thumb. He didn't want to talk anymore. He felt their relationship slipping away. He wondered if that's what he wanted.

He reached over and turned on the hot tub jets. They roared back to life and the churning water exploded to the surface, drowning out the sounds of the city as the bubbles covered their nakedness.

For the moment, blinded by the final rays of the setting sun, the only thing he could see was Geneva, and he wondered what lay beneath the surface of their relationship. It was complicated, and he was tired and emotionally drained. The whys behind her behavior would have to wait. Simple answers would have to do for now. He draped his arm around her neck and caressed her breast. He hugged her close and turned to face the darkening sky.

47

Geneva gingerly plucked the strand of white hair clinging to her wet cheek. It had irritated her skin. *How did I miss that?* She was sure she had gotten rid of all of the strays when she dumped the wig shortly after the funeral. She had disguised herself to ensure she wasn't recognized sitting next to Cara.

She was shocked when she realized Beck had showed up. She hadn't expected him to fly all the way to Texas. It forced her to avoid the family visitation the night before to ensure she didn't bump into him. She had no doubt he'd recognize her up close, so she asked the ushers to seat him in the rear of the church for the funeral service, if possible, and she'd lucked out.

She looked up at Beck. His eyes were closed. He had a broad smile of contentment.

She rolled the strand discreetly between her finger and thumb into a small, manageable bundle and quietly flicked it over the edge of the hot tub.

Her movement aroused Beck's limited attention. He muttered something unintelligible, never opening his eyes, and drew her closer. Geneva felt comfort again, engulfed in the womb of hot water and Beck's warm embrace. She grasped his hand tighter against her breast, squeezing her affection for him into her soul and turned and kissed his cheek. His two-day growth of beard prickled on her lips and his eyes opened, acceding to her light touch.

They looked into each other's eyes. She thought she saw warmth again. It felt almost normal again.

She loved this man. He was honest and kind and complicated and undeservedly forgiving of her. They just needed time. She needed time. She would not risk losing him over something like this thing with Justice Castiglia. She would fix it. Somehow.

She wondered why he never asked her where she had disappeared to for so many days. She knew he would figure out her flimsy lie about an affair with Cara. The two of them had nothing in common. She'd erred there. She was upset and had made up the story on the spot to hide the truth. They both had pasts, and she knew Beck would never accept her having an affair with a woman and would do everything in his power to disprove it.

Eventually, she would have to tell him something, though she could put it off for now. *How can I explain it?* She had already come so close.

She had hidden her grief from him, staying away until she was emotionally ready to reenter his world—their world. The world she had wanted almost since the day she met him. Yet there was another life, a past life. And she had to admit she had fair warning several weeks ago when she eyed Beck's photos. She was startled at first, until she examined the photo closely and realized who she was looking at.

But that did not diminish her grieving for a former love. Although she felt an agonizing ache in her chest, she reminded herself that she had left that life behind long ago.

She would keep her secret from Beck.

For now. Maybe forever. Their future might depend on it.

After all, it wasn't Beck or Cara she was shocked to see when she had arrived uninvited at his condominium that day. No, Beck had gotten that wrong. She was shocked to see her current love Beck standing there shirtless next to a woman she had mistaken for her former lover, Denise.

48

Partners stopped Curtiss in the halls twice as he trundled back to his office. Both asked if he was okay. He looked ill, one said. Curtiss waved them off, saying he had gotten little sleep last night working on a case. All of the partners could identify with that.

When he finally shut his office door behind him, Curtiss pulled a bottle of bourbon from his bottom desk drawer, poured a double, and sat in his chair contemplating what he had just learned.

"Jesus," he growled to himself. "Jesus, I can't believe this." He shook his head and guzzled half of his drink. In his fury he'd forgotten to add ice. He downed the glass anyway.

What had Castiglia done? It wasn't like him. Howell was right. The cancer must have affected Castiglia's judgment.

Curtiss picked up his phone and called.

"Charles, how are you?" asked the voice on the other end of the line.

"We have a big problem, Mr. President."

"Oh?"

"Castiglia was dying of pancreatic cancer that spread to his brain. His judgment was impaired, and he contracted syphilis and hepatitis. There's a good chance he gave them to Cara."

"Oh."

There was silence on the phone. Curtiss waited for the president to speak. He knew what Cara meant to him. She was his link to the daily operations of the Renaissance Circle and she protected his political agenda. Curtiss knew President Harvey had been a member of the executive committee since the beginning. Years ago, his wife, Geneva, had attended their initial organizational meeting as his representative and recommended against him joining. But Curtiss lobbied him hard and Harvey quietly become a member behind her back.

Curtiss knew Harvey was fond of Cara and wondered if they had ever slept together. Harvey relied on her to run the organization's day-to-day operations. She made it all happen so they could keep their distance and never dirty their hands.

"I knew Castiglia was dying," Harvey said.

"You did?"

"I am the president. The Supreme Court is part of my daily security briefing."

"Oh. I see." Curtiss was an important figure in this town, but he was not important enough to receive that kind of information. The president had just put him in his place.

"That's why I didn't move earlier to remove him and put in our own man. I was going to let Mother Nature take care of the problem. But when I realized he was about to expose us, we had to move quickly."

Finally, Curtiss spoke up. "What about the syphilis and hepatitis?"

"That's news to me."

"You remember what Cara was supposed to be doing today, don't you?"

"Yes," Harvey said. "I got a message from her a few hours ago. Mission accomplished. Even got photographic evidence."

Curtiss heard a long sigh over his phone. He closed his eyes and rubbed his chin. *What are we going to do?* Two of the most important people in their revolution might have syphilis and hepatitis. The Renaissance Circle would have a difficult time accomplishing its goals if either of them were ill or incapacitated.

"Is it fatal?" Harvey asked.

"Can be. More likely, if left untreated, it would be debilitating. Neither disease is anything to toy with. Hepatitis is some serious shit, and everyone knows how bad syphilis is."

"Early treatment help that?"

"I believe so. But we need to let them know now."

"We'll make this work," said Harvey.

That seemed awfully optimistic, thought Curtiss. "What do you have in mind?" He heard coughing over the phone and wondered if he'd caught the president smoking a cigar. Then more coughing.

Harvey cleared his throat. "Let's not tell Cara or Dan anything just yet. There's still a lot of work we need to do before we let them know. I've been thinking about that liberal, Jim Andrews. What was he? Seventh in seniority on the court behind Castiglia? He's younger than all of the other justices and will be around a lot longer. I'd like Cara to give Andrews a late-night visit and take some pictures. And this time she can leave behind more than just a few photos."

"You're serious."

"Absolutely. And after Andrews, I can think of another dozen house calls she can make on Capitol Hill. This could prove to be a real coup. Of course, we can't tell her anything about her condition. Not just yet. And who's to say she's even contracted anything? She and Dan could be just fine."

"You're willing to take that chance? Don't you think that's a bit extreme? I mean, the vice president is a good friend of yours."

"Extreme is what happened to Castiglia. Wouldn't you say?" Harvey rasped.

"But that was different."

"Don't kid yourself. Who was it—Goldwater?—who said, 'Extremism in defense of liberty is no vice. Moderation in pursuit of justice is no virtue.'"

"Goldwater was a right-wing extremist."

"Was he? Or was he just insightful about wielding power?"

Curtiss couldn't believe Harvey was willing to destroy those closest to him—those who had been most loyal to him—to accomplish some political agenda. *What is this man made of? Is everyone expendable in Harvey's mind?* Curtiss fingered his empty glass and then spoke. "Our revolution focuses on ridding Washington of the extremist elements. If our tactics mirror those of the extremists, then what have we accomplished? Our revolution is as big a fraud as theirs."

"You still don't get it, do you? If we don't win, we don't rule."

"But at what price are you willing to rule?" Curtiss heard another long sigh. He felt the president's frustration growing. He imagined the president sitting on the Truman Balcony smoking a cigar and looking out over the lawn toward the Washington Monument—a blunt reminder of whose seat he occupied.

"It sometimes takes extreme measures to win," Harvey continued. "Wielding power is everything. But the Washington truth is this: It's all about winning. Nothing else really matters. Now does it?"

49

Beck kept his eyes closed and felt the warmth of the fading day on his face, the hot tub bubbles burst across his chest and Geneva's hand slip down to touch his crotch.

He was living the good life.

He had won the girl. He had figured out the case. He could chalk up another win on his tote board.

But at what cost?

His girlfriend had deceived him. Beautiful, smart, sexy Geneva—his ultimate male fantasy—had a dark side. *Can I really love a woman who has repeatedly lied to me? Or am I just in an eternal state of lust? Really. What kind of a relationship is that?*

Life, he knew, was a series of compromises. *How far am I willing to go? Is living in a luxurious penthouse and making love to a beautiful woman enough?* It was sure something, he had to admit.

He was beginning to show signs of the same kind of Washington behavior he despised, where winning power was everything. He needed to step back and find his moral compass again. He'd left it somewhere along the way during this investigation.

What would Red say? She wasn't much good at advising him on his love life—after all, she was a leather chair. But Red was damned good at pulling stories together, making Beck see the links and consequences that told the entire narrative. And the first thing Red would impress upon him now was the public's right to know—a moral imperative. Beck felt it was his ethical duty.

Yet he knew in his heart he would never find the whole truth and he had to learn to live with that. Truth in Washington, after all, was like a giant iceberg. Only a small portion was evident. Truth and decency were victims laid waste on the floor of backroom deals, unscrupulous compromises and money—lots and lots of money.

So now he had to decide. *How can I go public with the Castiglia affair when I have no evidence to back up my story?* He couldn't hand it to Giegerich at the *Post-Examiner*. Unlike the rest of Washington, his former employer's standards were high. Steve would demand hard facts.

He remembered what Geneva had said. The logical way to tell this story was to write a factual account and call it fiction. Even then, no one would believe there was a real threat in Washington to overthrow the government.

Or will they?

ACKNOWLEDGEMENTS

Thanks, Red. I'm amazed at what you can do on an oriental rug. And without saying a word. You know what they say about still waters.

Jill Howard, I continue to use ideas from your plot-twisted mind. I hope it stays that way for a long time. I look forward to many new adventures together.

And to Kelsey Laye. Thanks for the encouragement.

Thanks to my editor, Lorin Oberweger. You may not realize it, but you taught me how this is done. I am grateful.

Laurie Baker, editing is your hidden talent. Thank you for catching so many details in the manuscript early on when I really needed the help.

Kerry Devine, thanks for your insightful beta read on your iPhone (!). You've got better eyes than I. Impressive.

And to my good friends in the Royal Writers Secret Society, the smartest group of thriller writers I know. You have great insights over food and drink, and they're not all alcohol induced. I appreciate the many times you've critiqued pieces of this manuscript.

My novel writing career has been like this novel, filled with its share of twists and turns. Ron Sauder, of Secant Publishing, has corrected my steering on several occasions. This book would never have been published without your guidance and your advice on how this crazy business works. I am grateful beyond measure. You're a true friend.

Thanks to my editors, Joe Coccaro and Hannah Woodlan at Koehler

Books, for quickly pushing this forward, and to my publisher, John Koehler, for realizing the beauty in serial nakedness.

And a special thanks to Cherie, my auburn advocate.

ABOUT THE AUTHOR

Rick Pullen is a magazine editor and former investigative reporter. Although he was often accused of writing fiction by the targets of his numerous investigative stories, he never actually attempted until 2011. That's when he had the seed of an idea for his first novel, *Naked Ambition*. *Naked Truth* is the second in this thriller series. He is also author of the serial, *The Apprentice*.

In 2015 Rick was named to the *Folio 100*—the 100 most influential people in magazine publishing. The same year he was a finalist for editor of the year.

To learn more about Rick and his writing, visit his website at www.RickPullen.com.

Read an excerpt from Rick Pullen's first novel in the series,

Naked Ambition.

NAKED AMBITION

With his secret secure and brain afire, Beck was alive. Fueled by a rush of adrenalin, his mind would not rest. But it was not always that way. Like now. Oh man, especially like now.

Grateful to finally be home in the solace of his cluttered condominium after a turbulent morning flight back to Washington, Beck was cranking through a chilling novel and a second Corona Light. He'd suffered through five interminable days in a fleabag in Flyover, America. *And for what? The stale beer? The stench of cigarettes?* No, it was the lumpy bed and the low-pitched rumble of the sputtering air conditioner. Or maybe the all-night, rag-tag symphony of truckers braking at the intersection just outside his hotel. *Yeah. That was it. Has to be.* The price of admission to his world.

His cell phone rang. *Not now*, he thought.

He'd just reached the climax, where the hero discovered his beautiful accomplice was an enemy spy. Finally, Beck would learn . . .

The damn thing rang again.

He glared at it vibrating on his coffee table, willing it to shut up and stop dancing.

Caller ID was blocked. *Shit.* He looked back at the page, determined to finish the chapter, but his eyes refused to focus. His DNA was nothing if not emphatic. God, he hated that about himself.

"Yeah?" he grumbled into the phone.

"Beck Rikki?"

"Yeah."

"The reporter for the *Post-Examiner*?"

"Maybe. Who's calling?"

"Daniel Fahy, head of the Public Integrity section at Justice. Your office said I could reach you at this number. I'd like to speak with you privately."

"About?"

"I'd rather not say over the phone. Can we meet?"

Not another crackpot, thought Beck. He'd just finished a week of hounding false leads. He didn't need this right now. "Got a thing about phones?"

"It would be more appropriate to discuss what I have to say face to face."

"How do I know that?"

"You'll just have to trust me."

"Why should I? I haven't a clue who you are."

"I just told you."

Beck groaned softly. He needed to talk to the city desk about giving out his number. "Look, I've had a bad week. Lost my appetite for wild goose chase. Throw me a bone."

"Are you always this difficult?"

"Occupational hazard. You always this secretive?"

"Occupational hazard."

Beck leaned back on his couch and stared at the ceiling, waiting. Not another smartass government bureaucrat whining about his boss mistreating him. *Why do these loons always call a reporter instead of HR?*

Fahy fell silent, but Beck heard muffled laughter in the background. "You still there?"

"I'm thinking," Fahy said.

Beck heard more laughter. "That's okay. While you're at your party, I'm sitting here quietly engrossed in one of the best novels I've read all year. I've got nothing better to do with my time than to listen to silence on *my* end of *your* phone call."

"Okay. Okay. I think I've run across a bribery scheme involving a very important public official—a *very important* public official. Interested?"

Beck sat up straight. "I could be. How important is important?"

"Near the top of the Washington food chain."

"Meaning?"

"He looks in the mirror every morning and imagines he sees the president."

"That's half of Washington."

"He's already taken the measurements of the Oval Office and ordered new carpet."

Beck felt his brain spark. It was like striking a match. Then, just as quickly, the familiar refrain of his defenses jumped in to douse the flames.

"Why tell me?" he asked. "I thought you Justice guys liked to do this sort of investigation in the shadows. You hate the press."

"I've got my reasons. I'll make you a deal. I'll not only give you what I think is a story, but I'll explain my motivation for calling you when we meet. Fair enough?"

"Not fair, but it's enough." Beck had to play ball. He'd just about gone crazy over the past several months. It had been too long since he published a significant investigative piece. His editors had been hounding him. One even suggested he be assigned to a regular beat again. A beat? For the most decorated investigative reporter at the paper? How humiliating.

Fahy suggested breakfast the next day and gave Beck directions to a restaurant south of Old Town Alexandria on old US Route 1, a good ten miles outside of Washington.

"How will I recognize you?"

"Don't worry," Fahy said. "You will." And hung up.

2

Beck eyed his cell phone for a moment. *What the hell? Who is this guy Fahy?* He'd heard a rasp, maybe a hint of an Irish or Scottish brogue? Languages weren't his thing. Even his exasperated journalism prof once told him English was his second language.

No mind. He grabbed his laptop and Googled Daniel Fahy. Sure enough, the director of the Justice Department unit that prosecutes dirty politicians, graduated fourth in his class at Georgetown Law and, according to an old Nicky Allen *POLITICO* story, had a reputation as a Boy Scout — a government do-gooder. *An oxymoron, at best, in this town*, Beck thought.

A couple of clicks later, he pulled up some old *Post-Examiner* stories from the newspaper morgue. Same thing. A feature a few years back mentioned Fahy's reputation for prosecuting wayward politicians. His investigations didn't make him popular in Washington but did make him politically untouchable.

"Red?" Beck did not look up at his writing assistant sitting in the far corner of his living room but continued scanning his computer screen. "This guy might be legit."

He checked the article's byline. *Shit. Kerry Rabidan.* Her newsroom moniker was "Rabid Dog"— she was that good. But lacking enough seniority to own her job, the paper downsized her a year ago. Union rules. She now worked for the rival *News-Times*, Washington's other daily newspaper. *Damn*, he thought, *can't call the competition for background.*

"Red, why is the head of the Justice Department Public Integrity Unit really calling me at home?"

Beck stood and walked back into his living room. He sank into the soft brown couch and felt the expensive, speckled leather cushions sigh beneath him.

He shoved a week's worth of old newspapers into a pile atop his crowded coffee table and created a soft landing for his feet. He noted his Italian shoes were badly scuffed. *Must have been from dogging dead ends around Flyover*, he thought. It was all he had to show for a week's worth of hard labor.

Beck leaned back with his neglected Corona Light and took a swig. *Good*. It was still cold. He wiped his mouth and mustache with his sleeve.

Red faced the fireplace near Beck's "Whodunit Wall"—a floor-to-ceiling collection of autographed Lawrence Block mysteries, as well as first edition Dashiell Hammett and Raymond Chandler detective novels. Beck especially liked his Michael Connelly novels, but he recognized himself more as a character in one of Carl Hiaasen's offbeat beach capers. Five hardback copies of his own nonfiction work were scattered in no particular order on the bottom shelf along with several Jimmy Buffett books. *Thank god the maid is coming tomorrow*. She'd make order of his chaos.

Beck stared at Red as she sat in silence. He thought about the possibilities of the phone call. If Fahy really did have the goods, Beck knew he and Red might quickly be back on top. He wanted nothing more. A big story meant he would not face the agony of backsliding into the mundane trappings of covering a beat like most of his newsroom colleagues. And, most important, there would be no threat of anyone finding out about Red. A big story meant they could continue to work together in private, here, in his man-cave sanctuary. He had worked too hard with too little talent to get this far. He needed a big score and he needed Red's help to make it happen.

God, he was glad they'd met. Even if they hadn't collaborated in months, without her clandestine assistance, he would have never become one of Washington's most successful investigative reporters. Beck had never shared a byline with her, but he credited Red with organizing his thoughts, two Pulitzer

Prize nominations and two *New York Times* best sellers. She was always the first one he acknowledged in his books.

Twelve years ago, his career was in the toilet. No Justice Department officials were calling then, requesting secret meetings. He was a snarl of dangling participles and disjointed gerunds demanding industrial-strength editing from the city desk.

But then, thanks to a half-price Labor Day sale on all-leather furniture, Red entered his life.

Their accidental partnership began about a week after he brought her home. He paced the floor, wearing a path in his oriental rug and reading a draft out loud, struggling to craft a story for the weekend national news section. He then turned his attention to Red for a moment, and something suddenly clicked. The words flowed easily. He didn't realize it at the time, but he had found his muse—and a half-priced one, at that. Considering his level of writing talent, maybe that was appropriate. It wasn't poetry, but it was close enough. He was suddenly welcome on the front page. It was embarrassing—no, outright humiliating—but Red saved his career.

He gazed across the room at her—his empty leather reading chair nestled comfortably in the corner. Beck felt that queasy sensation in his stomach, the one he got when he wasn't certain of his facts. "Red, you think Fahy could be setting us up?"

3

Daniel Fahy hung up and slipped his cell phone back into his suit coat pocket. He worried if he'd overstepped by calling a reporter. Then he glanced up, toward a commotion across the hotel lobby. The doors to F Street swung open, ushering in a whiff of steamy summer downpour, followed by a strong gust of Senator David Bayard. Bayard strode across the plush lobby of the W Hotel, two young aides drafting in his wake.

Fahy felt desperate. He knew he was losing his battle to rein in Bayard before the senator won his party's presidential nomination. If he didn't do something quickly, Bayard would likely escape justice forever. Fahy took a big breath and felt helpless watching his target from afar.

The lobby was unusually crowded. Dozens of bangle-laden tourists huddled boisterously near the first floor alcohol supply to escape the violent afternoon thunderstorm that had cleared the rooftop terrace lounge. Halfway across the lobby, Bayard stopped suddenly to greet a designer couple dressed in black and white and clinging to martini glasses filled with unmet expectations. The trio created a traffic jam in the boutique hotel's packed corridor. Bayard gave the woman a peck on the cheek and pumped the man's hand, shaking his martini far more than the bartender ever intended.

Perched across the room, cradled in a cushioned velvet chair near the Fifteenth Street lobby entrance, Fahy felt silly about his feeble attempt at amateur sleuthing while watching his prey with a bit of awe. The alpha male was establishing his exceptionalism.

The senator stepped back from the couple, nodding in a well-practiced farewell gesture, and slipped away into the glittering, damp-haired crowd, heading in the direction of the lobby bar. Unlike the throng, he showed no signs he had just stepped from Washington's summer steam bath. His groomed, graying hair—turned premature blond at some high-priced salon—along with his crisp, tailored suit hugging his slim, athletic frame, belied both his age and the weather.

Bayard shook three more bejeweled hands as he eased through the throng of slinky summer dresses and brass-button sports jackets, each time grabbing a forearm and practically jamming its reluctant hand into his palm.

Fahy recognized the insatiable urge for political sustenance. So far, he had remained immune to the Washington epidemic—the incurable need for recognition that seemed to accompany political power. He preferred to wield whatever power he possessed quietly and remain anonymous.

He studied his quarry. Bayard appeared obsessed with grabbing the ultimate brass ring, preaching God, family and lower taxes—all the while using his elective office to grow his personal wealth. Bayard's government financial disclosure reports suggested it. Fahy needed to somehow prove it. And he needed to prove it quickly before Bayard took down the entire Republican Party.

Bayard slapped another back and finally slithered next to a whale of a man sitting at the end of the bar. Built like a former college football player—"former" being the operative word—the Whale wore a crumpled, navy, chalk-stripe suit and hovered over his latest round. *How many tumblers is it?* Fahy had lost count.

The senator talked briefly with the man, and then motioned with his thumb over his shoulder toward the well-heeled couples behind him. Both men laughed, but Fahy could make out none of it above the genial roar of the raucous crowd, whose volume had risen with their alcohol consumption.

The Whale stood, as big a man as Fahy had imagined. His belly cascaded over his belt as he reached into his trousers pocket and withdrew a shimmering money clip. He extracted two bills and slapped them on the bar.

Bayard turned briefly to his two young aides, told them something and swiveled, briefly resting his hand on the big man's shoulder. The two men then walked together across the black-and-white marble lobby to the nearby elevator and slipped through its ornate doors, leaving the two young assistants at the bar.

Fahy eyed the electronic display on the lobby wall above the elevator. The elevator did not stop until it reached the rooftop lounge. He rose from his chair, folded the newspaper he had used as a prop, and strode toward the elevator, dodging several small gatherings. It was not unlike his morning commute, darting in and out of traffic on the Beltway, always in a rush to get to the Justice Department.

He needed to hurry. For what, exactly, he wasn't sure. But he felt he was running out of options.

In moments, he sat unnoticed and uncomfortable under the still-dripping canopy shielding the rooftop terrace, posted in a chair far across the expanse of damp, empty tables and chairs from the Whale and the Republican senator from New Jersey. He smiled to himself. Thanks to the storm, the empty rooftop lounge offered not only an unfettered view of the presidential candidate but also a stillness that enabled him to make out bits of their conversation—even from across the steamy patio.

Thank god for Mother Nature, he thought. *She's a Republican.*

Bayard nursed a glass of clear liquid on the rocks. The Whale appeared to have arranged for another tumbler of brown liquor. Fahy suspected single malt scotch, the preferred drink of the power elite. Washington was so cliché—a city of red-tie conformity and uniform egocentric comportment. The drinks rested on the high-top table between them, mere props as both men leaned in, engulfed in conversation.

Fahy partially hid behind his wilting copy of the day's *Post-Examiner* as the waiter brought him ice tea. Spy craft, he had to admit, was not his forte. He strained to hear and bit his lip, hoping for something—a clue of some sort. He wiped his brow. His suit was starting to stick to him. *Am I just nervous or is it the loitering humidity?*

He looked up again over his newspaper. *Will they recognize me?* But the two men—busy chatting and laughing—paid him no attention.

The Whale made a grand gesture, extending his arm out over the balcony's iron railing toward the White House, whose roof and top floor loomed a block away. Fahy felt he could reach out and touch the executive mansion from his chair. He imagined Bayard did too. But this had to be as close as the senator got.

Bayard looked toward the White House and smiled.

It might as well have a For Sale *sign planted on the South Lawn,* Fahy thought. Bayard had slithered through his fingers again and again, and now the Republican convention was just days away. If Bayard got the nomination, he would be placing a substantial down payment on the First Family residence. If elected and subsequently exposed, Fahy was sure Bayard would destroy the Republican Party. Fahy could kick himself. Had he done a better job, the New Jersey senator would never have gotten this close.

Bayard must have intentionally chosen his seat next to the rooftop railing. Literally, nothing stood between him and the White House.

"Shoot! You're kidding. You're killing me, man," the Whale cackled. The words echoed throughout the empty lounge.

Fahy smiled and immediately looked at his watch, marking the time. *Maybe this time,* he thought. *Just maybe.*

Bayard leaned on the railing and spied the White House as if affirming his future ownership.

Perfect, thought Fahy. *He has no idea the White House is spying right back.*

CPSIA information can be obtained
at www.ICGtesting.com
Printed in the USA
FFHW02n2216090918
48243125-52009FF